THE
HAMMETT
HEX

VICTORIA ABBOTT

BERKLEY PRIME CRIME
New York

BERKLEY PRIME CRIME
Published by Berkley
An imprint of Penguin Random House LLC
375 Hudson Street, New York, New York 10014

Copyright © 2016 by Berkley Publishing Group

ISBN: 9780425280355

First Edition: October 2016

Printed in the United States of America
3 5 7 9 10 8 6 4 2

Cover art by Tony Mauro
Cover design by Rita Frangie

This is a work of fiction. Names, characters, places, and incidents either are the product
of the author's imagination or are used fictitiously, and any resemblance to actual persons,
living or dead, business establishments, events, or locales is entirely coincidental.

PUBLISHER'S NOTE: The recipes contained in this book have been created for the
ingredients and techniques indicated. The Publisher is not responsible for your specific
health or allergy needs that may require supervision. Nor is the Publisher responsible for
any adverse reactions you may have to the recipes contained in the book, whether you
follow them as written or modify them to suit your personal dietary needs or tastes.

If you purchased this book without a cover, you should be aware that this book is stolen
property. It was reported as "unsold and destroyed" to the publisher, and neither the author
nor the publisher has received any payment for this "stripped book."

ACKNOWLEDGMENTS

Many, many thanks to the wonderful Linda Wiken (aka Erika Chase) for her help with this manuscript and her friendship over the past twenty-six years. We'd also be lost without the eagle eye of John Merchant trained on our manuscript.

This year we want to express our appreciation to the organizers of the Bony Blithe Award (for mysteries that make us smile) for awarding the 2016 prize to *The Marsh Madness*, the fourth book in the Book Collector series, thus allowing us to be in a terrific mood for who knows how long.

At Berkley Prime Crime, we are always grateful to Tom Colgan, our editor, for advice, enthusiasm and support, and to Allison Janice for cheerful efficiency and, of course, to the unseen copy editors who make such a difference.

Our agent, Kim Lionetti of BookEnds, always has time to listen to an idea, fill us in on the news and give us a boost. We love that!

Victoria and Peachy would like to thank Duane and Natalie Holmes for their support and allowing them to share five acres of paradise.

Thanks to Luc Lavigne who has brought endless creative inspiration, years of tutelage in the medium of film and for being our "Sam Spade" in our latest trailer.

Every week, our colleagues at Mystery Lovers Kitchen and The Cozy Chicks blogs are amazing sources of information, expertise and friendship. We'd be lost without them and their books, because, naturally, we are readers too.

To all those of you who cherish the great and mysterious traditions of this genre and to the legions of fans, librarians, booksellers and reviewers who help keep the mystery world going, may you live long and read much.

We truly appreciate the many readers who reach out to tell us how you feel about our books. Thanks for lifting our spirits. You make a difference.

Closer to home, we thank Giulio Maffini for being a rock and keeping his head when all around him are losing theirs as deadlines and edits loom.

Last but not least, we thank Peachy the Pug for mood elevation, and Daisy and Lily, the princess dachshunds, for napping helpfully under the desk.

IT'S ALL DOWNHILL
FROM HERE

SQUISHED INTO A cable car, hurtling down a steep hill, clinging to a rail with the wind rushing in your ears amid the clang and clatter of metal and the shrieks of fellow passengers might not be everybody's idea of a romantic moment, but strangely, it was working for me. Sure, my knuckles were white, but I felt happy because I was wedged up against Tyler "Smiley" Dekker, the occasional man of my dreams. Plus the cable car we were riding on gave us a view of San Francisco Bay. The half-dozen squealing schoolgirls—black asymmetrical haircuts with weird-colored tips, shredded jeans and selfie sticks—couldn't diminish the experience.

After all, you're only young and pink-tipped once. One of them rolled her eyes at me.

I had also managed to tune out the puffy, bickering couple next to us. Who knew that you could sustain a twenty-minute dispute about the flavor of gelato? Chocolate or nocciola? Obviously these two would never run out of things to fight about, and yet, they'd miraculously agreed to the same 49ers T-shirt.

We'd bumped into them before on the tourist walks in the area near Union Station. They always had plenty to argue with each other about.

The hulking guy right behind me was a bit harder to ignore. His large, pink, moon face was damp with sweat and his short-sleeved, blue-checked shirt strained at the buttons. He had clearly forgotten his deodorant this morning. Worse, he didn't appear to comprehend the idea of personal space.

Smiley turned and flashed his grin. I loved that little gap between his front teeth and the way his blond hair blew in the wind. I loved that we were here in this romantic city. I loved that I could still make him blush.

Two silver-haired ladies wearing Birkenstock sandals and Tilley hats nudged each other and smiled at us in approval. I recognized them from our hotel. I'd noticed their bright toenail polish in the lineup at the restaurant in the morning. Even though I was a bit jealous that they'd found seats on the cable car, I smiled back at them.

They each gave us a little wave as they eased their way to the exit behind me.

All the world loves a lover, as they say. Loves a lover! Imagine that. Smiley and I had taken a few sharp detours in our relationship. It was still hard to believe that we were on a getaway alone without hot and cold running relatives and the persistent, gravelly voice of my employer, Vera Van Alst. Could a cop with ambitions to be a detective and a girl who was the first person in her family to go legit have a chance at happiness?

So far, it was looking good.

Powell Street, he mouthed. Smiley had a thing for Dashiell Hammett, and Powell Street was important to him too. He brought up the name every few minutes. He had also mentioned something to do with Sam Spade every few minutes on our cable car ride. As far as I could see, he'd watched *The Maltese Falcon* once too often as a child. It seemed that his grandfather was to blame. I knew all about fascinations with fictional characters and settings. So I got that. But I had just discovered this classic noir detective and I was reserving judgment about Hammett and his gang.

Today, Smiley was also busy snapping pictures. I was equally busy hanging on to my gray fedora because of the bouncy ride and the stiff breeze. That fedora had been the perfect vintage find that morning and just right for San Francisco. It was sort of inspired by Sam Spade (see reserving judgment, above), but mainly I wore it because the foggy damp air turned my mid-length dark hair into wild frizz. It was either the fedora or a brown paper bag.

It was our third trip on this particular line. We had three-day visitor passports and Smiley wanted us to get our twenty bucks' worth on every form of transportation.

Much of it had to do with getting to know the city of Sam Spade. Smiley had a strong desire to visit Burrett Alley, off Stockton, where there was supposed to be a sign commemorating the shooting of Miles Archer in *The Maltese Falcon*. Pulp and noir were not my thing, and to tell the truth, I'd been a bit surprised that Smiley was such an aficionado. I preferred the gentle sleuths of the Golden Age of Detection and, of course, any book with Archie Goodwin in it. But if he wanted to see that memorial to a fictional murder, I was fine with it as long as I could keep my hat on.

Smiley had managed to turn full circle as we proceeded to the next block. There couldn't be a building he hadn't captured for posterity. There were plenty of shots of me too. That was fine as my hair was covered and I had lots to smile about.

"Seafood tonight?" he shouted, suddenly serious.

Well, how about that? I had yet another prospect to smile about. "We're in the right city for it."

My response was lost in the racket.

We shuddered to a stop again and people pushed onto the cable car. I tried not to get separated from Smiley as passengers squeezed their way through the car and a short, bullet-shaped man with crisply gelled black hair attempted to shoulder his way between us. The cable car lurched forward. I steadied myself by grabbing Smiley's belt with one hand. I held on to my hat with the other. "Sorry," I said to the bullet-shaped man, who seemed determined to take up more space.

I guess I'd been in the friendly, civil society of Harrison Falls, in upstate New York, for a bit too long. I wasn't used to jockeying for position in tight spots.

Bullet-man flashed me a bleak look and eased behind me. Good. Let him experience the big stinky guy firsthand.

Smiley was pointing now, his enthusiastic words carried away on the wind. No question about it. He was adorable. And he wasn't the first person to develop a fascination with Sam Spade or the Continental Op. I'd get my turn too. I couldn't wait to get to Haight-Ashbury and its vintage stores.

I gasped as my hat flew off. As I reached for the airborne fedora, something slammed hard into my back, knocking the breath out of me. I lost hold of Smiley as I tumbled forward. When I managed to steady myself, a second sharp slam accelerated my fall. Panicked, I tried to grab at nearby arms and legs, but too little too late. With a roar of shouting voices behind me, I plunged, screaming wordlessly, from the lumbering cable car toward the pavement, my head set to meet Powell Street the hard way.

But I'm getting ahead of my story.

Let me start at the beginning.

CHAPTER ONE

Tell them what they want to hear.
—THE KELLY RULES

IT BEGAN ON a sunny June morning, over a delicious breakfast served at eight sharp in the conservatory of Van Alst House, the crumbling mansion where I'm lucky to live. Birds were trilling from the mature trees surrounding the expansive Van Alst property. A vase of French white lilacs scented the air, and from the windows we could see clusters of pink, white and red peonies beginning to bloom.

Walter the Pug was dancing around and wagging his little stump of a tail to show his appreciation for the day and the breakfast leftovers to come. Walter belongs to my friend Karen Smith, who married my uncle Lucky not that long ago. As their life appears to be one long mobile honeymoon, Walter now spends most of his time with me. That's a good thing.

But once I polished off my plate of sizzling golden French toast with whipped cream and mixed berries, plus a bracing serving of espresso, I had the nerve to ask for a week off. What was I thinking?

Vera Van Alst glanced up from the *New York Times*

crossword. Her glance turned to a glower. Although the sun was beaming through the windows of the conservatory, I felt dark clouds gather.

Uncle Kev paused in the middle of raising his forkful of French toast and grinned. Vera's cook and housekeeper, Signora Panetone, gasped. I did my best not to grimace, even though exaggerated facial expressions seemed the order of the day.

Vera pushed back the fraying cuffs of her drab beige sweater. "Absolutely not, Miss Bingham. I do not pay you to take vacations. What do you think this is? A charitable institution?"

I opened my mouth to give a calm and reasoned summary of why I should be entitled to a week off. "Obviously you're not a charity," I said. "But as I have been working steadily for nearly two years and I—"

Those dark clouds began to drift across the bright June sky.

"We can't lose sight of the Hammett purchase. Time is of the essence." Vera turned back to her puzzle and raised her hand to cut off a rebuttal from my end.

This kind of discussion wasn't all that unusual for breakfast at Van Alst House. I'd grown accustomed to Vera's bad temper, ghastly wardrobe and unreasonable demands. I didn't let her get me down. She might be rich, living in a stately home with staff to look after her whims. She might indulge her passion of book collecting with a single-minded lack of concern for other people. She might always expect to get her own way. Still, I had it good. My job came with a charming and cozy attic apartment and the best food I'd ever had. I had a flexible schedule, a job I loved and a chance to make a bit of money on the side. Life was great. I'd even adjusted to having Uncle Kev, that charming time bomb, sitting across from me in the conservatory in the mornings and in the formal dining room in the night. Kev worked as our maintenance man, gardener and "other duties as required" guy. So far, no real disasters, if you don't count the exploding still, but I knew our peaceful days were numbered.

There was no way I could let Vera prevent me from taking my first vacation in I couldn't remember how long. Let's just say, I'd been beyond broke before I started here, and since my first day on the job, we had been remarkably busy. In case you don't know, my job was finding first editions of mysteries from the Golden Age of Detection and brokering deals that enhanced Vera's collection. Generally pleasant work although occasionally saving Vera's life seemed to fall under my duties. I could be spared for seven days. I wasn't an indentured serf, after all.

"Fine," I said, stiffening my spine and looking straight at Vera. "I'll take the time off without pay."

It wouldn't do my savings much good to lose a week's salary, but if Vera actually had the nerve to accept the offer, it would still be worth it. After all, Tyler Dekker had anted up for two airline tickets to San Francisco and a hotel, his way of making up for a few rocky patches in our relationship. We'd both had a bit too much murder in our lives and this trip was supposed to help us get back to normal. I had found myself dreaming about a relaxed pleasant vacation without a care in the world.

San Francisco was the old haunt of my uncle Seamus, now living as legend only, possibly in Rio or Tahiti. I'd heard stories about Seamus since I was a child. Although Seamus vanished from our lives before I was born, his sage advice continues on in our family as "the Kelly Rules." I would get to visit and see the spots where he'd pulled off some spectacular jobs. Perhaps I wouldn't make too much of it in front of my favorite police officer.

Vera was staring at her crossword puzzle as if the conversation had ended.

"You really shouldn't trust that Dekker guy enough to go away with him, Jordie," Uncle Kev said, before stuffing his mouth again. "What do you really know about him?"

What did I know about Tyler? I knew he was honest and stubborn and extremely neat. I knew we had rescued each other from disaster and near-death more than once. I knew he'd been willing to change jobs to keep our romance going. I knew we both loved dogs and chocolate. And apparently—although this was new information to me—he also had a thing for classic noir mysteries.

I hoped we could work past our misunderstandings and different values, because I also knew the spark was there.

"He is a cop, Kev, not a serial killer."

"Police officer. That says it all."

Kev's point could have been made by any of my uncles. I was the first person in my large, larcenous family to take the path of honest work. My relatives had put a bit of a strain on my relationship with Smiley, but we had worked past it, mostly. It was my side that couldn't trust a cop, even if he had left the job he loved and moved to the next police jurisdiction to avoid conflict of interest issues.

I said, "Don't worry."

Kev shrugged and reached for the maple syrup. "Be very careful is all I'm sayin', Jordie. That's the other side of the country and people get sucked out of planes all the time."

"For the record, Kev, people do not 'get sucked out of planes all the time,' and even if they did, which they do not, what would that have to do with Tyler Dekker?"

"Like I said, he's a cop."

There are some arguments that just go round and round. Most of Uncle Kev's, for instance.

Vera had upgraded her expression to a full-fledged scowl. She glanced up and met my eyes. "You are needed here, Miss Bingham. End of discussion."

I said, "Hold on a minute—"

Bingha...

I felt like...
needed the job...
That wasn't asking...

I was pretty sure...
bluff? This position w...
to get back to grad sc...
modations and that cha...
I was able to save almost...

Vera was spoiled and d...
She could have remembere...
reputation and her books more...
she was being funny. She was...
points of humor.

I glanced at Kev and then back to Vera, but they were both gawking at the signora.

Signora Panetone is tiny, round and black-clad with an unlikely ebony bun that looks like it's been painted on her scalp. She will never see eighty again. At this moment she was hovering with a pale green platter and was just about to transfer a piece of French toast onto Vera's plate. Getting food to our boss usually takes planning as Vera never willingly eats anything. The signora jerked back the platter, pivoted and walked away. Vera, Kev and I regarded her broad, black-garbed body lumbering toward the kitchen.

Time ticked by as we sat there openmouthed. Such a thing had never happened in my time with Vera. The signora has worked at Van Alst House since Vera was a child. She is devoted. The door to the kitchen swung closed behind the wide black behind.

We may have still been staring two minutes later. The signora emerged with two little red spots glowing on her wrinkled cheeks. Her hands were on her hips.

"*Ragazza viziata!*" She turned and the door swung closed

...ount of Italian in
...s a new one. I thought

...vatory. I could hear Uncle
...re he was worried about losing
...square meals a day if I got fired.
...too, losing out on all the food and
...of Jolly Ranchers that Vera kept in the

...s thrilled by this unlikely ally. Unless I had
...ood what had upset the signora, Vera had crossed
...nd, in fact, she *had* crossed a line. Not only was I
...al employee, but I had *also* put my life on the line for
...ra more than once and I deserved reasonable treatment.
And I needed to seize the moment.

"So," I said, "back to my question. I'll take the week off
with no pay, if you'd like, or I'll make up the time before or
after the trip and take the pay. What will it be?"

But Vera was watching the door. Could she have been
nervous? Not possible. No history of that whatsoever.

"The Hammett item takes precedence over everything,
Miss Bingham." Obviously, she was prepared to stick to her
guns although I thought I heard a wobble in that gravelly
voice. But I was also sticking to my guns. Smiley had bought
nonrefundable tickets, which might not have been the most
practical plan as he'd done it before I'd agreed. It was a big
deal for him. San Francisco might have been a romantic
city, but Smiley was such a fan of Sam Spade and the Continental Op that—oh, what was the matter with me?

"Exactly," I said, smiling triumphantly.

"What are you jabbering about, Miss Bingham?"
Vera said. She'd lost a bit of her fire when the signora
stormed out.

From the kitchen came a one-sided conversation in
Italian.

"*Cattiva! Schifosa! Bruta!*" What? Ugly? Wicked? Bad? Wow.

The kitchen door swung open and the signora emerged, empty handed, arms crossing her round body. She gave Vera what is known around here as *malocchio*, the evil eye. I'd just never expected to see that directed at Vera. It suddenly occurred to me that Vera had learned her scowling from this unexpected teacher.

They glared each other down. The musical score from *High Noon* hummed in my brain. Walter whimpered and pushed up against my leg. Good Cat and Bad Cat, the unpredictable and ever-present Siamese, were nowhere to be seen.

"You let *la povera ragazza* go to vacation, Vera."

Generally, I wouldn't like to be thought of as the "poor girl," but these were desperate times.

Uncle Kev's baby blues almost popped out. I'm sure my own eyes were hovering in midair, like a frame out of *Roger Rabbit*.

Vera opened her mouth slowly and ominously.

This was not a light moment.

I said in what I hoped was an up-tempo voice, "San Francisco was Hammett's town, Vera. He's a legend there, part of the culture. Surely that's where we'll find a signed first edition of *Red Harvest*, right there in Hammett's old neighborhood. And with the shipping on someone else's dime. It's settled."

The signora viewed with me suspicion. Probably there was little she'd have understood in that sentence.

Vera nodded slowly. You'd almost think she was grateful for my Hail Mary pass.

The signora spoke. "Jordan needs vacation. She saved your life, Vera. You pay Jordan, Vera. Don't take 'vantage."

Vera sputtered. Keeping face had always been important to the Van Alst family, and now there was only Vera to uphold the tradition. "Fine. Suit yourself, Fiammetta."

The signora's black eyes shone victoriously. Her cheeks were flushed with triumph. She smoothed her vast floral apron like a general dusting off his epaulettes. I hoped I wasn't dreaming.

"Don't let things get behind. I won't tolerate that. Twelve hundred, tops. Negotiate. I'll give you cash," Vera muttered in my general direction. That sounded like the real Vera. I took her words to mean my vacation to San Francisco was a go and I would pay the price for it on my return.

"That's good then. I should go make arrangements."

"You know I can't stand chirping, Miss Bingham."

"I couldn't agree more," I chirped.

The signora emerged again with the French toast, and Uncle Kev reached happily forward with his plate. The signora beamed at him like he had just cured world hunger. Vera turned back to her crossword.

Peace and harmony fell upon our land. Except I had not the slightest idea how I was going to get that signed first edition of *Red Harvest*. But you only live once. And I'd cross that golden gate when I came to it. I was going to San Francisco.

Only one more mountain to climb before it was time to pack.

CHAPTER TWO

Don't trust anyone except maybe family.
—THE KELLY RULES

V ERA WAS NOT the only obstacle to a blissful vacation
and not even the main one. You can quit your job, but it
would be hard to quit your family. There was still Uncle Mick
to contend with. Fortunately Uncle Lucky was still in New
York City with Karen. At least I wasn't outnumbered.

"But to think what he does for a living!" Uncle Mick
moaned as he put the finishing touches (mustard) on fried
baloney sandwiches, a specialty of the Kelly kitchen. He
wiped his hands on his Kiss the Blarney Stone apron with
the downward-pointing arrow. His ginger hair seemed to
grow redder and his ginger eyebrows wilder.

"He's a police officer."

"Exactly, the police thing, and what does that tell you,
my girl?"

"It tells me I'll be safe with him, among other things. Oh,
and he probably won't take my wallet while I'm sleeping."

Change of tactic from Uncle Mick. "What kind of family
sends their boys to the police?"

"First of all, Tyler is not a boy, and second, the same kind of family whose boys become . . ." In my family we call them independent business people or entrepreneurs.

No way was I telling Uncle Mick that Tyler "Smiley" Dekker was estranged from his parents over becoming a police officer. I didn't have the full story, but it seemed that being a cop was too big a step down the social ladder for them. Over time Uncle Mick might have been able to come to grips with the "police thing" but estranged from family? That would be a deal breaker.

I bent forward and let stars shine in my eyes. "San Francisco was Uncle Seamus's town. I've always wanted to visit."

Mick leaned back and grinned happily. "Ah, our boy Seamus, now there was a lad."

"I grew up on those stories! Remember?"

"How could I ever forget our Seamus and his shenanigans?"

"Remember when he 'liberated' the emerald and diamond choker from the twenty-sixth floor of that five-star hotel and he scrambled all the way around the building from balcony to balcony?" As a girl, I had imagined Uncle Seamus to be like Spiderman only with red, fuzzy eyebrows and a gold chain in his ginger chest hair.

"And him afraid of heights! He was a scallywag!"

A fool more like it, but now I was on a roll. "And wasn't there some great story about a maid?"

"Indeed, all the ladies loved our Seamus. He was like catnip to a calico."

"Was he?"

"He always got away right under the noses of the police."

"How did he do that?" Of course, I could have told this and a dozen other Uncle Seamus stories myself without any prompting, but it was more fun this way.

"Talked the silly girl right out of her uniform, he did, and wheeled the cart down the hallway. The *po*-lice even checked in the cart to see if anything was hidden and they still didn't notice it was him pushing it."

"They couldn't have been trying very hard if they didn't spot he was a man, Uncle Mick."

"Indeed, our Seamus was always a bit delicate in appearance, had to be small and agile in his line of work. And anyway, he knew the cops wouldn't even give a second look to that poor girl. No one sees past a uniform. You should know that."

"And I suppose he didn't have a five o'clock shadow."

"Scrupulously groomed at all times was Seamus." He paused, probably wondering if he should say, "Rest his soul." We'd never been sure of what happened to Uncle Seamus in the aftermath of a heist that involved a diamond necklace belonging to the second girlfriend of a minor mobster named Les "the Bat" Blatt, known for his interrogation techniques with an aluminum baseball bat. We often say "rest his soul" in this family, but when it comes to Seamus, we go silent.

"And the maid, what do you think she did without her uniform?"

"What any sensible female would do! Took some clothing from the room she was cleaning and walked right outta there."

Not everyone lived by the rules of the Kelly family. I hoped the chambermaid in the story wasn't made to pay for her mistake.

Uncle Mick was on a roll now.

"So you see," I said, "this trip would be like a pilgrimage for me."

Before I left, he had me doubled over retelling the famous story of Uncle Seamus, his pockets stuffed with cash, racing through a hotel kitchen, flinging pots of water behind him to slip up his pursuers. Being Seamus, he managed to score an excellent meal on his way to freedom. In some versions it was a plate of caviar, but in this one, it was a chateaubriand for two and a bottle of brandy.

I changed the topic briefly on my way out. "Vera needs me to get a copy of *Red Harvest* in San Francisco."

"And that's a book?"

"Bingo. It's a book by Dashiell Hammett."

"Why can't you get it here?"

"Well, it's an old book and she wants a first edition signed by the author. And she wants it from his old haunt of San Francisco. It's not my type of reading but she claims it was an important piece, the transition of a genre from pulp into mainstream and I quote, '*The absurd violence seems to captivate people of a lower distinction*.'"

Mick shook his lionlike mane. "You must admit that thing for these old books is awful weird, my girl."

"It's the way I make my living, Uncle Mick. I can't bad-mouth her."

"Good for you. No one else in Harrison Falls can stand the woman."

And that wasn't entirely fair to Vera, the sins of the fathers and all that. "So I wonder if you have any connections in San Francisco that might help me to find a copy."

"Through unorthodox channels, you mean?"

"No," I said firmly. "Through regular legitimate business people only. I wondered if you knew someone who is familiar with the rare book community there. I'd be grateful if you had a lead."

"Well, there might be someone. Leave it with me, my girl, and I'll keep you posted."

Of course, I was capable of tracking down that copy, but now Uncle Mick's mind was off Tyler and his family for the time being. He had a project. And I was good to go.

SOMETIMES YOUR FRIENDS can be tougher than your family. My two best friends, Tiffany Tibeaut, currently on a nursing gig in the nearby town of Grandville, and Lance DeWitt, reference librarian and heartthrob at the Harrison Falls Public Library, both felt entitled to opinions on this and, in fact, all aspects of my life.

Tiff's text kicked off with an emoji of an engagement ring and an instruction. Don't get pressured into it. It's a huge step.

Really, Tiff? Pressured into it? Whatever you can say about Tyler Dekker, he had never pressured me. For sure, he'd hung around, causing great anxiety in the uncle sector, but he wasn't pushy except for that time he arrested me. He was relaxed, if you didn't count the occasions where he thought I was mixed up in something criminal. All misunderstandings, currently cleared up.

Tiff was not alone in her disapproval.

Lance was having none of it when I dropped by the Harrison Falls Library reference department to share my exciting plans. I waited in a lineup of Lance's octogenarian regulars to get my turn. As usual, he was drop-dead gorgeous and I was not the only person who thought that. As I waited patiently, I wondered what would have happened if my old buddy relationship with Lance had ever progressed past the crying on each other's shoulders to something more serious. I shook my head. Now Smiley was the man in my life, and Lance was one of my two best friends.

It started off well enough. "Hey, beautiful lady," he said, smiling that ultra-white smile of his. Lance looks like a movie star and sounds like a matinee idol from the forties. I broke the news to him before Tiff did.

"San Francisco? With Dekker? Are you out of your mind? What do you really know about this guy, Jordan?"

"Be serious."

"Excuse me, young woman, but other people need to talk to the librarian too, you know."

I knew better than to argue with any of Lance's posse. Lance took me by the elbow and led me out of the reference room and along the hallway to the safety of the staff room.

"You've had some betrayals and a lot of serious and dangerous events in the last couple of years."

"True, but—"

"Just sayin', take your time. Who knows what his motivations could be?"

My voice rose to an unappealing squeak. "Right. What motivations could he have for taking me to San Francisco, Lance? Couldn't he betray me in a less expensive way by staying home? It's a ridiculous allegation, which, by the way, is also light on detail."

He shrugged. "Your family, maybe."

"What do you mean?" I lowered my voice to a whisper as one of Lance's colleagues had come into the room.

"Sorry," she said. "Didn't realize you were here."

"No problem at all. I was just leaving."

Back in the hallway, Lance caught up to me and put his arms around me. "Don't be mad. But *you* are a route into relatives and their secrets—not that I know anything about them and those secrets—and *he* is an ambitious police officer. Just be sure you know what you're getting into. I'm your friend, beautiful lady, and I don't say this lightly."

"You say everything lightly."

But although I laughed, Lance's words stayed with me, even when I reached San Francisco with Tyler.

DASHIELL HAMMETT WAS known for a lot of things, relationship counseling not among them. Smiley and I had embarked on a cross-country trip with two flight changes and a three-hour time difference. We had never been anywhere together before, if you didn't count being trapped in a locked cellar in a burning building, facing down several killers or otherwise staring death in the face, but this isn't the time to talk about that. Sure, we knew all about stress, but we didn't know how to take a vacation as a couple.

One canceled flight had resulted in a trickle-down effect. Our thirteen-hour bargain trip ended up closer to twenty-four. In that time, we'd sprinted through JFK Airport, missed one connection and wished we'd also missed two very rough landings. We'd been rerouted on an extra leg, lost half our luggage and more than one meal. We'd spent our time on the flights we did make with our knees near our noses. Did there always have to be someone who insisted on putting the seat back as far into our space as possible? And what was with the kid kicking our seats in the back? Since when did potato chips stand in for lunch? And how was it some passengers managed to eat them so loudly?

But none of it mattered because we were both in a mood for Dashiell Hammett and we were each reading different books. We each had our own favorite detective. I was getting to know the Continental Op for the first time. I was new to Hammett's world and characters. Smiley was revisiting his old hard-boiled hero, Sam Spade, in *The Maltese Falcon*. I supposed we could go for joint custody of Nick and Nora Charles when the time came. In the meantime, having a good book can make a trying time seem pleasant. Hammett had that right sense of suspense. As for me, I decided I liked the idea of the fat private eye. Hammett liked to borrow from real life, and when he was a Pinkerton operative, he'd worked the Virginia Rappe murder investigation and film star Fatty Arbuckle had been the prime suspect. It must have sparked a bit of an obsession as many of Hammett's characters were nameless fat guys. I admired his keen sense of observation but found his gloomy view of human nature a bit of a downer. I lived with Vera. I already got my daily dose of downers. I turned my book over and gave Smiley a hug. At least I could count on him to do the right thing.

THE GREAT THING about travel is that, no matter how dragged out you are when you get to your destination, after a shower and a rest, you feel like a normal human being. I reveled in the excitement of being in this amazing city from

the moment we left the airport. Even the air was different
in San Francisco. I loved the hills and the houses that seemed
to be perched on them precariously. I enjoyed the rush and
roar of the traffic. It felt like an exotic country and we hadn't
even arrived in the city. I guess we made the right decision
not to rent a car because I couldn't imagine driving here
after sleepy little Harrison Falls. Smiley would have been
okay, but we'd already decided to use our feet and transit in
the city and maybe rent a car for a day if we wanted to visit
wine country. We'd lost nearly a day of our planned visit
because of the flight delays so we needed to pack stuff in.

I was glad all I had to do besides indulge on this vacation
was to get that Hammett book for Vera.

Smiley had many plans, most of them also connected in
some way to Dashiell Hammett. I had my own list of To
Do's. Locating and purchasing *Red Harvest* was the easy
one. But I wanted to get something special for my guy to
compensate for the trip.

Smiley knocked on the door that connected our two
rooms. Have I mentioned that part of the deal was separate
hotel rooms? If our trip didn't work out and for sure everyone
was warning me, I still wanted to have a room I could sulk
in. Maybe it meant I still wanted my freedom. Whatever, it
wasn't like we were in any kind of a race.

My phone buzzed. Tiff texting. All good?

Trip was a bit of a nightmare, but we made it. LOL.

Have fun. Send pix. Winky face.

I will.

LA PERLA, A charming independent hotel, was on the
small side, only nine floors, with well-appointed rooms most

with a balcony that ran the width of the room. I have a thing for balconies. Call it my Juliet side. And of course, Uncle Seamus once made a daring getaway with a bed sheet from a balcony without dropping his bag of loot. Although I'd never told him anything about the legendary Uncle Seamus, Smiley knew I loved balconies. He'd made sure our rooms had perfect examples.

The reception staff seemed friendly and the other guests pleasant enough. A pair of silver-haired ladies wearing Birkenstocks and Tilley hats were in the line to check in after us.

"Your first visit?" the taller one asked.

"Yes, we've only been here in movies," Smiley said.

They both grinned. The shorter one said with a wink, "I'm sure you'll find real life in this city very exciting."

Smiley and I exchanged glances. I wondered if whatever Smiley had in mind would be exciting. Or romantic. Whatever San Francisco had to offer would be perfect. A vacation, after all, didn't just happen every day or, in my case, every year.

Our side-by-side rooms when we got to them were clean and attractive, renovated within recent memory and stocked with artisanal soap and hair products and wonderful hand lotion that smelled like roses. My bed was perfect with a crisp white duvet and masses of pillows. I pulled back the drapes and the sheers, to let some light into the room, then unpacked and took a deep breath. After a rest, a shower and a change of clothes, I stepped out onto the balcony. Smiley had stepped out onto his. He was looking even more relaxed than usual. Of course, with Smiley, looks can be deceiving.

From either of the balconies, we could experience the fog and hear the gulls. A row of potted trees provided privacy on each one, and probably meant that the small white table and lounge chairs would be well used by guests. You could even catch a bit of sun if there had been any.

We couldn't actually see the bay through the thick mist but we felt it.

"Come on over," I said. "The party's started."

"I'll get some wine and put on some fog screen," he said.

I'd been told that one of the nice things about San Francisco is the mild weather no matter when you go. Never too hot to walk for hours and miles up and down hills, and I do mean hills. Even on the road in from the airport to the center of the city, I'd seen streets that seemed to be on forty-five-degree angles.

Despite the fog, it wasn't cold. I'd read enough to know that it was rarely too chilly to sit outside on a balcony. Our June weather was perfect. I had a long loose cable knit sweater scarf draped over my shoulders, mostly just because I liked the look.

He arrived with a bottle of crisp Pinot Grigio and two glasses.

On our small table between us I'd laid out the *Eyewitness Guide to San Francisco*. From that we'd be making plans for our days around town. Smiley's goal was to revisit Dashiell Hammett's haunts. I am a book person. He isn't. I am a vintage person. He isn't. I come from a family of beguiling fraudsters. His lifelong ambition was to be a cop. But we could agree on a few things: the crisp white Napa Valley wine, good food, especially when we hadn't prepared it, and the fun of exploring a city we'd only seen on the screen until this point.

He gazed out over the courtyard below us. Tourists were sauntering and locals moving purposefully to their destinations. After a day traveling by air, I was thrilled to be at my own destination. I'd had a chance to unkink from the flight. We'd planned to stroll out to dinner at tourist speed, say one mile an hour, and then amble along near the water after dinner. Things could not have been better.

I don't know quite when I first noticed that Smiley was

not entirely himself. I had made a commitment not to try to pry. Travel can be tiring, I decided, and he'd been very tied up in selling his small, immaculate brick house so that he could move to the next town over the county line for his new job. I couldn't help feeling a bit guilty about that, though I hadn't asked him to make this sacrifice. Having the Kelly family as connections would have meant career suicide in Harrison Falls, even though my uncles had never actually been convicted of anything, if you didn't count that unfortunate business with Uncle Kev in his youth.

I squeezed his hand. "I'm sorry."

He looked startled. "Sorry for what?"

"Putting you in the position where you had to move."

"You didn't do that. I made that decision."

I took a sip. "Right, but it was awkward for you."

"Life's full of awkwardness." He grinned. "It's nothing."

"I don't know. Giving up your house and your job with the Harrison Falls force, that was something, if you ask me."

"You know that there wasn't any future for me there, even leaving aside—"

"My relatives."

He shrugged and gazed off into the distance. "You know what they say. You can pick your friends, but you can't pick your relatives. I picked you."

There was no choice but to give him a hug over that. He had picked me. And I chose not to say that even though my uncles were as crooked as a bag of snakes, they had raised me and they were kind and loving, and if I'd had the choice, I would definitely have picked them. The problem was, I had also picked Officer Tyler Dekker.

"Don't forget," he said, "I'll be a detective when I start the job in Cabot. That's a step up. I call it a win."

That was worth a clink. "Congratulations. My hero."

"All I have to do is show up on time. If I'd stayed in Harrison Falls, I'd probably have had to wait for years for

Detective Castellano to move up to chief and Stoddard to die of boredom."

True. His superior officer and her sidekick hadn't been going anywhere.

I had no choice but to ask, "So why are you looking so down?"

He gave a little start. "What? Me? I'm not glum. I've been waiting for this chance to get—"

"Never kid a kidder, Tyler." I raised one eyebrow so he'd see I meant business.

He flushed to the roots of his blond hair. "Maybe it's better if I tell you the whole story over dinner."

I decided it could wait. I sipped my delicious wine and basked in the fog. My heart was beating just a wee bit faster than normal, though.

CALL ME OLD-FASHIONED although I prefer vintage, but I like to up my game for dinner. I kept my mind off whatever "the whole story" was by concentrating on what to wear. My charcoal cashmere sweater dress would keep me from catching a chill off the bay. I paired it with matching tights and scarlet ankle boots with little gold zippers. Even though the dress was years old, someone had loved it and cared for it and then I'd been lucky enough to snatch it up for a song at a vintage shop.

Smiley had found a large, beautiful seafood restaurant with a spectacular view of the water. It seemed extravagant to me. I knew he was juggling a move, selling his house at a time when the market in Harrison Falls favored buyers and yet the market in Cabot, a mere half hour away, seemed to favor the seller. If the Town of Cabot Police Department hadn't had a rule that officers had to live within the town limits, he wouldn't have had a problem.

"I don't care," he said. "This is our first night here. It's our first vacation after several brushes with death and I'm willing to use my savings to have a great time. Try to cope."

"Well, I'll contribute my share." Of course, I hated to pay the big bucks for upscale restaurants because I had a very specific goal for my savings, but it was the right thing to do. And I was spoiled rotten with the signora's cooking all year long.

"This one's on me," he said with a grin. "Humor me, Jordan."

Pick your battles, as they say.

EVEN THOUGH THE sun had finally peeked out, it was still cool. I was glad I'd worn the timeless cashmere dress as there were plenty of chic women there. Lots of people were wearing comfy touristy garb, but it was a place you could be happy if you dressed up.

There were candles glowing on each table and soft lighting and a haunting view of the water. Perfect. Smiley had managed to arrange for a table for two with what had to be the best view in the house.

Our waiter had recommended a jewel-like Napa Valley cabernet. It was almost hypnotic as it glowed in our oversized red wine goblets. I felt very grown up.

Next to us, two young couples flirted; the women tossed their long hair (almost certainly extensions) and jingled their gold bangles. They both spoke with their heads at an angle. The blonde played with a few strands of hair. The redhead traced little patterns on her date's forearm.

I figured both women had wasted quite a bit of time in tanning beds.

Tyler still seemed subdued. He gazed off in the distance, but not at the stunning view. All of sudden, it hit me. Was he really planning to propose? Was that the reason for his unusual mood? He is not known as Smiley for nothing. I have my ups and downs and my ginger-haired relatives are always flying off the handle about nothing important, but Tyler is resilient and usually pretty cheerful. As a rule, he's almost too good to be true. I couldn't figure out the reason for his mood. Maybe it was reading Hammett? The whole mean streets noir thing. For sure, Hammett's life hadn't been all roses and it was reflected in his writing. It was kind of the opposite of Tyler, who—despite the emotional limitations of his family—was optimistic, cheerful and expected a good outcome. He seemed immune to the evils of the world.

"A bit gloomy, I gotta admit, but fun to read."

He blinked.

"Hammett," I said by way of explanation.

"Oh yeah, he's great. I love the whole vibe."

"Right, me too."

So not Hammett, then.

He turned toward me and met my eyes, a searching enquiry I wasn't used to.

On the other hand, maybe it wasn't what he'd been reading. I had a sinking feeling this was more serious. He felt around his pocket. My heart constricted. What if this entire trip was the setup for a proposal? That was the last thing I wanted. I was still finding my way in this world. I'd just managed to get out from under my uncles' constant surveillance and "helpful" advice. I was still a way from achieving my dream of returning to work on my graduate degree in Victorian literature. I was barely healed after the worst romantic relationship in my life: broken heart, plundered bank account, maxed-out credit cards. Even though the breaker of my heart had gotten what was coming to him, I still had flashbacks. Still, Tyler Dekker was pretty terrific. I loved the way his skin could go from pale as snow to sunset red with just one kiss.

He was smart, kind, flexible and affectionate.

He loved dogs.

He loved chocolate.

It wasn't him. It was me.

It was too early.

I smiled tightly and raised my glass of cabernet.

"Jordan?"

"Mmm?"

"Would you—"

I took a deep breath. *Be brave*, I told myself. *You can do this.*

The waiter materialized, seemingly out of thin air. "Do you need a bit more time with the menu?"

We hadn't even looked at it.

Smiley looked bemused and nodded toward me.

I said. "Just a few minutes. Sorry."

"No worries. I'll be back."

"I suppose I should make a decision. It's actually getting late."

The sun was beginning to set, leaving a rosy glow over the water. We watched as the glow spread along the horizon. It seemed a waste to turn our eyes away to the menu, but as the brilliant light faded, we did.

I went for seafood chowder and the spicy crab cakes. He decided on pistachio-crusted halibut with no appetizer. "Not that hungry. Maybe it's the time difference. I don't usually eat dinner at midnight our time."

Of course, he didn't spend all his time at Van Alst House, where the signora was likely to spring a pile of food on you at any time, including midnight. I'd been in training for nearly two years.

"So there's something I've been meaning to ask you," he said.

I couldn't help shifting my gaze to the next table, where a fiftyish couple had been sitting almost as long as we had. He had taken out his smart phone and she stared out over the glittering water. So far they hadn't spoken to each other or given each other a glance. Each of them pointed to their choices when the server came by and then returned to their solitary activities.

I leaned forward. "Married too long," I whispered, giving a sideways nod in their direction.

Smiley blinked.

I mouthed, *Bored to tears.*

He shrugged. "Maybe they're business colleagues and they just can't stand each other."

"No," I insisted. "They're married."

"Sure. Not every ending is happily ever after." He clinked my glass. We were very clinky on this trip.

"Or at all." Geez, why did I say that? Leave it to me to find a tiny gap in which to insert my foot.

He put down the glass and frowned a bit. "Is something wrong, Jordan?"

"Of course not. I was just observing things."

"But are you having a good time?"

"Absolutely. I love San Francisco and it's a great trip. So relaxed. No big deals about anything."

He blinked. "True, I guess, although I was just about to make a big deal about something."

Gulp. I drained my pricey cab.

CHAPTER THREE

Everybody's after something.
—THE KELLY RULES

*H*ERE GOES NOTHING, I thought with my heart thundering. I didn't want to hurt Tyler. There was no one in the world I cared more for, except maybe my uncles on Christmas morning. But I had no idea what I'd respond if he asked what I thought he was going to. The thought did flutter through my mind that I didn't have many positive role models for happy marriages. I knew very little about my own parents. My uncles had all played the field (except for Mick's two Russian brides, but never mind them). But then Uncle Lucky had married my friend Karen Smith just last year and you could practically see the pink hearts floating in the air around their besotted heads.

"Jordan?" Tyler said. "You're miles away."

"Another glass of cabernet?" the waiter asked, having materialized out of nowhere, it seemed.

"Why not?" said Tyler.

I did my best to chill out. I wasn't sure how lovely he'd think I was at the end of the meal.

When my seafood chowder arrived, Tyler was fiddling with his bread.

"So," he said. "Can I just get this over with?"

"Shoot," I said.

"Really? Shoot?"

"Don't know where that came from. Maybe it's the grape talking." I raised my glass and took another sip.

"I'm going to shoot. Would you like to meet my grandmother?"

A bit of wine dribbled down my chin and onto my cashmere dress before I could stop it. "But you don't have a grandmother."

"Apparently, I do now. Would you like to meet her?"

What a relief! It was only a previously unknown grandmother, not a lifetime giving each other the silent treatment in restaurants.

"I really would."

"Me too. She's here."

I glanced around. "In this restaurant?"

"In San Francisco. Not all that far."

"And you are just finding this out right now?"

"Not right now. But, um, not long ago."

"You are as red as a beet. I'd like to know why."

"She got in touch."

"And you didn't know you had a grandmother?"

"No. *You* didn't know I had a grandmother. I just knew very little about her for the last twenty years and the bit I did know wasn't flattering."

I thought about my large, loud and intrusive family. I knew about fifth cousins in Dublin and the legendary Uncle Olaf from the tenth century who brought red hair and ginger eyebrows to the family from Scandinavia. I knew more than I should have about my own Grandma Kelly, who drove a mean getaway car and could roll a smoke with one hand.

The Binghams were another story altogether, but not a topic for today.

"Not flattering?"

"Well, she was estranged from our family. She cut us off."

"But why?"

"I don't know. I think there was something about my father she didn't like. When I was a kid, I remember her sending me lots of gifts and there were visits and phone calls and . . ."

"And?"

"And then it just stopped. My parents wouldn't talk about her. I figured she'd dropped us."

"That's . . ." I stopped short of saying reprehensible. "So, how did this come about?"

"She sought me out and asked to see me."

"But why didn't you mention it?"

"I guess I felt weird about it. She offered to pay my way."

"Did you accept?"

"That felt wrong. I said no. I still have bad feelings about what she did. She might be an old lady and she might want to make amends, but I didn't want to feel obliged. If I needed to walk away, I wanted to be able to do that."

"It's kind of weird that she contacted you around the same time you and I planned a vacation here, isn't it?"

"Not really."

"Oh, I think you'd better explain."

The waiter arrived with our entrées and slid the plates onto the white tablecloth in front of us with a flourish. Perhaps he'd been a magician in another life.

"Fresh ground pepper?"

As our meals were peppered, I grinned at Smiley. "And make it good."

The waiter withdrew with a strange little half bow and Smiley leaned forward. "For many years, I've heard from her on my birthday. I've never responded, but maybe that was what put the idea of San Francisco in my mind."

"You never responded?"

"She started up more frequent contact after I joined the police. Maybe she found out I was estranged from my parents." There it was again, that estrangement. What was with these Dekkers?

"And you didn't—"

He shrugged. "I guess I had trouble getting over her just leaving me when I was a child to go to San Francisco with her new husband."

"Oh, right. I can see that. But you're an adult now. Did you just ignore her?"

"Yeah. She sent a card every year."

"That was it?"

"Just a sentimental card. And her address."

"Huh."

"Well, what would you do?"

"But isn't she your only relative?"

"There are my parents, who don't speak to me."

"So then, you're nearly her only relative too?" I turned and gazed out the window. "I don't know what I'd do. I think I'd be very curious."

"I was. For one thing, how was she always able to find my address?"

"What do you mean?"

"I was away at college. I didn't live with my parents. Then I went on to the police academy and then I moved to my first couple of jobs, just temporary security things, and then on to Harrison Falls. But on my birthday, the card always came."

I tried not to react to the goose bumps. "That is, um, odd. It's like your grandmother is stalking you." To be fair to Grandma Stalkington, these days with social media, just about anyone could creep you.

"Exactly. Maybe that's why I resisted."

The waiter emerged from the ether again to inquire about our dinners. Those would be the dinners that had been rapidly cooling in front of us.

"Good," Smiley said without glancing at his untouched halibut.

"Excellent," I said with a fake smile. The waiter's eyes flicked from my face to my virgin plate. He matched my fake smile and departed.

"We should eat," I said, "midnight or not. I'll try not to badger you about your stalker grandmother. Hey, you know with all the kinds of things that have happened recently, do you really know she's your grandmother? Could it be some unscrupulous—"

"She is my grandmother. There's nothing unscrupulous about the approach. She has nothing to gain financially from me, as you know. And she is who she says she is."

"How do you know?"

"You may be aware that I am a police officer?"

"Right, I'd heard that."

"I did my due diligence."

"What kind of 'due diligence'?"

"You know, the usual, checked out records, online and all that. I have my ways."

I sat back and gasped. "You mean you stalked your own grandmother right back?"

There was the telltale flush, right from the collar to the hairline. I loved that.

"I did not stalk my own grandmother as you so ridiculously put it."

I couldn't hold back the laughter anymore. "Not sure what's worse, your granny stalking you or you stalking her. Next-level creepy."

Conversation had kind of died down around us. The long-married couple had stopped ignoring each other and started staring at us. One of the pretty girls with the extensions and the bangles said, "Ew." Oops. I didn't want my teasing to turn into some viral incident with people snapping shots on their cell phones.

Under the table I gave Smiley a little kick on the ankle and then stared straight at him. Somewhat belatedly, our would-be detective had realized that we were the entertainment in our section of the restaurant.

I said, "That's absolutely hilarious. It still needs a bit of work for your stand-up routine. You'll have everyone on the floor when you get the rough bits worked out. I think it would be funnier if you wanted your granny to be a bank robber instead of a stalker, you being a cop and all. Or you could invent a grandpa who spends all his time in his underwear smoking cigars and talking trash politics. Still it's your time at the mic."

People around us seemed to lose interest after that.

I grinned at the rose-colored police officer and lowered my voice. "So when do we meet her?"

He leaned forward and whispered. "Tomorrow seems like a good idea. I planned to phone and see what she wants. I don't know anything about how she spends her time. She could be pretty old and maybe's she sick. I wasn't able to find anything personal about her."

"She might not be that old. You're nearly twenty-nine. She is probably only in her eighties or even younger. She might pass you jogging for all you know."

He frowned at me.

"Oh, right, you don't jog."

He said, "Maybe we should try to enjoy our dinner?"

"You're right. It's a shame to waste this." For a couple of minutes we did justice to the food and hoped we were now very boring to everyone seated near us.

Tyler didn't manage more than half of his, but I did better

than that. Finally I couldn't resist asking, "Is it far from here? I'm betting that you know."

"It's too far to walk. Maybe we can sightsee in the morning and then go later. Or should I get it over with? What do you want to do tomorrow?"

"I think I mentioned how excited I am about exploring the vintage shops in Haight-Ashbury."

"Hardly more than a dozen times. But who am I to talk after all my prattling on about Sam Spade and the Continental Op?"

"We can each explore what we want. We have plenty of time here. Maybe you should find out what works for your grandmother first and we'll plan around that."

"Of course. It's actually planned." He exhaled.

I guess I hadn't realized he must have been holding his breath. "What is it?"

"I feel so relieved. I've been carrying this thing around in my head. Why does she want to meet?"

"Maybe she feels bad about abandoning you."

He shrugged. "I wasn't feeling too friendly towards her. She reminded me to call her 'Gram,' but I can't do that yet."

"And now?"

"There's a lot of water under the bridge. I'll see what she has to say. It's set for tomorrow morning."

I raised my glass. "Here's to reframing the past."

Clink. Clink. Yet again.

He said, "I guess we're doing that for ourselves too."

Well, that was an understatement.

CHAPTER FOUR

Stay out of dark alleys.
—THE KELLY RULES

THE STROLL TO the hotel was as romantic as it could have been for two people who had each had more wine than they were used to and who found themselves feeling their way through the fog in an unfamiliar city. We took a shortcut through a short alley, walking hand in hand, leaning against each other and feeling like this was turning into the perfect holiday together after all. Note to self: Do not tempt fate.

We weren't paying attention to our surroundings, to this city steeped in the history of adventures, gold rush and disaster. The alley captured the mood of the town. But we weren't giving it much thought. We were only thinking about each other.

I was teasing Smiley about the effect his stalker grandmother had made on our section of the restaurant. He was taking it well, showing that he had the strength of character to be a police detective. Neither of us minded the cool night. We needed the fresh and foggy air to wake us up a bit. In the gloom, I could almost imagine the Continental Op gaining ground on some hapless criminal who didn't realize that the fat and ordinary little man was the best in the business.

"Feels like we're in a Hammett novel right now," he said, probably wanting to change the subject.

"It does kind of feel like that. Maybe I want to be one of those girls in Hammett's world."

"What do you mean?"

"You known, the kind of woman who isn't quite who she seems to be. The type who would steal your heart and then your wallet and then leave you alone to face the music."

"Remember that you are dealing with a highly trained professional," he joked back.

"So sorry, sir. I had forgotten."

"Better keep it in mind, miss," he said.

Never one to be told what to do, I waggled his wallet under his nose. "You call that highly trained?"

His eyes widened.

"You should never challenge me," I said, handing it over. I felt the mood change a bit. Of course, lifting a wallet while you have distracted someone who wouldn't have suspected you is a bit of a parlor trick in our family. We pick each other's pockets at every opportunity. It's a game. Christmas is musical wallets and funerals, well . . . You don't even want to know. But of course, Smiley wouldn't see it that way

"Sorry," I said. "I was just being silly. All the Kellys do that to each other all the time. But I won't do it again if you're going to have that particular expression on your face."

"As long as you can take it as well as you dish it out," he said.

"Of course. I—where did you get my phone?"

"You think you're the only one who knows how to divert attention?" He planted a kiss on my cheek.

We resumed our slow stroll, arms touching, no need to talk every minute. I found myself imagining future scenarios, but none of them involved having him shout "Look out!" and pushing me forward into a concrete planter. Smiley was flattened against me. I looked ahead to see a black Prius rocketing off the sidewalk past us toward the end of the block and, with a screech of tires, around the corner and out of sight.

"Are you hurt?" Smiley said. "Don't move in case something's broken."

"Seriously? We were almost run down by a rogue Prius? That doesn't even make sense."

"Yeah, yeah, a Prius, so unlikely, but are you okay?"

I shook my slightly addled head. "Nothing broken. Skinned knees maybe. I tore my favorite tights, though, and they matched so well with my dress. Are you okay?"

"What?" Smiley was obviously a bit addled too.

"Did that car hit you?"

"Missed me. That guy must have been hammered."

"Guess so."

"I hope he doesn't kill someone driving like that."

We talked about calling 911, but in our state of tipsiness, reporting being nearly wiped out by a Prius might lead to even more embarrassing conversations or hysterical laughter.

"I'm feeling more like a Hammett novel every minute," I said. "Should we call the police?"

"And tell them what? I didn't get the plate, did you?"

"No."

"I suppose there are a gazillion Priuses in this town."

"We're not hurt. Let's let it go."

We may have leaned on each other a bit more on the stumble home. I was glad that I had a guy who would put

his life at risk to toss me into a cement planter, even though
I normally like to look after myself.

THE NEXT MORNING, I snuck into the bathroom with
my cell phone to receive a secretive call from Uncle Mick.
Uncle Mick is conspiratorial by nature. Smiley and I had
lovely adjoining rooms but with the connecting doors open,
there was no privacy and I really wanted to make a few calls,
and in addition to talking to Mick, I wanted to surprise Tyler
with something special, say, a highly collectible Guy Noir
Bobblehead. How cool would that be? I could give it to him
when he came back from seeing his grandmother. It could
be a celebration or a compensation, depending.

Uncle Mick is a man of magic and he had located a copy
of *Red Harvest*. He "had a guy," an old friend of the family.
This guy had slightly unconventional business practices. Of
course he did. Apparently he owned a rare book and curiosities shop that not only had a signed first edition of *Red
Harvest*, but Uncle Mick was sure he'd have a Guy Noir
Bobblehead, whatever that was, or he could get one fast.
Mick would make the contact right away. I was ecstatic
about both. Since Smiley would be getting reacquainted
with his grandmother, all I had to do was make my way to
Farley's Finest. It was somewhere near Mission and Valen-
cia, a trendy, mostly Hispanic neighborhood. That made it
even more attractive, since Tyler and I hadn't gone there yet
and I heard tales of lots of funky inexpensive shops.

"What are you up to today?" he said.

"Shopping," I said.

I left a tip on the pillowcase, something I'd done ever
since I read about the life of hotel maids in a mystery by
Elaine Viets. Another reason why mysteries make the world
a better place. I checked myself in the mirror and left the
room. I passed a cheerful chambermaid in the hallway and

stepped into the waiting elevator. Outside, I flagged a cab to the street corner that was nearest to my destination, Farley's Finest. The neighborhood was just too interesting not to walk through but my instructions on how to find Farley's included turning right at the mural of Salvador Dali and down the alley past Puerto Alegre but before the lady selling puppets. Not exactly Google maps but I didn't care. As soon as I stepped out of the cab onto the curb and looked up at the colorful buildings against the bright blue sky, I was enamored with this spot. Every wall had eclectic street art and every storefront was crammed with bright and exciting items, promising hidden gems in back and worlds begging to be explored. I would, of course, have to control my spending until I got my mitts on that *Red Harvest* and Tyler's Guy Noir Bobblehead.

My phone chimed with a text from Uncle Kev.

Whatever you do, don't mention Sea World to Farley!
Trust me.

While I was fairly certain I would be able to steer conversation away from Sea World, trusting Kev was a stretch. Why was he getting involved anyway? Sounds and smells filled my senses, making it even more difficult to concentrate. For example, I was now craving a churro on top of everything else. So, I let it go. "Kevin can wait!" as we say in our family. I spotted the Dali mural, the artist's upturned mustache pointing down the alleyway. The street art continued on the walls. A pair of elderly men sat on stools sipping steamy coffees from tiny china cups. Beside them an orange rusty door was slightly ajar, the sounds of Spanish speakers and the chaos of a commercial kitchen emanating from within. The men nodded at me solemnly as I passed. I was glad I brought my sweater scarf in my tote bag, because out of the brilliant sunshine, only feet away, it was cold and damp. I gave the cozy scarf another loop around my neck and walked on, my footsteps echoing off the narrow space.

Farley's Finest was literally a hidden treasure. At the end of the alley around another corner, there it was. A small sandwich board announced my arrival. The parameters of the space were difficult to comprehend, and merchandise had obviously spilled out of the closet-like shop into the alley, adding to the whole magical quality. Maybe six feet wide and five feet deep, the place was stacked with books to the ceiling. Two teetering curio cases flanked the door inside. They were jammed with twinkling vintage jewelry, collectibles and what appeared to be a pair of stuffed peacocks crowned this display. My eyes couldn't take it all in. I could see dozens of things I wanted. I would have stepped back for a better view, but there was nowhere to step to, only another brick wall painted in years of old graffiti. There was no one in the shop. There was no room for anyone to actually be in the shop.

A velvety "Jordan" at my back scared me right out of my boots. I pirouetted to see the shop's namesake. He was not much taller than me, but his shoulders were broad and straight. A little shock of silver through his dark, thick hair was "silver fox" sexy. He wasn't imposing, though, and sparkly black eyes peered over chiseled brown cheekbones at me. I recognized that twinkle of mischief from my own uncles' gazes and felt instantly at ease. Mischief makers in mysterious shops down dark alleys? These are my people. I extended my hand from under the many layers of scarf.

"Farley Tso."

"Jordan Bingham."

"Ah yes. I've been expecting you for a while, Jordan. So, Bingham. Not Kelly?"

Waiting for me?

"Um, well, no. The Kellys are on my mother's side. As you know, Uncle Mick sent me and there's Lucky and Kev—"

"And Seamus?"

"Oh yes. Seamus." I was surprised he knew about Seamus.

He looked at me long enough that we could have boiled an egg. Finally having sized up the situation, he nodded. "Bingham. Okay." He gestured toward his inventory so I could continue to browse. Just trying to keep focus in this dizzying array of items was hard. There were books stacked on a steamer trunk that varied in subject matter from *The Far Side* to *The Cold War.* Sitting atop that stack was a precariously balanced mini-Eames Rocker in all its bright yellow, molded fiberglass glory. I wanted it, for no other reason than it existed. Much like the turquoise "squash blossom" necklace that looked very authentic to my eye. I dabbed the drool from the corner of my mouth.

As I sniffed about the goodies, Farley pulled a brown bag from under the smallest curio cabinet. It smelled of cigars and leather. Inside was a Guy Noir Bobblehead, in its original packaging.

"And don't you worry about that *Red Harvest*, I've got one for you, it's just going to take a day or two to be delivered." Farley's eyes shone with pride, seeing my obvious excitement. I wasn't even trying to hide, knowing that Mick, his name and reputation would have already secured me the best price.

"Half now, half on delivery?"

"That will be six hundred dollars then, Miss, um, Bingham, plus the bobblehead." I paid for Smiley's gift and then fished half of Vera's cash out of my trusty orange satchel, and pressed the bills into his leathery hand. We shook again and smiled.

"Are you sure I can't interest you in the necklace?" Farley teased, with a strange undertone in his comment.

"Oh, I'm interested! But I hardly have the money for

that." Even with my basic knowledge of authentic Southwest turquoise, I knew that piece had to be worth at least two grand. "But I might have to take home that antique French handkerchief box." Again, Farley looked at me for a really long time. I started to twitch under his gaze. He picked up the six-by-six-inch flat wooden box, with the faded early-twentieth-century embellishments and turned away. I heard the crinkling of tissue paper.

"Please." He said, pressing another small bag into my hand, "It is a gift." Farley's deep brown eyes fixed on mine. I could not say no.

"I will be sure to tell Uncle Mick how helpful and kind you were. Thank you so much, Mr. Tso."

"Please give my best to them all, Mick, Lucky, Kev, and of course, Seamus," he said as I turned to leave. I did jump a little when he mentioned Seamus's name again. I guess because we really didn't speak about my uncle often in recent years. He was merely the stuff of whispers and legends from my childhood.

I bundled my purchases and gift into my bag and strode back down the alley toward the busy street. The older gentlemen had taken their coffees and gone inside, maybe because of the two tall burly men flanking the mouth of the alley when I got there. I wondered if they were some kind of "store security." Something in my lizard brain told me not to strike up a conversation with these guys. Maybe it was the long black leather coats or perhaps the cold dead eyes. Minutes later as I flagged a cab from the street, I turned back to get a better look but they had evaporated into the crowd.

I WENT OFF to meet Tyler for the next phrase of our adventure. San Francisco and cable cars: what a magic combination. Tyler and I agreed on that much when we finally connected. Not quite right for a heart-to-heart about the grandmother, but what a way to see the city, with the thrill of steep hills up and stomach-dropping descents. We couldn't wait. Soon I was squished into a cable car, hurtling down a steep hill, clinging to a rail with the wind rushing in my ears amid the clang and clatter of metal and the shrieks of fellow passengers. We were loving this adventure, smiling at the others, including a few familiar faces from our hotel and not smiling at a very large, sweaty man standing too close and a bullet-headed guy who seemed not only too familiar but too pushy as he wedged his way into the car. Minutes later I was lying on the sidewalk, wondering who had given me the hard push that sent me flying through the air and cost me my dignity and my new fedora. Such a weird accident. But then, why didn't it feel accidental?

CHAPTER FIVE

Put your feet up whenever you can.
—THE KELLY RULES

SMILEY WAS STILL fussing over me an hour later. We'd made a quick return to the hotel to clean up and assess the damage. Tyler had insisted.

"I told you I'm okay. What will it take to convince you?" I said.

"Confirmation from a doctor."

"No way am I sitting in an emergency room because I have bruised knees yet again and my palms are scratched."

He got his cop face on. That always makes me resist more.

"If you find a doctor who can replace my lost fedora, then we might have a deal," I said.

"Never mind the stupid hat. What about your head?"

"What about my stupid head?"

"I did not say 'your stupid head.'"

"But did you think it?"

"I thought that if you hit your head, you could have been seriously injured. You could have a concussion or a brain bleed."

"Charming. But by some miracle I didn't hit my head. I only scratched the palms of my hands and lost my beautiful hat. My knees were already beat up from last night and the Attack of the Midnight Prius."

"Hmm."

"If you want to worry about something and it appears that you do, how about the fact that I think someone may have actually pushed me deliberately."

He patted me on the back, in the patronizing way people do when they think you're being an idiot.

"Don't do that," I said. "Someone pushed me, from behind obviously, and that bothers me. I've already said that."

"I didn't see anyone push you."

"Just because you didn't see something happen doesn't mean it didn't. As a police officer, you should be well aware of that. While you were pointing out sights, someone gave me a very hard, sharp shove. I think whoever did that meant business."

His forehead furrowed. "But what business?"

"No idea. I still think it was weird."

"More than just weird. We're going to the police."

"We are not going to the police and we are not going to the hospital. We are going to continue on our vacation and we are going to have a good time. Don't bother arguing. You know the police won't do anything about that. This is a huge city and that was only one *possible* assault."

"Why don't you think about it?"

"For the same reason you didn't think about it last night on our way home from dinner."

"That was different. We'd had a few drinks and it *was* a Prius."

"Right. They might have laughed."

"Could have been worse. Could have been a bicycle. That would be more humiliating." He checked out my scraped palms. "But you've really scratched up your hands, Jordan."

"Yep. They sting like crazy. And I broke a nail too."

"Again, who would want to push you?"

"Nobody has any reason to hurt me or us. And as I wasn't killed or badly hurt, I'm not going to let it bring me down."

"The main thing is to be very careful from now on."

"No. The main thing is that I didn't ruin another good outfit and I don't have a concussion."

"Um, that's two main things."

"True. Three if you count that I'll definitely have to shop."

"Maybe later. My grandmother is really keen to meet you."

"When?"

"Today. Remember?"

"Right. So now I'm going to get changed. I want to look good when I meet your grandmother. So glad I don't have a concussion for the occasion."

SMILEY HADN'T BEEN kidding about walking off our meals. On our way to his grandmother's place, we took in a lot of this city. Apparently, Smiley's grandmother lived at the edge of Pacific Heights, a ritzy part of town at the top of a serious set of hills.

We combined seeing the city—walking and cable cars (keeping our backs covered and our eyes opened)—and we got to see a lot of the vibrant bustling city that was well outside of the tourist area. We rattled down California Street on a cable car as cars whizzed by and buildings towered.

Every now and then we'd get off and walk to get a sense of the area.

Have I mentioned there were hills?

The hills of San Francisco made me appreciate the steep flights of stairs to my attic apartment in Van Alst House. If I hadn't gone racing up and down those three flights of wooden steps at least a dozen times a day (frequently dodging Bad Cat's good aim with claws), I might have collapsed in a heap as we climbed toward our destination.

I wasn't alone in this.

"Good thing I've been going to the gym," Smiley said. He looked like he might have been ready to huff and puff anyway. We both knew he could have gone to the gym a bit more often. I had my own exercise program (aside from the stairs) although lately it seemed to consist of running for my life and dodging the police, too often including the man at my side.

I said, "You couldn't help but be fit if you lived here."

"I am fit," he snapped.

"I mean a person couldn't help but be fit, not you in particular." I hadn't realized that was a sore spot. Live and learn, as Uncle Mick used to say after a close call with a cop. "Take a look."

The look registered plenty of pedestrians, mothers with strollers, dozens of cyclists and more than a few skateboarders. I didn't envy the cyclists or the skateboarders on those hills.

"Yeah, okay."

"Hey, not everything is about you," I said, giving him an affectionate poke in the ribs.

"Maybe it is." He grinned.

With the mood lightened, we kept walking.

"Not far now," he promised.

"Great area," I puffed. "You've got a bit of everything here from Victorian to mid-century modern to contemporary. I love it. You never mentioned that your grandmother was rolling in money."

"She's not. Now."

"Don't be mysterious," I said, trying to keep up.

"Her second husband, William Huddy, made a lot of money on some kind of invention that improved the performance of plastics. They used it to modify the design of plastic extruders and—"

I held up my hand. "More than I need to know."

"Me too. When Gram and this new husband came out here, he was trying to sell this process he'd invented. The people who bought out his patent went on to become billionaires, according to Gram, and then William invested the bulk of his share in some tech stock that sank like a stone."

"So she was left with nothing?"

"Not at all. They had a nice house, in her name, and William had paid Gram back for everything she had invested plus a share of the sale of the patent. She had that. He died not long afterwards. She was devastated, but not penniless. She still has the house and I guess enough income to support her in comfort. She has live-in help."

"Nice."

"Maybe 'nice' isn't the word. She's alone and has some mobility issues. And that so-called help of hers takes a bit of getting used to. But you'll see."

"Okay. Well, I really love this neighborhood. I'm sure I'll like your grandmother too and I'm prepared to keep an open mind about the help. Keep in mind that I'm the help when I'm at home."

He stopped and threw back his head and laughed. "Not how I think of you. And I'll remind you of that remark later. We're not that far away."

"Good." It's a bad habit, I know, but everywhere I go, I find myself wondering what it would be like to live there and comparing an imaginary new life to my tranquil existence of books, food, vintage clothes and cuddly critters (including Smiley) back home. I was spoiled, no question. But San Francisco had a magic quality. My vintage look fit in, although maybe not with the yummy mummies in their high-end active wear, and so far the food had been excellent. I saw no shortage of pampered pooches and I assumed there would be equally pampered cats lurking somewhere. As for books, well, we'd already found one strange source and there had to be others. The only fly in this pot of ointment was real estate, although I thought of it as Unreal Estate.

"What do you think these places would go for?" I asked Smiley. As a cop, he likes facts. I might moon over the pictures in, say, *Architectural Digest*, whereas he would get the price, square footage, tax rate, cost of utilities and a report on possible exposure to radon before he gave anything a second look.

"There are all kinds of different places, some rentals, but they'd be scarce. There are condos and co-ops and massive old houses. You might get a one-bedroom condo unit for eight hundred thousand, but then again, maybe not."

"Huh." Next to my free accommodation, that was as likely as landing on Jupiter. Smiley had bought his fixer-upper, fixed 'er up and sold the tiny immaculate brick house and made a profit. He'd bought a small two-story Cape Cod for one hundred and twenty-four thousand and was slowly whipping it into shape, all for a fraction of the cost of this alleged one-bedroom condo. "You know, if you can just flip another fifty houses, you might be able to get one of those."

He snorted. "Don't exaggerate. It wouldn't take more than ten."

"I don't know. There are the condo fees too."

"Might not be a lot of cops living around here."

"Even fewer book researchers."

"That's a safe bet."

"So, that's us out of the market. We're either living in splendor sponging off elderly eccentrics or sleeping in our cars."

"Your car is very uncomfortable."

"Don't knock my Saab. It's practically an antique."

We deked to the left to dodge a couple with a velvety gray Weimaraner and a stroller built for two. They required a sidewalk to themselves. On this outing we'd dodge a number of baby strollers and toddlers. They were everywhere. The parents all appeared to be puffed with pride. I glanced at Smiley and found he was staring with interest at another couple in their late thirties with a fat, pink baby in some kind of carrier on Dad's chest and a curly-haired toddler being herded by Mom. They seemed to have a mountain of gear. I didn't understand any of it and was just about to whisper that to Tyler when I caught a new expression. Interest had upgraded to fascination. I hoped it was the gear, but I feared it was the children.

Weird. He'd never shown an interest in kids. I hoped he wasn't going to get all domestic on me. First you find your grandmother and then you want a houseful of kids. Was that a thing? If so, it was way too early.

I said, "I guess the people who live around here must have made a bundle in the tech sector to live in this neighborhood and bring up a family."

He blinked.

I said, "It's just that I read somewhere that on average it costs nearly a quarter of a million dollars to raise a child. And that's if they don't decide to go to some Ivy League college."

Smiley's blink had turned to a stare.

"Have I just grown horns on my forehead?" I said.

"What?"

"Spinach in my teeth?"

"No."

"Revealed myself as an alien?"

"What are you talking about? Why would you even—"

"Just the look on your face."

"Okay, it's just that I think kids are about more than money. People love them. For themselves."

Tough one. And of course, I knew that people loved their kids. I wasn't suggesting that they shouldn't. It was just that I wasn't ready to start thinking about children, and from the look on his face, Smiley was.

I chose to keep walking along, not saying much of anything and hoping he got it out of his system. I still wanted to travel and to find the life that would suit me. I knew it wouldn't be one with a lot of money, and even if by some lottery winning miracle it was, children were for the distant future. I decided we should try to avoid them for the time being.

Easier said than done.

A young mother pushing a pricey-looking stroller passed us while jogging up the last long hill before his grandmother's place. I figured her casual activewear cost a bomb too. She pushed the stroller with one hand and held her Starbucks cup in the other. Her honey-brown ponytail swayed as she ran.

"Did you notice that baby carriage has two cup holders?" he said. "She doesn't need to hold that latte or whatever. She's just showing off."

I shook my head. I knew nothing of babies or strollers, although I am familiar with Starbucks and high-end activewear.

"Police training," he said. "Let's us observe details."

"How much do you think her outfit cost?"

"No idea, but I bet that stroller is over a thousand."

"You're kidding."

"Nope. One of the guys at the new station was pricing them. His hair was practically falling out when he'd check the bottom line."

"Who knew? And who can afford something like that?"

He shrugged. "People in finance, banking, real estate, and around here, high tech."

"Lots of money in this city."

I knew that the headquarters for Google and Facebook weren't far. I'd heard that many of their young and hip employees lived in the city. It was hard to imagine how different this bustling trendy city was from sleepy little Harrison Falls and the equally dozy Town of Cabot.

The woman with the carriage had stopped to stretch and we gradually caught up with her.

As we strolled past, she gave us a big, unexpected smile. Smiley smiled back. He pointed at the covered-up infant and asked about the baby.

No wonder he was smiling. The yummy mummy had pale luminous skin and flawless teeth to match. She was a naturally beautiful woman who looked fabulous in her exercise gear and simple hairstyle. I imagined the child would be photogenic too. "Harry's sleeping," she whispered. "The little beast kept us up all night."

"Really?" I said, secretly pleased.

She shrugged. "Teething. Nothing to be done but wait until they're all in."

Smiley, who probably knew even less than I did about babies—so nothing—nodded in agreement.

At least he hadn't insisted on peering under the blanket at the tiny sleeping being. I knew no one with a baby, had no baby cousins or even distant relatives and not a single friend who was longing for babies. I knew the little creatures were out there and could be very appealing. I even understood that they were important to the continuity of the human race, but that was about the extent of it. I understood nothing of teething or the other surprises of parenthood, but was happy to be standing still and not climbing the rest of the hill.

After a few minutes of pleasant chat, she excused herself to go into a small shop for "supplies." "See you soon!"

We waved good-bye and continued our slog. I was doing my best to look energetic. Even Smiley's face was getting flushed. More training was obviously required and we were definitely trudging as we neared the top of the hill.

As we approached the block where we expected to find Smiley's Gram's home, the young mother passed us again, waving with her free hand when she jogged by and crossed the street in a diagonal without breaking stride. She stopped and managed somehow to pull the stroller and its teething inhabitant up the wide stairs and through the door of a substantial house that looked to be from the early nineteenth century. As we watched, impressed, she waved cheerfully and vanished.

"Well," I said, "I feel like a tree sloth after that performance."

He shrugged. "Me too. Maybe I've been eating all wrong."

"Right. Maybe you should try eating green smoothies and taking cleanses."

"Be careful."

I was still chuckling at my silly joke when we approached Gram's house.

Tyler's grandmother's house was on the high ground. It was a grand Victorian style, like the famous Painted Ladies but without the vibrant color. This one was a sedate mauve and gray with a charming set of turret windows in front as well as a set of bay windows. Tyler stopped talking as we approached. He was clutching a gift-wrapped puzzle featuring five thousand pieces of Antarctic ice relieved by a few lonesome penguins. I really hoped this visit went well for him. I'd had second thoughts about accompanying him. But he wanted it. So I was there, bruised knees, scraped palms and all. I'd have to remember to call her Mrs. Huddy after the new husband and not Dekker.

As I'd also been dipping my pedicure into the dark and shady land of Hammett, I knew that in that world, no one was to be trusted. That included sweet little old ladies. Just ask the Continental Op how they can pull the rug out from under you. Smiley was such a bundle of suppressed excitement that I couldn't quite bring myself to mention this.

We walked up the well-maintained wooden front steps to the covered veranda with a solid purple door. I smoothed my navy romper with the cream lace detail (back in fashion yet again) as we stood at the door, and did not let myself peer through the turret window. Smiley pressed the doorbell and we listened to the pleasant chimes that announced our arrival. A small smile played around the corners of his very nice mouth. The door was opened by a tall, whippet-like, dark-haired woman who looked to be mid-thirties. Her wide silver eyes were full of wariness. Her hair was pulled into a stylish topknot with little strands artfully framing her face. With high, broad cheekbones like that, she didn't really need any artful assistance.

"Comb in. Mrs. Huddy iss expecting you," she said, flatly. I tried to place her accent. Russian? Latvian?

She turned to me. "I am Zoya. And you are . . ." She could easily have been straight out of a noirish thriller.

Tyler said, "Jordan Bingham. My grandmother is expecting her as well."

She shrugged, gave a contemptuous sneer at my taupe desert boots and turned on one of her shiny black heels. "Zis way."

We kept up. The foyer was on the dark side with dated teal and pink wallpaper and dark mahogany tables every few feet, including a console table I would have killed for, even without the stunning sterling bowl. A massive chandelier hung from the ceiling but it hadn't been turned on. I was trying not to think that silver-eyed young women in Hammett's world were inclined to betrayal. But this wasn't Hammett's world. It was Hammett's town, but this, in some strange and soon-to-be-discovered way, was Tyler Dekker's world.

We followed our guide past a long formal parlor, then a vestibule with a substantial dark mahogany staircase. Before we hit the library, I peeked into the dining room with rows of botanical prints (heavy on the pink), a massive sterling candelabra on the glossy table and a magnificent Chinese lacquered screen. This entire house was a delicious crowded dream. A half-opened door off to the right showed a second staircase, a narrower flight of steps to the second floor that must have been for the servants back in the day. We turned right opposite the kitchen to arrive at a sunroom of sorts. It had beautiful windows looking out over the fog shrouding the possibly spectacular view below.

Inside was a different story. For starters, there was enough furniture to fill three rooms. Most of it was well-worn white wicker: chairs with flowered cushions, tables crowded with African violets, several ottomans with woolly throws, and a sideboard with teapots and small china figurines, heavy on the shepherdesses and smiling dogs. Not to forget the plant stands with a community of Boston ferns. A small pug glowered at us from beneath a wicker love seat. Clearly, we'd ruined its day.

But the dominant aspect of the place was the noise and its source. The sounds of birds were almost overwhelming. I noted at least seven cages: Uncle Kev used to have a thing for birds so I knew who was who here. A yellow cockatiel with bright orange cheeks made the sound of a cell phone ring.

Trill trill trill.

A small green parrot that I thought was a Quaker said, "Hello."

In the corner a pair of bright-eyed lovebirds snuggled on their swing together.

A second cockatiel showed off a doorbell imitation. Very nice.

"Who is it?" the parrot said with dangerous overtones.

I laughed out loud.

I loved this place.

In the far corner with at least two pastel throws on her lap, an elderly lady watched us with what looked like glee.

Tyler and his grandmother glowed at each other.

She had a little gap between her two front teeth, and yes, she was blushing from the neck of her baby-blue polyester top to the scalp that showed pinkly through her soft white waves. A serious cane rested by the chair, the only dark item in the room. The metal bird on the handle stood out next to the mahogany finish.

"Tyler!"

"Gram."

He dashed across the room, dodging ottomans, small tables, standing lamps and a brass umbrella stand that held a collection of canes.

She gripped his hand and beamed. He beamed back. She said, "Oh, pet." Her voice held an echo of English origins, the accent worn by many years in the USA, but still there and still appealing. She patted the chintz ottoman by her feet. "Zoya will get you some cookies and milk."

Zoya's head jerked. She looked like she'd just as soon drop strychnine into the milk and add crushed glass to the cookies.

"No thanks," Tyler said with a nervous glance in Zoya's direction. He did perch on the ottoman, though.

"Oh, Tyler, make an old lady happy, have some. And your little friend too."

We glanced at each other.

Smiley said, "Gram, this is my fiancée, Jordan Bingham."

Fiancée? I looked down at my hand in case the proposal had just slipped my mind.

"How lovely. Welcome to the family, my dear." She beckoned me forward and squeezed my hand. Her grip was a lot stronger than I'd expected. Maybe she lifted weights when she wasn't bird-watching or smiling at the figurine collection. I got a pleasant whiff of her delicate lavender scent. Tyler didn't talk about his family. As far as I knew, aside from his estranged parents, the entire Dekker clan was standing in this room. That made it emotionally significant, that and the fact I'd agreed to spend the rest of my life with one of them, apparently.

"Jordan loves La Perla," Smiley said.

"It's a beautiful hotel. Was it your suggestion?"

"It came highly recommended from a relative. I'm so glad it worked out."

"Thank you. I really love it there."

"We all love a bride, my dear," Gram trilled. "This is such good news about your engagement."

Prior to that moment, I hadn't believed that people trilled outside of fiction, but this was a day of surprises. I blushed at her sweetness and at the awkwardness Tyler had dropped me into.

Zoya, returning with a tray containing cookies and milk, looked surprised too. The look didn't suit her any better than her other expressions: disdain, disinterest, dislike and so on.

Gram turned to Smiley. "When did you propose, pet?"

I was also interested to hear his answer.

Gotcha. He blanched. "Um, just on this trip actually."

Exactly, and that would be on the part of this trip that hadn't actually occurred.

She clapped her hands, apparently in delight. Zoya's eyes bugged out. Mine might have too. The pug's definitely did. "We must have an engagement party! We'll have to invite your new cousins."

I said. "What? No. We couldn't possibly—"

"Darling boy," she said. Apparently, she could only hear him. "I'm thrilled."

The Quaker parrot squawked, "Party party!"

Zoya pushed into the room. "No parties, missus. You are supposed to rest."

The parrot said, "Time to go."

I laughed at the little green tyrant, but I had no problem with the sentiment. We didn't stay long and promised to return as soon as possible. The minute we said good-bye, we found ourselves hustled toward the front door, while Gram called out, "Come back tomorrow! We'll plan the party." The pug circled our ankles yipping and snapping. The birds shrieked a variety of shrieks. Zoya merely scowled.

"Do not come back here again," she said, closing the door on us. "I know what you up to and you not velcome."

CHAPTER SIX

A locked door is a piece of cake.
—THE KELLY RULES

S MILEY GAWKED AT the closed purple door.
   I said, "We'll come back tomorrow."

He turned and stared at me. "You don't think that was strange?"

"What part? The bit where I'm your fiancée and the last one to know about it?"

"Oh, that. Well—"

"Oh, that?"

"It didn't come out right."

I stood on the steps to his grandmother's house and sputtered.

He said, "What I meant to say is that I've been thinking a lot about us."

I crossed my arms and stared across the steep street.

He said, "I think we should consider it."

How romantic. "I think you shouldn't announce something momentous like that without discussing it with me, your so-called fiancée. It's the kind of decision where I would get a vote."

"I do realize that. It just came out because it was such a nice moment and I wanted it to be true. I wanted to introduce you as my fiancée to my grandmother. Thank you for not saying it wasn't exactly true."

"Wasn't *exactly* true?"

"You know."

"I do know and it wasn't even a little bit true." I'm not over the top about engagement rituals, but I did feel a little bit robbed of a moment.

He looked so downcast that I started to feel bad for him, but really, springing an engagement on a girl? Not cool.

We walked along toward the intersection where we could get the streetcar, without either of us saying a word. Just as we got close, I said, "You never told me about any cousins."

"I never met them. They're on Gram's husband's side." I was surprised to see him grin. "I never had anyone, no brothers and sisters, no cousins. This is really good news."

We were both only children. My only cousins were in distant branches of the Kelly family, although you could say that Uncle Kev was like a perpetual child. I'd been the center of my uncles' lives. I wasn't sure I'd have liked having competition from cousins. As annoyed as I was, I decided to let Smiley enjoy his new-found semi-relatives.

"Tomorrow, we will go back and see your grandmother and you can find out more about them. As it's so important, I'll continue to be your fake fiancée."

He stopped abruptly, just as the streetcar slowed. "I'm kind of worried about that Zoya. I don't trust her."

I stopped too. "I hear you, but I then I don't usually trust people who tell me to go away and never come back."

"Can't say I liked her much either."

"She didn't seem to want us to like her, but maybe that's her way of protecting Gram. Who knows what kind of relationship they have behind closed doors." I thought of the infinitely complicated power dynamic between Vera and the signora back at Van Alst House.

"On the other hand, perhaps she didn't want us hanging around because things are not right with Gram."

"You mean because Zoya's taking advantage?"

"Maybe. Are you worried?"

By this point the streetcar had come and thundered by. "We may as well find out," he said. We trudged the long way back to the faded gray and mauve home.

The drapes were closed in the front windows this time. Smiley rang the bell. We waited. He rang again after a couple of minutes. Nothing. He hammered on the front door. I felt a bit of panic and expected a matching emotion from him, but I suppose his inner cop was taking over. He leaned down and opened the mail slot. He bellowed. "Open up! Police."

It was true enough in its own way.

Zoya did not materialize. Neither did Gram. But the little pug raced along the hallway and continued to run in circles barking.

"She might be asleep," I said. "She *is* quite elderly and—"

"And Zoya? Where is she?"

Of course, I'd thought of that. In other circumstances, I might have thought that the caregiver might have settled her patient into bed and then dashed out for an errand. There didn't seem to have been enough time for that. But what if Zoya had gone out and now Gram might hear the racket from the little dog and come downstairs (or out from wherever she was) and stumble, fall and then there'd be heartbreak. I touched Smiley's sleeve and said, "Either she can't hear us. Or she can't get to us."

He scowled.

"You'd need a warrant to go in, I suppose," I said, thinking I could read his mind. "And you're not here on a case.

It's personal. So I don't think you should try to kick the door in."

This time it was a glower. "Of course I wouldn't do that. But what if something's happened to her?"

I sighed. "Maybe I can help. It would be better if you weren't in on it, though."

"Go ahead. We'll just say that the door wasn't locked. Zoya can try to talk her way out of that one."

"I can't believe you actually said that. You're the one who's the stickler for proper procedure and not break-ing the—"

It goes without saying that I had not flown across the USA with my set of treasured lockpicks in my luggage. There are rules. However, this lock was almost laughably easy. A quick slide with a credit card was all it would take.

"Use my card," he said.

"Maybe you should avert your eyes."

"I'm a cop. I know how locks get opened with cards. I've just never done it. Not part of my training."

"Give me a little cover so the neighbors can't see what I'm doing. I'll pretend to bang on the door. When it opens, we both act like we're being greeted. And let's hope there isn't a security system."

A quick slide, a jiggle and we were in.

Of course there was no security system.

Smiley said, "I'll make sure to remind her to get one. It was way too easy to get in here."

"Let's get going." Despite my heritage, I really hate be-ing in a house that I don't belong in. Smiley had the confi-dence that cops have when they trespass. Maybe it's an acquired skill.

I tried the main level and found no Gram anywhere. The little pug was yipping around my ankles throughout. Not a relaxing search.

I headed up the stairs after Smiley. He was methodically going from room to room, softly calling "Gram" before opening each door.

"I don't want to frighten her."

"I think the master bedrooms in this style of house should be in the front, where the turret window is."

"I checked it."

"Fine. She'll have the best room, so maybe it looks down over the city in the back." We moved toward the rear of the second floor and knocked on the last door. No response.

Slowly and still calling her name, Smiley opened the door. I was holding my breath.

A vast round bed filled one wall. The vivid fuchsia and pink peony pattern on the bedspread and the masses of matching throw cushions would take a little getting used to. This room had obviously been renovated and sat over the sunroom. In the floor-to-ceiling window a floral reclining chair commanded a spectacular view. No one was in the chair.

Smiley ran his hands through his hair. "Where is she? What has that woman done with her?"

Usually the simplest answer is the best.

"Maybe she hasn't done anything with her," I said, moving toward the bed. Sure enough, a small figure lay there, camouflaged by pillows.

Gram was in the bed.

She wasn't moving.

Smiley bent over her, shouting, "Gram!"

He shook her. She moaned softly. He shook harder. I picked up the phone to dial 911 when her eyes popped open.

"What a nice surprise," she said. "Twice in one day."

Smiley slumped. "You gave me quite a scare. I thought you were—" He gave a little squeal. Her eyes had closed and she was lying back again, breathing shallowly.

"Drugs," I said. "Pretty sure."

The mirrored dressing table showed no signs of medication, just a glass of water. He checked her pulse and I picked up the glass using a tissue to keep my prints off it.

"Her pulse is . . . not bad."

I know nothing of pulses, so I said, "Great." I sniffed the glass. Then "Oh, that smells like—"

Smiley patted his grandmother's pale cheek. "I'm calling 911."

I said, "Maybe you should—"

A noise at the door caused the two of us to whirl like characters in a melodrama. It sort of felt like that too.

"Vat are you doing here?" Zoya said. "I vill call police."

Smiley managed to stay calm.

"Not if we call them first," I sputtered.

She grabbed the phone and made an attempt at 911. Her hand was shaking. "You vill not kill us and get avay vith it."

By my calculation, she was short of one "1."

"Kill you?"

"You think I am fool?"

Fool? I thought she was a bit of a villain. I supposed she might have been a fool too.

"I am not trying to kill my gram. We've just been re-united. We are family."

"Sure, *you* say that."

The telltale Dekker flush had rushed from Smiley's collar to the roots of his hair. Perhaps it was a bit brighter than usual. It's not every day someone accuses you of attempting to kill your grandmother.

"I do say that," he said. "And you will stop saying anything else. I am a police officer. But I'm wondering what you'll get out of it if Gram . . ." He mouthed the word *dies*.

Zoya gasped. We watched as she turned and loped from the room. I heard the clatter of heels on the hardwood stairs, then the slam of the door.

Gram's eyes popped open wide, and with the twinkle turned on.

"When's dinner?" she said.

Dekker folded her into a hug. "Are you all right?"

"Well, I'm starving and you almost broke my ribs, but aside from that, I'm right as rain."

"Right as rain," Smiley said. "You always said that."

"And I'm still saying it. Where's Zoya?"

"She, um, ran away."

"Why would she run away?"

"She seemed to think I had tried to kill you, and then when she learned I was a police officer, she took off. Are you sure she's—"

"Loyal as the day is long, although a bit high strung. But I'm happy with her. Don't meddle, darling boy." Gram reached over and pulled the long embroidered bell, like something out of Downton Abbey.

Smiley sat on the chair and leaned over his grandmother. "What happened, Gram?"

"Well, your parents were funny about everything, jealous of our relationship—"

"I mean what happened to you just now?"

"Nothing happened to me. I was having a nap and then there was all this commotion."

"A nap?"

"Yes. I have one every afternoon. I'm a little old lady, pet. We need our rest."

He picked up the glass. "Do you think that Zoya would have put something in it?"

"Just Beefeater."

"What?"

"Just a bit of Beefeater and tonic."

I laughed. No wonder it had smelled familiar. "I tried to tell you. It's a G and T." I'd made a million of those for my uncles.

She nodded. "Sure. It gives me a bit of a buzz and I'm out like a light."

"You leave her alone! Step away!"

Zoya was back but not with dinner. She carried the metal-headed cane and I was betting she'd have a mean swing.

"You go now and don't come back."

"Don't be a silly goose, Zoya. You know perfectly well that this is my grandson and his fiancée. They aren't trying to harm me. They were worried. They suspected you of ulterior motives, drugging my water glass." She managed a wheezy chuckle. At the end of it, a scarlet blush had spread from her neck to the top of her head as I could clearly see through her white waves.

"Drugged? Never!" Zoya's pallid face was fishbelly white by now. She swayed, but hadn't dropped the cane yet. I wondered if the swaying was just part of a dramatic performance. If so, it was a good one. Zoya was clearly very distressed. Her elegant hairstyle had become a bit undone.

Smiley obviously hadn't attempted to harm Gram. Gram had confirmed this. If Zoya had indeed given Gram that snootful of gin, she must have realized that the elderly woman might be groggy and that anyone normal, say Smiley and myself, would be concerned. Was she trying to deflect attention from the fact that she hadn't opened the door? Had she left Gram alone?

"Where were you, Zoya, when we arrived?" Smiley turned to her, crossed his arms over his chest and used his cop voice. It's one of the few things I don't like about him—that cop voice. I'd had it turned on me not that long ago. Apparently, Zoya liked it even less.

"I do not answer! Is not of your business." Again with the swaying.

We both glanced at Gram to see if she was about to chide her employee. But Gram was convulsed. I assumed she was having some kind of medical event and Smiley rushed to her side, but then I heard the wheezy chortle and understood she was merely having a good laugh. She was lucky one of us didn't attempt CPR before we figured that out.

Gram gasped for breath. Smiley sank into the chair by the bed. I watched Zoya. She seemed to deflate, hard as that would be for a person so whippetlike.

"Do you think I don't know you are watching soap operas while I have my little naps, Zoya?"

The chin went up. "Is nothing wrong, missus."

"That's right. There is nothing wrong, but all you had to do was say so. You're entitled to a break."

Smiley said, "You were taking a break and that's why you didn't answer the door."

Zoya managed a sullen nod. "Missus was sleeping. No need to disturb."

I exchanged glances with Smiley and slipped in a comment to Gram. "That's a relief. You had us worried. You too, Zoya."

I was staring at a strange appliance on Gram's bedside table. "What is this?" I said, worrying as the words popped out that I might have asked an inappropriate question.

"Iss tabletop humidifier," Zoya said haughtily. "Good for missus to breathe."

Gram shrugged. "Sometimes I have a little problem."

Tyler said, "Should we turn it on?"

"Not now. I have my radio plugged in and the lamp, and if I turn that on, it blows the fuse. Hardly worth being plunged into darkness while we find the fuse box."

Tyler looked prepared to argue in favor of unplugging the radio and turning on the humidifier. "I think you should—"

"I think you should stop fussing. I got to this ripe old age and I'm not done yet," Gram said.

I liked her even more. Smiley turned red, of course.

Gram said, "Now that's all settled, I suppose a person could have a snack then?"

She leaned forward. "Don't you worry pet, I'm in good hands with Zoya. She knows how to use that cane too."

It took another twenty minutes for Smiley to be convinced that Gram was all right. While Zoya departed to get the overdue snack, he grilled his grandmother. "Where did you find her?"

"A story for another time," she said, her blue eyes twinkling with excitement. "I find it absolutely charming that you are so concerned about me."

It was a nice moment. The eyes kept twinkling and she pointed to the dresser in her room. Like the rest of the room, it was a study in frills and flowers in pink, rose and fuchsia and cream, fresh from the planet Chintz. It suited her, right down to the feminine shades on the crystal lamps. The only thing out of place was the large glass apothecary jar filled with marbles, none of them pink, rose, fuchsia or cream.

"Remember those, pet?"

Smiley stared at the jar. "My marbles. One for every time I visited you. Hundreds of visits."

She beamed.

He said, with a catch in his throat, "You moved them all the way out here? You kept them."

"It was only twenty years. Of course I kept them. But I bet you thought you'd lost your marbles," she said with the wheezy chuckle. "I meant to get Zoya to bring them downstairs earlier, but I forgot. Losing *my* marbles."

"In more than one way," he said with a grin.

I resisted making any lame jokes, maybe because I found myself tearing up. Couldn't have that. Kellys don't tear up, and the Binghams wouldn't have either, whoever they were.

"Kept them for you because I knew you'd be back."

"You may have been hoping I was still a kid."

"I figured you wouldn't be too happy if your precious collection wasn't still intact. Come here."

He moved a little closer. She reached into the top drawer of her French Provincial bedside table and produced a deep purple aggie. It glinted gorgeously in the light. "Now you can add another one."

They smiled their identical gap-toothed smiles at each other. A beautiful moment. Smiley turned, walked to the dresser, lifted the lid of the apothecary jar and dropped in the marble.

Gram leaned back on her flowered pillow and yawned. Her eyes fluttered and slowly closed. Before we could get a scare, a ladylike snore reassured us.

Smiley perched on the side of the bed and watched her.

After a while, I signaled to Smiley that the beautiful moment was over and it was time to go. He stood up and beckoned me aside. "Do you mind if I stay here awhile?"

His grandmother issued another soft and ladylike snore.

He must have read my mind. "I know, but we got a scare and I realize I may not have that much time with her after being estranged all these years."

"Sure thing. I'll head back and give you some time to-gether. I'll be at the hotel."

I combined the cable cars and walking for the trip back. It was still broad daylight and the city makes you want to walk. It's also hard on the feet. I'd decided to put mine up as soon as I was back in my room, maybe with a glass of something refreshing on that great balcony. It was a vaca-tion, after all, grandmotherly scares or not.

AS I REACHED to put my key in the hotel door, I noticed it was ajar. Had Smiley had a short visit and made better time than I did by taking a cab back to the hotel?

"Tyler?" I said as I pushed it all the way open.

My brain tried to make sense of what I was staring at.

A cyclone would have done less damage. Every article of my clothing had been flung from the closet. I would have collapsed in a chair, but they were both tipped over. The bedding was off the bed and the mattress had been slashed. The pillows too, which explained the feathers flying around the room. My suitcase lining was cut. The liners had also been torn out of my good shoes.

The phone had been ripped from the wall.

In the bathroom, my toiletries were scattered, some broken. The shower curtain was ripped from the rod. Glass littered the floor. The cracked mirror reflected my shocked face.

I felt overwhelmed by a sense of menace and evil.

Come on, now, Jordan. This is the work of a burglar, not some unnamed evil. My sensible side thought that while the rest of me screamed, *But just in case, run!*

I backed out of the bathroom and then out of the room and stood in the hallway, getting my breath. Perhaps the hallway wasn't the safest place. What if the burglar was still making the rounds? I saw no hotel staff within sight. Where was our cheerful maid? I did have the second key to Smiley's room. That door was still closed. I inserted the key card and pushed it open. At least I could call the desk from there, with the deadlock on behind me.

It took a couple of seconds to let the scene in his room register. Half the room was torn up as mine had been, except he had two beds and the mattress was actually tipped off one. The other was still intact. That meant the burglar was still at it. In the bathroom perhaps?

I bolted through the still open door, pulled it closed and raced along the corridor toward the exit, reaching out to bang on doors as I passed and screaming at the top of my lungs. "Fire!"

I knew if you yelled "Thief!" people might hide in their

closets to avoid you, but "Fire!" might get them to the hall-way. It's an old trick from my uncles. It can also help to generate a crowd if you needed one to blend in with. I could have used a crowd, but the trick failed. No one came. As I reached the door to the exit stairs and pushed it open, I turned to see if the burglar was in pursuit. Part of me said, *For the most part, burglars are nonviolent. They want your stuff. Not your life.* The other part said, *Just in case this guy's different, put up the best fight you can.* I raised my fists, figured I could get a nose with one fist and a windpipe with the other. What the uncles called the old one-two when they were teaching a small child self-defense. But there was no time for that.

A bizarre spectral shape loomed over me. I couldn't make sense of it. As I tried to grasp what was happening, I stumbled back on the metal landing. I felt rather than saw the thick bedspread drop over my head and shoulders. Unable to see, I felt myself begin a slow tumble. Slow and painful. Someone gave me a massive push sideways. I reached out to grab where I thought the railing was and just met cloth. I heard the muffled clatter of steps rushing past me and down. My back hit the wall, and I slid down and sat, stunned. I pushed against the cloth and tried to raise it. Three attempts and I finally got my head out. The clatter of feet was distant now. I crawled to the railing and stared down the stairwell. Nothing. No one. Of course, I could hardly see straight with my head whirling and the wail of . . . a fire alarm?

I leaned back and closed my eyes, took a couple of breaths and got to my feet. The door behind me opened and an older woman gasped. "Is there a fire?"

"That was me. Did I say 'Fire'? I meant 'Thief'! Can you call the desk? Tell them to send security, please."

"What?"

An anxious chambermaid carrying towels rushed up

behind her. "What is happening? Are you all right? Is there a fire?"

I shook my head. "Not at this moment. Call security, please."

She pointed around me, "But what's all this?"

"I believe it's a bedspread."

"I don't understand," the woman said. "Why would you take the bedspread from your room?"

"I didn't. Someone else took it and dropped it over me so I couldn't see him."

"And did you see him?"

I shook my head.

"He tried to kill you!"

I gazed at her as my thoughts cleared. "I don't think so."

He, whoever he was, didn't try to kill me, just get me out of commission. He'd tried to make sure I didn't see him. He'd succeeded on both counts. One thing I knew, he'd taken care not to kill me. Or even to injure me seriously.

What had he been trying to do?

CHAPTER SEVEN

Watch what you say to the police.
—THE KELLY RULES

S MILEY WAS BREATHING raggedly when he blew in through the door of the manager's office in the hotel. Like me, he was not a welcome visitor. The manager, a short, thin, nervous individual with small eyes and hands and large feet, stopped pacing and glowered at Smiley. By this time, I was wrapped in a blanket and I foolishly hoped the bedspread would be bagged and placed somewhere secure, say, in an evidence room after forensics had checked it out before long. Of course, I knew better. There wasn't much chance of the attack on me being treated as a high priority as I hadn't been hurt. There was still no sign of the police. I felt there would be pressure from the hotel for them to deal with it. Unless they preferred to keep it under wraps. Having your guests robbed and pushed on stairways wouldn't be good for business.

"What happened?" Smiley said, running his hands through his blond waves. He wasn't blushing this time. In fact, he was whiter than the sheets that had been ripped from my bed. "I went to the room and there's CAUTION tape. Security told me you'd had an incident."

I snorted. "I guess you could call it that."

Smiley stared. I did my best to keep from shaking. The shock of the attack was catching up with me.

"Did you see the room?"

"What? No! I came down here as fast as I could. What happened to you? What kind of a place is this?" He took hold of my shoulders. I thought for a second he was going to shake me—which would not have been well received—but he enveloped me in a tight hug. I buried my face in his chest and tried to stay cool.

The manager, who was even redder than Smiley usually gets, interjected, "We take security very seriously in our hotel. Our policy is—" He practically stamped those large feet of his.

Smiley pulled away and turned to face him.

I said, "Someone broke into my room and trashed it. And when I say trashed, I do mean trashed. Whoever did it was gone. I was sure of that, but the phone was ripped from the wall. I went next door to your room to phone and he must have been in the middle of it. I ran for the stairs and"—I shrugged, embarrassed—"he caught up with me. He dropped a bedspread over my head and pushed me on the landing."

"She pulled the fire alarm," the smirking manager said. "We had to evacuate the hotel."

I rubbed my itchy nose. Perhaps I was about to have a fight. "I did not pull the fire alarm. Someone else did that. Possibly the burglar to create confusion."

"My staff says it was you, miss." His tone was growing more snide by the second.

"Whoever said that is lying."

"I don't think that's possible."

"If you had a staff member who saw me pull the fire alarm, can you please explain why this person didn't help when I was being attacked?"

Oh. Snap.

Smiley said, "Your duty is to your guests and my fiancée has been attacked."

I looked as solemn as I could.

"Perhaps it was a staff member who opened our doors." I turned to Smiley. "I have two keys, one to your room and one to mine. You?"

He reached into his wallet. "The same."

"Therefore, either someone else had a set and that was not okayed by us or more likely a staff member let them in." This was unfair as I knew from reliable sources that there are ways to get by key locks, but I just didn't know what those ways were. I didn't want some hapless chambermaid to get the blame. I'd let the manager push my buttons when my guard was down.

"Where are the police?" Smiley asked tightly.

"They haven't arrived yet."

"What?"

"Security is equipped to take care of this."

"I don't think so," Smiley said. "It's an assault."

"And are you a police officer?" the manager said with a sneer.

"Matter of fact, I am." Smiley's smile had not the faintest touch of warmth in it, as he reached back into his pocket for his badge. "There has been a physical attack on a guest in your hotel and you have chosen not to inform the police. Is that correct?"

"Since you put it that way."

"I do." Smiley picked up the phone and "called it in."

Once the call was made, I said, "We'll need new rooms."

"That is out of the question. We can't be giving new rooms to everyone who—"

I snorted. "Gets attacked in your hotel? Social media will just love that. We had our keys with us, so I'm guessing that it was with inside help. Yes, two rooms, please. Adjoining. I'd like to lie down now."

"You heard the lady," Smiley said in his cop voice. "New rooms. Now."

For once, I didn't mind the cop voice and all it stood for. I didn't understand this manager's attitude at all and I was glad Smiley was in my corner.

The manager looked like he was prepared to fight back on our demand. He stepped out of the room, leaving us to stew for at least five minutes. When he returned, he was a different critter altogether. As Vera might have said, *Butter wouldn't melt in his mouth.*

NEXT WE HAD to deal with the police. Not my best thing at any time. The less said to them, the better. Still, we did want them on our side in this case. I described what I'd seen in the room and what happened to me in the hallway.

I didn't know the name of the witness, but they'd be able to find her easily. The maid was probably still on the floor too.

No, I didn't know their names.

No, I hadn't seen whoever was in the room.

No, I didn't see who pushed me on the staircase because I had a bedspread over my head.

No, nothing seemed to have been taken.

No, I hadn't lost any money or my camera or my jewelry.

No, I had not the slightest idea what they could have been looking for.

Yes, I was all right.

No, I didn't want to go to the hospital.

Yes, I would get in touch if I thought of anything else.

Yes, also if I saw anything.

*   *   *

SMILEY DIDN'T CARE much for his interview either. I suppose it's hard to be on the other side of the law.

"You know what?" he said.

"I don't."

"They didn't seem to take the other two things seriously at all."

"Other two things?"

"The Prius and the cable car. Now that we've had this—"

"*I've* had this. And I was hurt by the Prius and pushed from the cable car."

"Sorry. I know you were attacked, but both our rooms were trashed so it's *we* in some way. The point is that three times in twenty-four hours can't be a coincidence."

"And the officer said?"

He said, "Asked about a plate number, asked about a description, asked about the cable car number—"

"Well, who would have that?"

"Not us for sure. We could narrow it down."

"There are people in this hotel who were on the cable car. We could ask them to speak to the police."

"That's a good idea. I wasn't paying much attention to who was there. Were you?"

"Yes, I—"

"I hope you'll be happy with these rooms," the manager said, rubbing his small, white hands together as he presented our new accommodations. "You've had a shock and we want our clients to be comfortable."

Who wouldn't be happy? We seemed to have scored the best digs in the hotel. I noticed he hadn't said "safe and comfortable." But comfortable was pretty darn good. I had ditched my security blanket in the office so I was able to stroll through the hotel with a bit of dignity.

"The Bay View Suite is our best suite and luckily it was

available. It should leave you with wonderful memories of our hotel." His eyes pleaded for feedback, or did I imagine that?

"Beautiful," I said, "and with its own living room and dining area."

"And the bar." He beamed. "Plus of course, you are high enough to have a spectacular view from your own private balcony."

As much as I wanted to crash on the bed and not talk to anyone, I followed him out to the balcony. He was right. The view of the Bay was unbeatable in between foggy patches. There was stunning architecture wherever you looked. I could only imagine how gorgeous it would be at night. A door from the living area led out to it and so did a door from each of the bedrooms. We could never afford something like this and all it took was having our rooms trashed and me being attacked on the stairs.

"I'll leave you then, will I?" the manager said, disappearing through the door.

Before I could say, "I wonder what changed his attitude?" he popped his head in and said, "Of course, your belongings have been shifted to your new rooms. You should find everything to your satisfaction. We will make arrangements for you to dine at Magari tonight at our expense, if that meets with your approval." I suppose he didn't really click his heels together, but just as good as. He left us nodding.

When the coast was clear, Smiley turned to me. I said, "Are they really that worried I'll sue over the break-in?"

"If they have an idea that an employee was involved, that might explain it. Also the attack on you in the staircase probably has them worried. I guess it has you worried too."

If I knew that look, Smiley was worried as well. "You could have been killed."

"Well, that's the thing. I don't think so."

"Pushing a person down a metal staircase is good way to do them in."

"Agreed, except that he didn't push me down the stairs. I've been thinking about what happened and he threw the spread over me, so I wouldn't see his face."

"And then he pushed you."

"Yes, but he pushed me sideways. He didn't push me down. I was stunned by the whole attack and I'm just starting to make sense of it."

"Are you sure? It's an act of violence to throw something over a person's head to obscure their view and then push them on a staircase when they'd be helpless to break their fall."

"I know that. I experienced it, remember? And I'm telling you that he pushed me sideways to the wall. And before you ask again, yes, I am sure. It was serious, no question, but I don't think he meant to kill me. He wanted to avoid being seen by me or anyone else. He needed to get away. I was probably a distraction too."

"But people might have seen him anyway."

"Why are you arguing with me? I'm the one who was there. And don't use your cop voice."

"Fine. So he didn't intend to kill you?"

"Good question. But why couldn't I see him?"

"Because you had a bedspread over your head."

"Funny. I mean what difference would it make if I saw him?"

"You could have identified him, given the police a description, which you were not able to do."

"Or maybe it was because I would recognize him."

"What?"

"It's not like we know anyone here, and you've told me how hard it is to get an accurate description of an assailant in a fast attack."

"You think you knew the person?"

"More like I would recognize him. Maybe."

Smiley leaned back and exhaled. "Someone around the

hotel? A staff member or another guest. That would make sense. But even if he didn't intend to harm you, that was a precarious situation. You could have been killed."

"Could have been. It was a risky move. What I'm trying to say is that he wasn't trying to kill me or he could have."

"So it wasn't personal."

"The ransacking of the rooms felt personal. He was looking for something. Something very specific."

"What did you have that he was looking for?"

"I have no idea, Tyler. Like I said to the cops, nothing seemed to be taken. He didn't take my jewelry or my tablet or camera. Then he hit your room. He must have still been there when I surprised him."

Smiley scratched his nose. He only does that when he's irritated. "Why you?"

"No clue. Why you?"

He shot me a look. "Let's take this seriously."

"I'm the one who got the worst of it. Trust me, Tyler, I am taking it very seriously. And I think we both have something to worry about because he didn't find what he was looking for."

Smiley stared at me without speaking.

I made my point. "Therefore, he's going to keep looking."

CHAPTER EIGHT

Someone is always listening to you.
—THE KELLY RULES

THE HOTEL STAFF had done a commendable job of putting my belongings back in order. The smiling young chambermaid knocked to deliver extra fluffy snow-white towels. I recognized her from the fourth floor. I supposed that she was the person who'd lined up my shoes precisely on the closet floor and arranged my notebook, camera and sightseeing books neatly on the desk. I was glad I'd left her a tip at our previous room. She or someone had shaped our fluffy facecloths into swans.

My toiletry bag was hanging on the back of the door in the huge marble bathroom. They were falling all over themselves to make it right.

"You're working long hours," I said as she backed out of the room.

"I need to," she said as she left.

I sat on the crisp white duvet on my new king-size bed and told myself to get it together. This was a vacation and one we both needed. It was a chance to rebuild trust. Even though we'd had our hotel rooms trashed in what seemed like a very personal way and even though I'd been attacked by persons unknown, I had to admit Smiley and I had been through a lot worse than this.

"Dinner," I said out loud, "will be the best medicine."

I HAD A little red dress I'd been saving for a special occasion and this situation certainly needed help. The dress was cotton jersey and required some serious undergarments to make it cling in just the right places. Plus it was just long enough to cover my battered knees, a very good thing.

A thin gold vintage belt hugged my waist. It made me feel like a femme fatale, so I was surprised that Smiley didn't even offer a "you look nice."

He continued to be silent on our stroll to Magari. I tried to get back to the buoyant frame of mind I'd been in before the break-in, but whenever I glanced at Smiley's closed face, the mood slipped. If this kept up, he was going to need another nickname. Surly perhaps or Grumpy.

We passed many restaurants full of happy tourists spilling out into the street, as we left the more touristy areas and ventured into the parts of San Francisco where people actually lived. So many places to eat and we were walking past all of them. I liked the looks of the bistros in old storefronts and the eateries in converted homes. They all seemed to be overflowing with twentyish trendy locals, eating, laughing and making noise. On the main streets, we passed a surprising number of gelaterias. I love gelato. On a normal night I would have suggested that we get gelato after dinner, but this night I would be having dinner in a lovely restaurant compliments of the hotel.

Officer Grumpy was walking slightly ahead of me, his head down, hands in pockets. If this had been our first date, it would have also been the last. But I figured Smiley was in there somewhere. As I didn't have anyone to talk to, I could spend my time speculating about his mood.

I didn't have time to do much speculating when after twenty minutes—much of it uphill—we arrived at the restaurant. Magari was a traditional restaurant, heavy on the dim lighting and velvet drapes. It seemed out of step with the city. It screamed vintage 1974, which was perfect for me, of course, although it was before I was born. And the price was right. Along with the low lights, comfortable leather chairs and crisp white tablecloths, red cloth napkins and bud vases with red carnations, there was a collection of older waiters, all of whom had a tendency to bow slightly and snap their fingers at each other. Inside we found only five other couples seated, all with a good thirty years on us. At least they were having a good time. I liked the quiet clink of wineglasses and the exclamations when food arrived. The couples within my view were smilers and chatters, all caught up in each other. In fact, they all looked like lovers, not old-marrieds. Only Grumpy and I would have given the impression that we'd been married for thirty years, all of them less than happy.

It was after nine by the time we were seated. The tall doughy waiter passed us menus with an old world flourish, bowed, lit the candle on our table and recommended an Italian red as their featured wine. Grumpy didn't put up a fight. The valpolicella sounded good to me.

I had a bit of nostalgia for the signora's dinners as each plate went sailing by to our fellow diners. My experience was that restaurants couldn't really compare. But I had decided to enjoy it anyway despite the sourpuss sitting across from me. Every now and then I used my phone to capture the restaurant's décor, the other diners and the hilarious waiters.

I went for the *gamberi in Sambucca*. I didn't recall the

signora ever cooking shrimp in Sambucca and cream, so I had no feelings of disloyalty. It did not disappoint. I oohed and aahed over it, camping it up a bit. "So creamy and with just a tiny hint of garlic."

Grumpy had the soup special and apparently not a word to say about it. It smelled wonderful from across the table.

All that lack of conversation gave me time to think about our break-in, about our relocation, about the strange inconsistent behavior and the over-the-top generosity of the manager, including dinner in this out-of-the-way time-warp restaurant.

For my second plate I opted for the *agnolotti* stuffed with butternut squash. I love all pastas, but especially stuffed ones, and Vera couldn't abide squash. We all know that what Vera can't abide doesn't turn up at Van Alst House. Once again, I could enjoy it with a clear conscience. My dining companion moved on to the lasagna, a safe choice.

The *agnolotti* were plump and stuffed with flavorful squash and a hint of what? Sage? Brown butter? Whatever it was, the dish was worthy, served as it was, alone with no distracting vegetables, but with large shavings of very good *parmegiano reggiano*.

Apparently, the lasagna didn't merit a single comment. In fact, Smiley didn't eat more than a third of it, pushing the rest randomly around the plate.

I, on the other hand, considered ordering a second plate of *agnolotti* for dessert. I didn't think the waiter would cope with that break with tradition, however, so I stuck with the dessert menu. Like the dinner list, there were no surprises. I went with *tartuffo*. Again, something the signora didn't serve.

As our large waiter bowed his way toward the kitchen with our orders, Grumpy stared at the table and drummed his fingers on it. I turned my attention to the other couples on the other side of the restaurant. One couple was head to head, foreheads touching as they shared a laugh, seemingly oblivious to the rest of us. I suppose I must have leaned sideways a bit to get a better look at them, maybe soak up a bit of that joyful spirit. As I did, my red napkin slipped to the floor. I bent over to get it, and for some unknown reason I lifted my head a bit too fast and banged it on the underside of the table. I gave the table a dirty look as if that made any sense. Of course, the way the evening was going, I could expect a bit more sympathy from that wooden table than from my dinner companion. I rubbed my head and did a double take. The waiter had hurried back, bowing, as I sat up straight in my seat. "Signorina! So sorry! Are you all right? More wine. Yes!" He snapped his fingers and a much smaller waiter came running with an emergency refill. He was obviously of the same school as the signora. I found myself shaking my head and saying, "No, thank you." It didn't work, of course.

"I'm fine really," I said, caving in to the extra wine. Why fight it?

Grumpy managed to ask, "Are you okay?"

I had just clearly said I was fine, but I let that go and nodded.

The waiter filled my glass and for good measure Mr. Grumpy's glass too.

Both waiters eased away from the table with a flurry of well-wishing, the older one giving the occasional bow. I raised my glass and smiled at him. *Thank you*, I mouthed.

"There's something I need to tell you," Mr. Grumpy said.

Uh-oh. What was up? Rethinking the relationship now that we were on the other side of the continent? "Can it wait?"

"It can't. And I am sorry." The old familiar blush was making its way to the roots of his hair. He still wasn't making eye contact.

I glanced over at the waiters, who were no longer paying

attention to us because they were busy snapping their fingers at the busboys, and then I turned my eyes toward to the laughing couple, who had never even noticed us in the first place.

Smiley leaned forward and opened his mouth.

I made the international sign for "zip your lip."

"Don't be like that," he said. "I'm trying to—"

Sometimes you just have to take action. I knocked over his water glass onto his lap. The look on his face almost made up for all the glowering.

"Let me help you," I said, grabbing napkins from the next table as well as ours. I moved to his side and began to "assist."

"Please stop," he said.

I leaned in as if to give him a peck on the cheek, as the other couple seemed to be doing again.

"Have you lost your mind?"

I whispered in his ear, "Don't tell me anything. There's a bug under the table, a listening device."

Already waiters were scurrying to address our problem.

"No problem," Smiley said to them. "We can manage."

"So clumsy of me," I said with a bit of a simper. I returned to my side of the table and swilled a bit of wine. I raised my glass to Tyler and winked.

He lifted his glass, shrugged and managed a weak grin.

I beamed at the waiter. "You know, I think I'll have the *tiramisu* as well as the *tartuffo*. One lonely dessert never seems to do the trick."

Before and during the second dessert, I filled the air with chatter, especially my hope of doing a boat cruise around the bay and maybe going to Napa for a wine tour. I babbled merrily about everything except what I was really worried about: the strange things that had happened since we'd been in San Francisco.

As for Tyler's big secret, I'd already known he was guilty

about something. He's a very ineffective liar, having missed the formidable training that growing up with my uncles provided me. Despite that, I preferred to be honest with each other whenever possible.

We finished our second desserts and ordered Spanish coffees. Tyler was starting to squirm, but I felt like running up the bill for whoever had arranged this dinner in order to tape our conversation. My money might have been on the hotel manager, but this whole day had been so full of unknowns. One thing I did know—that manager had whopping big feet and he wasn't the person who had dropped that bedspread over my head. The mic under the table of the restaurant he'd sent us to certainly made it look like he was implicated. But how? And who else was involved for whatever reasons?

Perhaps I'd know more when Tyler finally was able to get that confession off his chest. Whatever it was, I was hoping it wasn't a breakup.

We did at least leave a tip. After all, it's not every day you get all those bows and all that finger snapping. The other couples did glance up as we stood to leave. Tyler managed to preserve his dignity by folding his jacket over his arm and letting it hide the water stain on the front of his pants. Face it. Wet pants aren't a good look for anybody.

As we finally made our way out of the restaurant, waiters bowing and waving as we went, I leaned into him, this time without doing him any damage. He seemed to be feeling a bit better, all things considered, but something was still weighing on him.

I wondered if he could have hidden something in his hotel room that caused all this trouble and why he wouldn't have mentioned it. I could see how that would make a person feel bad.

We strolled past the many gelato shops on our way back, but even I couldn't have managed another bite.

"Whoever planted that bug didn't get their money's worth tonight," I said, giving him a little poke in the ribs, "but we sure did."

He nodded grimly. I took that to mean he would have enjoyed it more if he hadn't had the weight of the world on his shoulders. Sure I'd made a few remarks about Mr. Grumpy, but it really hadn't bothered me all that much, maybe because I eat three meals a day with a woman who has raised disagreeability to an art form.

I gave him a nudge with my elbow to follow up on the poke. "Sorry about the glass of water on your lap. I wasn't aiming for you but I did need you not to say anything you didn't want to have taped. Not that I know what you were going to say, but I'm sure you'll tell me in good time." I added a silent "or else" to that.

Figuring that I could wait, I linked arms with him and said, "When you're ready."

I decided to relax and enjoy the evening walk. Unlike our quiet town of Harrison Falls, the sidewalks were teaming with people, ambling along in twos and threes, walking dogs, wheeling bikes, relaxing in outdoor cafés, eating gelato, you name it. Some older women in uniforms trudged with heavy shopping bags, younger men and women jogged by in sleek sportswear. A place for everyone, this town.

"Tomorrow will be our gelato day," I said, leaning in. The thing was I still felt the tingle of attraction to my grouchy police officer. He didn't have the lean handsome face of the man who had robbed me of my college fund and maxed out my credit cards before leaving me high and dry. And he didn't have Lance's kooky charm and movie star looks. He was committed to being a police officer although that was the worst possible match for me given my family. He didn't always do what I wanted, but in the long run he was there for me. He'd changed jobs for me. He was ridiculously neat and organized and believed in the rules and doing his duty, but he'd still taken unpaid leave from the new job for this special vacation, to make a new start for us. No question that he was the guy for me. And eventually, I'd learn why he was being such a pain in the behind during that new start.

A silent but not unpleasant twenty minutes downhill and we were strolling along the boardwalk by the edge of the bay, along with a gazillion other starry-eyed visitors. We found a convenient bench and sat down to stare happily until we lost ourselves in the images of the glittering water.

Just as the evening chill was starting to sink in, he said. "I'm sorry."

"Oh well, people get in bad moods. Too bad it was during our free, no-strings-attached dinner."

"It's a good thing you spotted that device . . ."

I stopped myself from saying, "I know." No one likes an "I-know-it-all."

"Because I was about to tell you something."

"Oh yeah."

"I was keeping it from you."

As if I didn't know. I squeezed his hand.

"I think I know what they were looking for."

I waited. I felt a knot in my stomach that had nothing to do with two desserts and a Spanish coffee.

"It's something I had in the room."

I took a breath and thought, as Vera might have said out loud, "In our lifetime." Really, he was too much sometimes.

"I hid it under the mattress in the bed by the window. I guess you interrupted him before he got that far."

I couldn't stop myself. "And what was it? The Hope Diamond?"

"Don't laugh. It was a photo album."

"What?"

"A photo album."

That came as a surprise. "What photo album? You

carried an album with you? What for? Why didn't you mention it?"

"Which question do you want me to answer?"

"Pick one."

"My grandmother gave me the album."

"She did? When?"

"My first visit when I went without you. You were on your hunt for vintage stuff, I went to see her on my own. I'm sorry. I didn't mention the album. Don't know why."

"I know not a single person from the Bingham family. If I was given an album, I would want some time alone with it. I get it and you don't need to apologize."

"Thanks. I wasn't sure what was going on in my head."

"No worries. Tell me about the album."

"It was just an old family album, pictures of my dad when he was a kid, pictures of his father. Pictures of Gram. Some of me as a baby and as a kid with Gram before the family got . . . messed up."

"But that must have been wonderful."

"It was. Gram said some of these pictures were the only ones left. So, yeah, it's great. I intended to show it to you . . ."

"It's okay."

"I just needed some time with it."

"I get it."

"Alone. I guess that's stupid. I feel like a jerk about tonight. I get tied up in knots sometimes."

"Not stupid. Look, Tyler, there's nothing at all surprising in you wanting to look at this album alone. It's a big emotional load and of course you needed to keep it to yourself for a while. If someday you want to share it, I'd love to look at it, but you don't need to worry about that. Just get your head around this newfound relationship and enjoy it."

"Thanks."

"I'm glad they didn't find it."

"Yeah, me too."

"How did you get it from the room without anyone knowing?"

He shrugged and, for the first time since the robbery, showed his grin. *Welcome back, Smiley.*

"Sometimes it pays to be a police officer."

"Nice. And a bit noir."

He did his best to look noirish but, you know, with the blond curls, the little gap between the front teeth and that blush, it didn't come easy.

"Um. Did you slip it under the mattress again?"

He hesitated.

I said, "I hope you've decided to trust me."

"Right. I figured they wouldn't look twice. Although now that I'm saying it out loud, it does seem pretty stupid that anyone would turn over two hotel rooms and attack you over an old family photo album. I don't know why I thought that."

"Exactly. It's not like you were the Romanovs."

"I think you're right. I hid it because—"

I squeezed his hand. "Told you, I get it. It means a lot to you."

"I've been feeling more like a teenage girl than a cop over the whole hidden photo album thing. Glad it's out in the open."

"It's not really a Hammettish behavior, is it? Or maybe it is. I mean what would Nick Charles say?"

"He'd say that it's been too long between drinks."

I laughed. "Nora's up for it. But while we're sipping, we'll have to figure out why our table was bugged."

He stiffened. "It has to be the manager."

"Agreed."

"I can't figure out why he's involved but my gut tells me he is."

"He is pretty strange. On the other hand, we have that fabulous suite and we had a pretty good dinner—"

"Easy for you, you didn't get a glass of water dropped in your lap."

"That's true and I enjoyed every mouthful of dinner because *I* wasn't consumed with guilt over something perfectly understandable, but that's all behind us now."

"Maybe you were hiding something from me too."

"Maybe I am." There was that Guy Noir Bobblehead, saved for the right occasion. "I'm not consumed with guilt, but I am really wondering what there is about us that's attracting the wrong kind of attention."

"Chances are that some crook has one or both of us mixed up with somebody else."

"I should take notes. Option one: Mistaken identity. Sounds right for a Hammett adventure. Just add fog and stir."

"It does sound right."

"Then option two: How about someone thinks we have something belonging to them?"

"Like what? Not the photo album?"

"Well, that's the mystery, isn't it?"

"I don't see what we could have that belongs to someone we don't even know about."

"I'm just speculating because we don't really have anything to go on. You're a cop. Don't you come up with hypotheses during an investigation? What harm can it do?"

He said, "You're right. What about option three: Maybe a random burglar with a mean streak. Most likely in real life."

"That would be the hardest option, because we'd never find out, would we?"

"This is a big town, and as upsetting as it was, it's still a small crime and won't be big on the cops' priorities. We'll probably never know anyway. Although it seems unlikely that it's random considering the Prius incident and the cable car attack both involved—"

"Me. So it's got to be connected. Maybe option four brings us back to the manager."

"No question. Upgrading us to a suite, giving us a free dinner in a pricey restaurant, I wondered about that."

"What are you thinking?"

He rumpled his forehead. "A theft ring? Some kind of blackmail scam? Could happen, I suppose. I guess my idea about the album was just the guilt talking."

"No doubt. And maybe when this so-called ring found out you were a cop, they decided to treat you with kid gloves."

Our eyes met and we both found ourselves laughing. "That is a bit ridiculous," I admitted.

"More than a bit. Everything's a stretch."

"But even so, it is strange that we were treated like that."

He said, "My guess is that they were afraid of a lawsuit. If you could make the case that their room keys weren't secure and guests could be attacked in the stairwell. An unoccupied suite and then springing a couple hundred for dinner is a small price to pay to keep us from getting lawyers or cops involved."

"And don't forget the social media threat. But then how do we explain the bug under the table?"

Smiley said, "Same deal. They want to make sure that they know what we were planning. Take our measure."

"They went to a fair amount of trouble. Do you think they were hoping to hear something they could use against us?"

"Like I said, they'd want anything to steer clear of a lawsuit or a police investigation."

"Well, let's lull them into a false sense of security when we get back."

Considering we didn't know what was going on or who was behind it, we were in a great mood as we returned.

We made a point of stopping to see the manager to thank

him for the dinner and to test an idea. It was obvious he'd been working a brutally long shift. No wonder he seemed out of sorts. We laid it on thick.

"Excellent," I gushed. "We had fun and it was so good to have a chance to have a great meal and just think about what we're going to do next."

Smiley said, "Given the seriousness of the attack on Jordan and the damage done to our rooms, I am assuming that you have arranged for extra security to protect us while we're here."

I thought the manager might have paled.

"Of course," he said. I was surprised his pointed nose didn't grow another inch in front of us.

I burbled, "We'll head off to our suite now. And we thank you again for that."

It was hard not to collapse laughing in the elevator, but I managed to look like a normal person until we reached the ninth floor, opened the door to our suite and let the laughter out.

"I won't sleep a wink tonight anyway," I said to Smiley, five minutes later, shortly before stepping into my bedroom, keeling over on the bed and slipping from consciousness.

It had been quite a day.

CHAPTER NINE

*Use what you can find and find what
you can use.*
—THE KELLY RULES

"BAD NEWS," SMILEY said, knocking on the door.
I opened my eyes with a start. Like every morning it
took me a moment to figure out where I was.

"What?"

"No one got in when we were sleeping. So we're no closer
to figuring out the mystery."

"That's too bad and I suppose they didn't murder us in
our sleep either?"

"Correct."

"Well then, Officer Dekker, I suppose we have no choice
but to drown our sorrows in breakfast. Let me get ready.
Why don't we call room service and you can show me the
photo album without anyone else getting a look at it, in the
unlikely possibility that's why our rooms were trashed."

He scowled. "Room service? That sounds—"

"Decadent? Yes, it does, but in this case, also sensible.
Anyway, it can be my treat. Eggs Benedict and OJ? It's
supposed to be a specialty at La Perla."

A half hour later, we were sniffing the sea air and eyeing

the trolley that the room service waiter had maneuvered onto the balcony. I love the decadence of room service and this hotel did a beautiful job, from the snowy linen napkins to the large pot of coffee and the gerbera daisy in the little vase. We were instructed to take our seats on the balcony while the server uncovered our plates with a flourish. The Bennies were perfect with Canadian bacon and English muffins, the eggs medium, the way we like them. The Hollandaise sauce was excellent, buttery and rich with just a hint of lemon. Everything had survived the trip to the ninth floor. The meal came with a lovely fresh fruit salad—melon, orange and strawberries—and memorable sourdough toast with butter and jam.

We had no complaints about this meal, even though toward the end Smiley seemed to be getting a bit morose again.

"We agreed. No more secrets. Tell me what's bothering you now."

"It's just that my grandmother called when you were in the shower. She'd like me to go see her again today."

"You must go see your grandmother again. I realize how important this reunion is."

"And she'd like you to come too. I'm not sure that's how you want to spend your vacation."

"Well, it is now. She's part of the San Francisco experience. Are you going to waste that sourdough toast? Because I'm still here."

He laughed. "It's all yours and I guess you'll have plenty of opportunity to walk it off, but first we're going to the International Spy Shop. It's not far from here. Let's see what's new in bug sweepers."

"Oooh, and here I thought we'd be unscrewing lightbulbs and checking behind smoke detectors and maybe taking off the trim . . ."

"I've already looked everywhere. These are modern times, Jordan. Let's see what we can turn up."

A half hour later we were at the cashier of the International Spy Shop with a small laser bug detector and a small batch of cameras ready for purchase. I loved this shop. My uncles would have approved of the detour, provided they were on the right side of the camera, if you get my drift.

The equipment set Smiley back a few hundred dollars but the damage could have been much more worse. Anyway, he was in a Nick Charles extravagant kind of mood, even though it was the wrong town. There were many other types of detectors and some ran into the thousands, but Smiley said we had a good chance of finding any of the simple types. "We'll make do with what we have. After all, our burglar and my assailant weren't the most sophisticated of criminals—they didn't care if we knew they'd been there."

"No kidding."

"If someone is checking out our room, they won't be expecting this."

I had invested in a miniature video camera, which I thought would capture anyone who was prowling around in our living room, and one for the bedroom too. And I'd found an adorable and chic little pen camera that I thought Uncle Kev's special friend, Cherie, would just love. Cherie hadn't been on my gift list until the moment I saw the perfect item for her.

We left the shop with a spring in our steps, laughing and nudging each other.

It was a great start to the day as Smiley installed his unit in the living room and I happily placed mine behind the thermostat in my bedroom.

If someone managed to get in there again, we'd have a record of it.

WE SPENT SOME time strolling on the Embarcadero, soaking up the atmosphere and walking off the Bennies.

Unfortunately, the stroll and the air on the waterfront made us hungry. We fixed that with the gelatos we'd missed the night before. Smiley went off on a Hammett tour and I fiddled about in fun little shops. It was a rough life.

THE INVITATION TO Gram's was for a late lunch: a crab casserole and green salad. Very nice.

I played with the little dog, whistled to the cockatiels and avoided the mean parrot while they chatted. "Come here," it said. I didn't.

"Pet, could I get you to take care of some business for me while you're here?" Gram asked.

Smiley said, "Name it."

Perhaps he spoke too soon because Gram had a prepared list that involved him dropping papers off here, getting signatures there and even going to her bank to sign documents that added him to her accounts.

"It's all set up. You only need to turn up and sign. And I've arranged a quick meeting with my financial advisor, just to introduce yourself. I'm not so sure about him and I'd like you to give me your opinion as a police officer."

Quite the list. I got the impression that Gram had been waiting a long time to get these things sorted out.

WITH GRAM PLANNING a nap and Tyler on his errands, I was off the hook and I was itching to continue exploring the city. So everyone would be happy. I might be happier than Smiley because I would be having fun and not doing boring tasks. But I had a nagging bit of worry about Gram. I didn't know why. She'd obviously done just fine without us all these years. But maybe it was Zoya's nervous ways. And my own nerves were jangled over the things that had happened to us since we'd arrived. I knew it was silly.

On my way out, I spotted the television flickering in the kitchen. Zoya had her TV addiction, I'd already heard. A local news item about a murder was on the screen and I stopped in my tracks. A photo of a familiar face flashed across the screen. There in better days, the victim looked horribly familiar. I knew those twinkly dark eyes and that dramatic hair with the silver streak. Still, somehow I wasn't surprised that it had been a mug shot.

Zoya switched the channel just as the announcer intoned, *Police said that the victim—*

"Get the channel back, please!"

"Vat? I don't know vat channel. Too late. Go avay."

It was too late. And I did go away, but I had a heavy heart as I thought that perhaps the twinkly Farley Tso might be no more. A mistake, I told myself. Not at all likely that it was Farley. There are plenty of handsome men in late middle age with splendid manes of hair. And there was one way to find out.

AS I LEFT Gram's, I was happy to spot the pretty young neighbor across the street, sporting a new active wear outfit, aqua and gray. She was either heading into or out of her home.

She lit up when she saw me and waved. I crossed the street (not that easy mid-block) to chat. She gushed. "It's so nice that you're moving in. I told Michael—that's my husband—and he's so happy too. Everyone on the block is at least a hundred. So, no kids of your own yet?"

"What? Oh. I'm not—"

"I know you're not a hundred. I can't wait until you're here."

"I'm not moving in."

Her lovely luminous face fell. I felt like I'd told some innocent child there was no Santa Claus. "You're not? But you and your hus—"

"Not my husband."

"Sorry. Partner."

"No. Not even partner. Well, maybe, it's early days. Anyway, we're just here on vacation. We're visiting his grandmother. She lives here." I pointed up the stairs.

"Oh."

"It's a really happy visit for my, um, friend. And his gram can't be a day over eighty-five."

She giggled. "Better than the rest of them then. Well, it's too bad. We just moved in last week. I was looking forward to having friends on this block. And Harry would have liked little friends too."

"Harry?"

She rolled her eyes. "The little beast was up every hour all night long. We are bushed. And now he's quiet." She pointed to the stroller where Harry was covered up and sleeping off another awake night. He'd be waiting a long time before I provided him with playmates.

"Well," I said, "I hope you find some friends in the neighborhood soon."

"Hmm. It can be quite boring."

"You're very friendly. I'm sure it won't be long."

"By the way. I'm Sierra."

"Jordan."

"How long are you here, Jordan?"

"Another four days."

"Oh well." She seemed to lose all interest in me. I figured maybe I wasn't worth the investment of time as I wasn't moving into one of these multimillion-dollar properties. *Easy come, easy go*, as Uncle Mick would say. She yanked up the stroller and prepared to open the glossy black door with the antique brass knocker.

But I had an idea. A fairly good one with no downside that I could see.

I said, "It must be so difficult taking care of a child all the time. I had something I wanted to ask you but—"

"More like so boring, but anyway . . ." She lifted her perfectly sculpted eyebrows in question.

"Right. I just wondered. We are a bit worried about Gram, that's Tyler's grandmother, of course."

"Only eighty-five," she said.

"Yes, but we are worried about who might be trying to influence her and all that. Would you . . . oh really, I shouldn't ask."

"Would I what?"

Of course, she'd said she was bored.

"Just keep an eye on the place."

Her mouth turned down. From our previous conversations, I gathered that old people were not her cup of tea. "You mean visit?"

"No, no, no, of course not. Just observe."

"Well, I'd like to help but I don't really . . . well, I can't be tied down. I have obligations. Harry and Michael and other things."

"Of course you do. I shouldn't have asked." *What obligations?* I thought. *To get those perfect nails done? To jog to the gym? To think about finding a nanny for Harry?*

She said, "I'm really sorry."

"Don't give it a moment's thought. I was out of line to even ask. Forget I mentioned it."

I waved and stepped away to start my walk to the cable car.

"Wait," she called out.

I turned, not wishing to utter another batch of groveling apologies.

"What exactly would be involved?"

By now I was feeling ridiculous. "Nothing really. Just keep an eye on anyone coming and going."

"That wouldn't be all that often really."

"True. And I'd only ask if you were comfortable doing it."

"I see. Because it *is* kind of spying on the neighbors."

"I hadn't thought about it that way. I thought it's more like keeping an eye on a vulnerable"—I paused, not wanting to say "old lady" because I knew that wasn't a selling point—"and charming person." The charming part was true and possibly the vulnerable part was too.

"Hmm."

"Look, don't worry about it. I was out of line even suggesting it. I just thought you could give me a call if someone who wasn't the housekeeper or me or Tyler came to the house."

"Tyler is your partner? The one I met when you were walking up the hill?"

"Yes, sorry. I guess I never mentioned his name."

"I know what he looks like, so cute with those baby blues and the smile. But I've never seen the housekeeper."

I described Zoya as kindly as I could in words that Sierra would appreciate "Dark red lipstick and nails, dark hair in a bun, very slender, well-dressed and with a tendency to wave her hands in the air. And shout."

"Would there be any risk?"

Risk? What risk could there be letting your eye rest on someone just long enough to describe them and then calling me with that description?

"None," I said with what I hoped was an air of gravitas. "*Absolutely* none whatsoever. Not a scintilla." That was rather a bit of verbal overkill, but she seemed to buy it.

"That's good," she said.

"All I'd want would be for you to call or text me *if*—and it's a big if—you saw something. You might say, um, write,

'The postal carrier was here with something today,' or whatever, from the safety of your own home, by phone. First of all, no one would be at all worried about you or suspicious of you." I gave my biggest fake smile. Who knows why it was so fake when it was all true? "We're just a bit worried that some people may be trying to intimidate her."

"That's awful."

"Yes."

"Who are they?"

"We don't exactly know."

"What do they look like?"

"There you have me. I have no idea what they look like. I don't know why I'm worrying." Of course, there had been no suggestion of anything wrong at Gram's, but I worried that perhaps we might be bringing trouble to her. There was, after all, the photo album, which Smiley had returned at lunchtime. It was probably silly to connect these events, but for some reason I chose not to tell Sierra about the Prius, the cable car and the trashed room.

"I'll do it."

"There's a good chance that you'll never see a single human at that door and that will be fine too."

"I guess you better give me your cell number before I change my mind."

I jotted my number down on a paper, got Sierra's and made a big show of thanking her before heading on my way.

"Thank you!"

Sierra was no kind of security system, but because I'd done something, I felt better.

I HAD JUST reached La Perla after a fun bit of exploration when my cell phone rang and Sierra's breathless voice floated out.

"I see someone!"

"Who?" I realized that was a ridiculous question even before it was out of my mouth. How could Sierra know the answer?

"I'm not sure. Actually I have no idea. I mean, how would I know?"

"Silly me. Not sure why I said that."

"Anyway, they went in!"

I barely stopped myself from shouting and managed to keep my voice calm. "Was it a man or a woman?"

"Two men, I think. It's hard to tell sometimes."

Really? "What did they look like?"

"Like ordinary people. Maybe thirtyish. Tall. Not too thin, kind of big . . ."

"And not too fat," I interjected nervously.

"Well, this is San Francisco."

"True. Fair? Dark?"

"I couldn't really tell. They had umbrellas and hats. And raincoats, like, you know, trench coats."

Umbrellas as well as hats? Trench coats? If that wasn't suspicious, I didn't know what would be. And what thirtyish couple wore hats? Of course, this was, as we'd agreed, San Francisco so maybe trilbies or fedoras or were those no longer hip enough? Anyway, it all sounded like a B movie or maybe a scene from a Hammett page turner.

While we were talking, I was struggling into my denim jacket and desert boots using one hand. In case I had to leave in a hurry.

"Did the housekeeper turn them away?" That was my hope. Zoya to za rescue.

"I didn't see the housekeeper."

"Oh. Did they leave yet?"

"No. They just went in. The door opened but I didn't see anyone behind it and they just disappeared inside."

"No one answered? But you can see the door from your place, can't you?"

"Oh sure, but I didn't see anyone come to the door and I don't think anyone was there. I mean why would the house-keeper be hiding?"

"Right. When was this, Sierra?"

"Just before I called you."

"Great. Keep an eye on the house, and I'll get up there and see what they want."

Sierra's voice rose. "What could they want? She's a lit-tle old lady, isn't she? It's not like she could get into any trouble."

What a foolish statement. Vera might technically qualify as a little old lady, but she got (and got me) into boatloads of trouble on a regular basis. The same might apply to Gram.

"I'm on my way." I sprinted down the hotel corridor to the staircase and clattered down it, trying not to think about having a blanket tossed over my head. My head was thun-dering as I hit the ground floor and exploded into the foyer. The concierge looked up in surprise. "Taxi," I said, "and it's urgent."

"Did you say urgent?" Sierra squeaked. Oops. She was still on the phone.

"No no. Just a cab. I'll get there soon and check on her. Probably nothing at all." I raced after the concierge, who had somewhat magically made a cab appear. These people had power.

Sierra twittered, "I always use Uber. Don't you have the app?"

"No time."

"Right. Of course. What could it be?"

"Exactly. What indeed? I'll let you know. Call me if they leave again," I launched myself into the backseat and gave the address to the bored-looking driver. "I'll be there soon."

"Oh, this is exciting," Sierra said as I hung up. I practiced deep breathing all the way up the nearly vertical hill to California Street.

Hats and umbrellas and raincoats, I kept repeating to myself. Hats *and* umbrellas *and* raincoats. Of course it's not nothing. *Naturally.* I also kept repeating, *Smiley, where the hell are you?* With shaking hands, I called him. It went straight to voice mail. Perhaps he was in one of those meetings? My message was clear: *Get to Gram's now. Strangers in the house.*

I thrust the fare into the cabbie's outstretched hand and exited. I took the steps to Gram's house two at a time. The front door was not quite closed and it wouldn't take a detective first grade to figure out it had been jimmied.

Jimmying front doors in broad daylight is not the behavior of medical professionals, sincere relatives, government officials or anyone else with good intentions. It meant that whoever was inside wasn't to be trusted and was most likely dangerous.

I made another call to Smiley. I had to leave another message. It went like this—although in a quiet voice: *I am at Gram's place. Someone has jimmied the door. Sierra saw two people enter about twenty minutes ago. Wherever you are, you'd better just come back now.*

I called 911, gave the address, and stated there was a possible break-in where a vulnerable senior lived and I was just about to go into the house. I hung up as the dispatcher said, "Ma'am, I need you to stay outside. Do not enter the dwelling."

I called Sierra and asked her to keep an eye on anyone who left the building. She squeaked with excitement and promised to do it.

I finished our conversation with, "Make sure the police know you called me and I entered and that the door had been forced."

I figured I could count on Sierra if for no other reason than she welcomed the drama.

But I had a few other things going for me: I knew that

there were two people in the house, that they had entered illegally, and that they did not know that I was coming.

I nudged open the door and eased through it, making sure as little of me as possible was visible to anyone on the inside. The massive foyer chandelier was not even turned on. With just the light from the bay and the turret windows in the parlor, I could barely see, but I did remember the large silver bowl on the hall console. It was still there. Odd for a burglar to miss that. Touching the wall with my right, I scrunched down and felt my way along in the dim foyer. I was grateful for the soft soles of my desert boots. Not a squeak. The cushiony Persian runner muffled my steps. I stopped and listened for voices. Nothing. Where would Gram be at this time? In the sunroom with her birds? That seemed a good enough place to start. Or was it nap time again? And where was Zoya? I'd been very suspicious of her, but the signs of break-in suggested that she was not complicit in the strangers' arrival. Unless the break-in was intended to divert suspicion from her. That kind of thinking was probably linked to reading a bit too much Hammett in too short a time. Still, I was glad to have the tool that reading provided: Don't trust anyone.

I continued to grope along the corridor toward the rear of the house, where I could see a bit of light. A sound? My heart rate shot up. Was that a moan? I paused. Got my breathing under control, tried to be able to hear. The image of Gram, terrified or injured, flashed through my brain. I inched farther along the hallway. Another groan came from nearby. Was it coming from the dining room? I felt for the opening of the wide pocket doors and followed the low moaning. It seemed to be coming from the floor.

Zoya was curled up moaning softly on the rug, partly hidden by the lacquered Chinese screen. A tea tray lay beside her, its contents scattered: a broken cup, cookies, a napkin. Her eyes were closed and her hands and feet tied.

A telephone rested by her side, and it had clearly been severed from the jack, the cord cut. The sterling candelabra from the table had been dropped behind her, probably by her attacker. I reached down and touched her head, whispering "shhh" as I did. Her eyelids seemed to flicker. My hand came away sticky. I stared at it and gasped at the sight of blood. I backed up against the wall, needing desperately to wipe that blood away.

I bent over again and tried to undo the ties that bound her, without luck. I said, "Try to be quiet. Help is on the way. I will go to check on Gram." I patted Zoya's shoulder. I wasn't sure whether that would do any good, but she must have been terrified and in pain. The candelabra would have made a good weapon, but I couldn't bring myself to touch it. Then I raced to find Gram. *Smiley, where are you?*

CHAPTER TEN

Almost anything can be used as a weapon.
—THE KELLY RULES

I FOUND NOTHING and no one in the sunroom. Birds screeched, flapped and fluttered nervously. I exhaled, partly in relief. But the relief didn't last long. The place had been trashed. Puzzles were scattered, papers tossed. Cups broken. It looked like the intruders had taken their time. Books had been flung from the bookshelves onto the floor. What had they been looking for if not the silver? I did locate the wooden cane with the metal bird's head handle and took it with me.

Never mind. I needed to find Gram before they did. The first responders would be on their way. The cops could figure out the motive. I needed to act. Gram must have been upstairs. I would be a sitting duck on the main staircase. But would the invaders—whoever they were—know about the back staircase?

I scrambled toward the back staircase. Once again, I gave thanks for my upbringing. I went up the stairs on hands and knees.

I bumped my head on the door at the top. Could they have heard that? Again, I held my breath, stood up wielding the cane, ready to bean the first villain to open the door.

The door squeaked as I opened it. It seemed very loud to my ears, even louder than the thundering of my heart. I slipped through it and left it open in case the next squeak attracted their attention.

But no one came. Might I add that "no one" included the police, who should be showing up. What was going on?

Gram would almost certainly be in her bedroom. I was more than a bit disoriented. Which way was Gram's bedroom from this staircase? Right? Left? Right seemed to be the answer. I edged out into the hallway. A murmur of voices drifted from down the hallway.

I heard a man's muffled voice. "What room is she in?"

"I thought it was the front, but it must be this one." It wouldn't take them long.

I tried to keep in the shadows and crept toward Gram's room. This floor was less dim, perhaps because the curtains weren't drawn.

A small dog yipped. Fear? Pain? I heard it scamper down the front staircase. I felt a flash of anger that overwhelmed my fear. *Forget that, invaders. You'll be dealing with fight not flight from me.* I wasn't sure the cane would do the trick. But what else could I use? There were flowers, cushions, books, ladylike chairs on this level. A thought flickered in the back of my mind. Something useful.

I dove toward through the door to what I hoped was Gram's dimly lit bedroom, encountered the round bed and whispered, "It's me, Jordan," in her ear. "Someone's in the house. Can you hide in the closet?" Why not use every cliché in the world? But never mind. There are very good reasons why people hide in closets. I have no objections to hiding in closets myself.

"I can see you, my dear. No closet for me," Gram said in her normal speaking voice. She snatched the cane from me. It was hers after all.

I heard the intruders whispering and the whispers appeared to be getting closer. I pressed myself against the bedroom wall and ducked down on the far side of Gram's dresser. That was it. That's what Uncle Mick and Uncle Kev would do. But it wasn't enough.

Sometimes it's good to have been raised by people who often needed to know how to be soundless in the night. Soundlessly, I bounced up, moving quickly and switched off the light, a tactic I'd picked up from the Continental Op. Of course, I wasn't packing a gun so the rest of that scene would have to play out differently, but I had another stunt up my vintage sleeve. As the intruders came through the door, I felt on the dresser top for Smiley's marble collection. Next I hurled the giant glass jar of marbles to the floor.

There was shrieking then silence and then fresh yelling.

The light snapped on and I found myself facing two faceless faces. I screamed. Couldn't quite stop myself in time. Uncle Mick would say that's the oldest trick in the book, putting a stocking over your face, but I had to say it was also the creepiest. He also always used to say, "Don't scream like a girl," and I just had. Never mind, they were intruders and their lack of features sent shivers down my spine. The fedoras on their heads should have been funny, but they weren't. No one would ever be able to identify them. You couldn't see their hair, and with those black leather gloves, there would be no prints anywhere. The plastic booties they wore over their shoes didn't bear thinking about.

One of the faceless ones was sitting on the floor rubbing his head. He was surrounded by twinkling marbles and jagged glass from the broken apothecary jar and there was blood on his trench coat and hands. His weapon had fallen out of his reach and slid under the bed. Unfortunately, that didn't make him any less scary. The other one had some kind of serious-looking gun. It was now aimed at me in a way that meant business. I'd used my one weapon, the jar full of marbles. Gram had the cane out of my reach and there wasn't much in this room that could be used to protect us against a gun fired at close range.

I'd tried to save Gram and now I'd probably get both of us killed. They wouldn't let Zoya live either if they killed us. Where were the cops?

"Where is it?" the standing one said.

"Don't know what you're talking about," Gram snapped.

I shook my head. I really didn't know what they were talking about.

"I guess we'll just have to encourage you to remember then," he said in that eerie stocking-covered voice.

"We won't remember much if we're dead," I said.

"You won't be dead. You'll just wish you were. Look, Ma, no safety."

Gram clutched her heart. She uttered a rattling gasp. "I need my humidifier. I can't breathe." She pointed at me. "This girl doesn't know anything. But if I die, you'll be out of luck." She managed another strangled rattling gasp and pointed at the tabletop humidifier.

The muffled voice instructed, "Plug it in. Hurry up."

Bleating pitifully, Gram leaned over the bedside table, fumbling with the plug of the humidifier. Then the room went black again. Of course! The overloaded circuits. After losing a second to stunned surprise, I scrunched down and hurled myself forward toward the standing figure. He screamed and toppled. I figured he must have encountered a shard of glass. The room echoed as the gun went off. The smell of cordite filled the air. The bullet must have hit the ceiling because what seemed like bits of plaster rained down. I heard a soft thunk as the gun hit the floor.

The intruders were still shrieking from meeting the glass.

Thank you, glass shards. The only way to keep from getting cut or rolling on marbles was to keep perfectly still. They weren't doing that.

"Good one, Gram," I said, feeling around for the gun near where I thought I'd heard it fall. If and when one of them reached the hallway and found a light source, the odds would be somewhat different. Speaking of odds, what did it take to get a cop car in this hip burg?

The sound of sirens getting closer helped ease my fear. I thought I heard Gram getting out of bed and then a flash of light as the door to the bedroom opened. One of the intruders had managed that. I found the gun and gripped it. I told myself I was just going to have to fire it if it came down to that.

I said in my deepest voice, "Hear those sirens? I did take the time to call 911 before coming up the stairs. They could have been faster but looks like they're here now."

A whoop of a siren outside confirmed that.

"Good luck explaining your presence here wearing stockings over your faces and those idiot getups." Stall. Stall. Stall. "Remember, I have the weapon and you don't. I'll get you before you get me. Don't think I don't know how to use it either." This was not strictly speaking the absolute truth, but the moment called for it.

I heard a few colorful swear words and some scrambling, more swearing as the marbles and glass did their work. Would I have to shoot? The first one said, "Let's get out of here. There must be a back way out."

I weighed my options: Holding them at gunpoint would mean that one of them could launch himself at me to get the gun. I had no idea if I could actually hit either one of them if I needed to. The second one yelped and swore again and scrambled after the first one through the door.

"Here's the staircase," one of them yelled and I listened

as they thundered down it. Damn. Why hadn't I closed that door to the stairs?

"You okay, Gram?"

"Never better. They sure are making a lot of racket."

I ran into the hallway heading for the stairs, still holding the gun. It was unpleasantly heavy. I called back to Gram, "I'll try to figure out where they're going so I can tell the police. I don't want them to run into Zoya again." I didn't get far before a firm female voice said, "Drop your weapon and get on the floor."

CHAPTER ELEVEN

Always make friends.
—THE KELLY RULES

I KNEW BETTER than to argue with the officer. My uncles had drilled me on how to behave before I went to school. If you are carrying anything that might be interpreted as a weapon, say a comb or a pencil or a loaf of bread, drop it and get on the floor. That won't kill you. Resistance might.

I was carrying a gun.

I bent down immediately and put it on the floor. The cop kicked it out of my reach.

I couldn't help but worry about my chiffon snagging as I lay on the floor. Would I get blood on this outfit? Not that it was important in the scheme of things.

I thought I might try explaining to the cop. "Mrs. Huddy is my fiancé's grandmother. She was attacked by two male intruders who escaped down the back stairs. By all means, keep an eye on me. I'd do the same in your situation, but please get your colleagues after them. They'll be on the run. Stockings over their faces, fedoras and trench coats."

"Don't even try yanking my chain."

"Believe me, I know how idiotic it sounds, but those would have been intended to terrify a helpless senior citizen."

A reedy and not in the least helpless voice escaped from the darkened bedroom. "It didn't work the way they thought it would, but you'd better hustle after them."

I called out, "She has to watch me, Gram. It's standard procedure. I might not be who I say I am."

Gram said, "Is she alone? How can she—"

The officer bent down and snapped a pair of cuffs on my wrists. Her name was Jennifer Martinez. "Don't worry. My partner's downstairs and there's backup on the way." She spoke into her radio and gave a word-for-word description of the intruders. I could have gotten out of those handcuffs in two seconds flat—that had been a Kelly family parlor game when I was growing up—but I wasn't foolish enough to try it.

I added, "They seemed like males, one about six feet and the other over six feet. Heavyset. No way to tell race or ethnicity. From their movements I'd put them both in their thirties, give or take. One or both will be bleeding."

"Bleeding? Why bleeding?"

"They experienced a snag in their plans," I said. "We had to fight back and we used what we had, which was a massive collection of marbles in a very big glass jar."

She glanced around, gun still trained. "Who's 'we'?"

"Told you. Me and Gram, that's Mrs. Huddy. When the lights were out, I dropped the marbles. She managed to trick them and blow the fuse. That's how we got the gun. Gram was pretty brave."

"I'm in here and I knew you were the right girl for my Tyler. We put the boots to those two SOBs, didn't we, Jordan!"

"We sure did, Gram." I tried to lower my voice. "Officer,

there's an injured woman downstairs. Zoya is Mrs. Huddy's housekeeper and she appeared to have been hit on the head, I assume by the intruders, who were looking for something. I found her when I came home and I called 911."

"Is Zoya all right?" Gram said with a shake in her voice for the first time. There was nothing wrong with her hearing.

"I hope so," I said. "She seemed to have been knocked out but she was still breathing."

"Why would they hurt Zoya and try to scare us? What were they looking for? Not much chance they'd get anything here," Gram said weakly.

I thought it would be very interesting to find out exactly what they had been looking for, and I wasn't alone.

"So what were they looking for?" Martinez said.

"I have no idea. But they didn't find it, whatever it was."

"What they found was some glass in their keisters. Check the hospitals." Gram's voice was getting weaker, but she managed a wheezy chuckle.

"She's eighty-five and she's had a shock. She needs medical help and so does Zoya," I said. "I'm okay, though."

"Maybe not. Your hands are bleeding," the cop said.

Again. Just a bit of new damage to my palms. At least the knees hadn't met any glass shards.

"Just a flesh wound as they say. I didn't even feel it."

"Shock," she said. "You're gonna feel it later."

"Oh." It was tricky talking to her from my position face-down on the floor.

She shrugged. "Things happen."

"I guess so. They sure did happen here. Do you think anyone is going to try to catch up with those two? They might have split up. That would be smart."

"How do I even know you weren't behind the whole thing?"

"What whole thing?"

A sound at the bedroom door took our attention away from that little squabble. Gram was leaning against the door frame and gasping for breath. How had she gotten past those marbles and glass without injuring herself? She was holding the cane and I had to admire that spirit.

"Ma'am," Officer Martinez said. "Let me help you back to bed. The ambulance is coming."

"Help me back to bed? I don't think so. Do you want to get killed by those marbles? I almost did."

"What? Oh. But you—"

"What you should do, young woman, is uncuff my grandson's fiancée, who just saved my life and was extremely resourceful and brave . . ."

Her voice had started to fade away. I said, "No, you're brave, Gram. You did that amazing thing with the lights."

Gram swayed. "I guess I do need my bed."

"We'd better not go back in there, Gram. But you need to lie down until you've been checked by the paramedics. Where's the best bedroom for you now? Yours is way too dangerous with all that glass and the police need to check that for evidence."

"No DNA." Gram slowly pitched over. The cop caught her in time. I couldn't do a thing from the floor and in handcuffs. Gram added, "Masks, hats, leather gloves, plastic booties over their shoes."

"Professionals, maybe," the cop said, steering Gram toward the next door.

Gram said, "I'll move to the front room, if you don't mind. It was my husband's. Best room in the house."

I said, "But luckily those crooks did cut themselves, so you will get DNA. Perhaps including mine."

The cop said, "Right. That and fifty cents won't get you a shoe shine," she said. "You know what the waiting time is for DNA results?"

Right. Maybe six months if no one had been killed.

"Now if you'd been killed, we could pick up the pace."

"We were almost killed."

"Not good enough."

Gram put up a bit of a struggle, "You really have to let Jordan up. This is nothing short of police brutality, keeping my grandson's fiancée on the floor. It's the kind of thing that makes the news."

I said, "It does appear that I am on good terms with the victim and, in fact, am a victim myself. Perhaps that will merit a twist of the key. As you pointed out, I am also bleeding."

A thundering on the stairs caused us all to stop and stare. A blond head appeared at the top of the staircase and a familiar voice said, "What the—"

"Pet!"

"Tyler!"

"What the hell happened? Gram? Jordan? Zoya's lying downstairs and—"

"Oh, we had quite the visit," Gram said. "Can't wait to tell you about it. Jordan's a cracker in an emergency."

"Very true," he said.

I squirmed to get a good look at him. "Is Zoya getting help?"

"There's an officer downstairs with her and the paramedics are on the way."

"My partner," the officer said.

Smiley bellowed, "Why are you cuffed, Jordan? Are you hurt? Is that blood? Why is she cuffed?"

Gram said, "You bet your fat fanny she's hurt. She fought off two thugs and now this . . . *official* . . . refuses to take off the handcuffs, even though I have carefully explained she's practically family. And she saved my life."

This was not strictly true. Gram had actually saved my life. I said as much.

Gram said, "But if you hadn't come into the room and you hadn't known about the contents of the apothecary jar and you—"

Smiley—who wasn't smiling—turned to the officer and gave her his name. He also produced his badge, not that the hallowed name of Town of Cabot would cut much ice in the City by the Bay. "This is my grandmother and this is my fiancée. Can you tell me why she's in cuffs?" He reached down to help me struggle to my feet. I may have hammed it up just a bit.

"There was a lot of confusion here. I'm just following procedure. You know that." The officer did have two little red spots on her cheeks, I was happy to note. She had been following procedure, but even so, I was glad if she was the tiniest bit embarrassed. After all the stuff that's happened to me in front of Smiley and various other officers of the law over the past three years, I am well beyond humiliation. So my no-doubt bedraggled hair, the dust on my lovely clothes, the handcuffs and the bloody hands I hadn't seen yet wouldn't be enough to bring spots to my cheeks. I was immune.

Smiley said, "Keys, please."

Although I was pretty sure it wasn't procedure, she handed them over. "I'll need to get a statement from her at the station."

I took a leaf from Gram's book and swayed ever so slightly. "We better give that statement here or at the hospital," I whispered as he unlocked the cuffs. "Aren't we the victims?"

"Better sit down," Smiley said gravely. I noticed his lips twitched.

Luckily there was an overstuffed chintz chair in the corridor for me to plop into. I tried to keep my hands from leaving gory marks on it. Of course, the pink and fuchsia print was so busy, who would ever know? I stared at my palms, which did have a few new cuts on top of yesterday's scrapes and one small gash that was bleeding freely.

"That might need stitches," Smiley said.

"Oh boy. I was hoping it was nothing."

"And what's that about an apothecary jar?"

"You're going to hate this part," I said.

"No he's not," Gram interjected from the doorway. "He'll love it. It means there was a cosmic reason that we kept those marbles."

"My marbles? You're kidding. That is—I don't even know what to say."

"Don't worry. We'll pick them up. But you're going to need another jar." I know how much childhood treasures can mean to people so I reached out to reassure him.

He threw back his head and started to laugh. "Brilliant!"

"Well, they were going to shoot us, and I couldn't see another possible weapon in the room unless we smothered them with flowered throw pillows. But Gram was the brilliant one. She shorted out the circuit by plugging in the humidifier."

The next feet up the stairs belonged to the paramedic, who took a serious interest in Gram, now reclining in the four-poster in the huge front bedroom. If I hadn't known better, I'd have thought she was having the time of her life. Gram did not want to be transported to the hospital or anywhere else. She was staying in her home.

Tyler made his way to the door of the front room. I edged up behind him. I was a bit shaky but that was all.

Gram told the paramedic, "I am perfectly fine and I value my independence. And I don't think you can force me, young man. What would your mother say?"

The paramedic had a bit of trouble keeping the grin off his face. He'd probably stop trying after five minutes with

Gram. The second paramedic arrived shortly after, apparently having taken care of Zoya.

"How is Zoya doing?" I asked. "The woman with the head injury."

This paramedic was a cheerful woman with bright red hair and the freckles to go with it. She looked at me and said nothing in answer to my question. I said, "Sure, sure, privacy, I know, but we need to know. She took a conk on the head. That can be serious. We're worried about her."

"They want to take her to Emergency for examination by a neurologist and scans. She's refusing."

Gram called out from her new room, "She's scared about the money. Tell her I'll pay whatever it is."

Tyler said, "I'll tell her."

I added, "One of us should go with her unless she has some family around."

Gram called out, "Zoya has no family. Just me." And then to the paramedics: "What? Oh, all right. I'll be still, but we have a situation to deal with. Zoya's very high strung."

I said, "Maybe I should go, although I don't think she likes me much."

Smiley said, "I'll go with her, once I know that you and Gram are all right."

"I'm all right. Like I said, just a flesh wound. Who knew this town would be so tough?"

The paramedic said, "Glad that's all settled. Zoya will need someone with her. She's pretty shaken up. Now, before you go anywhere, let's have a look at that hand."

"I was lucky. It could have been worse. There was glass everywhere."

"What all happened?"

After I'd told the story of the cable car and the Prius and the home invasion, she said, "I guess you were lucky. What did they want?"

"We have no idea. Mrs. Huddy doesn't know. It might be some kind of mistaken identity."

"Huh. Well, I hope you're planning to get an alarm system."

Smiley said, "You bet we are."

I said nothing. There was almost no chance that the attack on me in the hotel, the push from the cable car and this bizarre home invasion were not connected, but how? And why? And what the—

The paramedic inclined her bright red head in the direction of Gram's room. "You can't let her stay here."

Gram called out, "I'd like to see someone try and make me leave."

Smiley grinned. "I told you she was stubborn."

I said, "But Zoya does need to go to the hospital, no matter what she says."

"No! No hospitals." Zoya somehow had made it upstairs, but she was leaning against the walls and even I—no medical expert—could see that her pupils were dilated, the left more than the right.

The paramedic who'd followed her up the stairs said, "You need to be seen. You need a scan and a doctor."

"I will stay here."

Gram raised her voice and showed her steely side, not for the first time in this memorable day.

"Zoya, you will go to the hospital with the ambulance now. I will cover your costs and you will not refuse if you know what's good for you."

Strangely, that did the trick.

IN THE END, the police were brought up to speed, we were all relatively comfortable again and Smiley was deputized to accompany Zoya to the hospital. I'd volunteered, but that got shot down. She had taken a strong dislike to me. That was okay. I was hardly crazy about her either, but she had definitely started it.

I was elected to stay with Gram until Zoya returned. I put clean sheets on the four-poster bed in the vast front room. I loved the feeling of the high-thread-count bed linen. Luxury.

Smiley poked his head in before they left and said, "Don't be brave. Just stay safe and keep Gram company. I'll be back as soon as possible. I'm used to emergency rooms. I'll talk it up. Don't investigate or snoop or try to be smart."

"Smart? I have no idea what you mean."

"Officer Martinez is still here. Let her know if there's any issue at all," he said as he headed out with Zoya.

I stared around the room. "This is an amazing room. It must be thirty feet wide."

"Yes, we knocked out the wall for William when he was ill, so he'd have a sitting room and space for visitors. He spent the last year of his life here. He loved the windows and he had two beautiful ones with a view of the street. That was his recliner. He loved that too. He kept all the family albums in their own special case. He enjoyed the old photos. All those albums and even a box of spares."

"And do you like them?"

"Not so much. I like the ones of Tyler because he's dear to my heart. But there weren't many photos of my family. My parents left England in the nineteen thirties when my father's business went under. There were only a few pictures of them and a handful of me as a child. I was an only child too. And I have no idea about any relatives we left behind. No great ties there."

"I have gaps in my history too," I said, almost to myself.

She didn't seem to hear. "I suppose I should move in here permanently myself. Zoya thinks so, but I like to keep it as it was when William was here. He made me truly happy and I love his memory. Now let's see, what can we do that will be fun?"

Gram was in unusually good spirits for someone who'd survived a violent break-in. "Nothing wrong with me at all," she said with a gleam in her bright blue eyes. "Well, nothing that a G and T wouldn't fix."

"Oh I don't think—"

"You're not here to think, my dear. You're here to look after me and keep me happy."

"I believe I'm supposed to keep you safe."

"I'll be safer with a gin and tonic. Now, hop to it. I'm not getting any younger. Supplies are in the butler's pantry. By all means, have one yourself."

I headed downstairs to mix her drink. She seemed better than she'd been before the home invasion. Maybe the hits of adrenaline had been good for her. In fact, she hadn't been injured. As I recalled, she hadn't even been all that frightened. Unlike me.

We spent a few pleasant hours together, although breakfast and lunch had long worn off. Eventually, I decided to hunt for something we could have for an appropriate light meal after a home invasion. Nothing in the fridge or pantry called to me, maybe because everything was in the ingredient stage for dishes I didn't know how to cook. But in the freezer I found a box of ice cream sandwiches. Sandwiches are always soothing. I made a pot of tea in a pretty china teapot with a pink flower design and found some matching cups and saucers. Tea made for a bit of extra soothing. I put it all on one of the many trays stored in the kitchen and headed upstairs.

Gram and I had two ice cream sandwiches each and left a few for Tyler and Zoya. We enjoyed the treat and the pot of tea. They were the kind of comforting snacks that help after a trauma. I am pretty sure we both catnapped several times in between long chats. The topic was usually how wonderful Tyler was and how much she still missed William. Occasionally, it veered into how glad she was to get to know me or how Zoya was really loyal and kind. There was still no sign of Smiley and the loyal Zoya, although the sun had now set.

Gram's eyes popped open and she smiled at me. "I usually have a nightcap."

I headed downstairs again to get her another G and T.

I could hear the squawk of anxious birds as I approached the butler's panty. I veered off to the sunroom, where birds were sounding distraught and squawking. In all the chaos, nobody had covered them for the night.

"Bet you guys all want to go to bed." A short hunt later in a cupboard, I found the sheets that must have been to cover the cages.

"Get lost," said the little green parrot.

"No, you get lost," I chuckled, flipping the first sheet over his cage. With a mutter and flutter of feathers, he settled down.

Next I covered the cockatiels, who both chirped in appreciation. The lovebirds were last, snuggled together on their perch.

"Good night, everyone."

I stopped. Not quite everyone. Where was the cuddly pug? In all the drama, I hadn't even thought of the poor creature. And there was no Zoya to fuss over her. I checked the pink chintz wicker armchairs, the sofas, under the tables and ottomans, behind the plants. No bug-eyed little dog.

That was weird. And troubling. Asta would have been traumatized by the intruders, for sure. Aside from Asta yipping down the stairs when I was on my way up, I hadn't heard any dog sounds after I'd reached the upstairs when the intruders were there. I couldn't even remember how long ago. It seemed like a lifetime. My heart rate shot up. I searched the downstairs area including the sunroom again, but found only plants, birds, pillows and chintz. Had Asta escaped when the thugs got out the back entrance? Or was she like Good Cat and Bad Cat back home, with plenty of secret places to hide? I stuck my head out the back door and called. Nothing. I did a halfhearted job of mixing the G and T. I rushed back upstairs and handed Gram her drink. I waited until she'd had a sip or two and then asked her if Asta had a favorite hideout.

Oops. There was panic I might have expected to see during the home invasion. One hand shot to her chest. "Asta! Where is my little dog? And the birds! What has happened to my birds?"

"They are all there. I covered all your feathered friends and they are snoring away. Asta is probably hiding from all the noise and fuss," I said, but I was worried. If we'd been invaded by police at home, Walter would have yipped at them, but still managed to be around begging for handouts. Maybe Asta had a different disposition. "You stay here and relax. I'll check again."

I checked the other bedrooms, except for Gram's. The police had closed Gram's own bedroom door and marked it off with tape. Asta hadn't been in there when they did that. Still, it had been quite a while since the police had left. I felt that if Asta had been around, she would have found Gram. Downstairs again, I peered through the back windows but there was no way to see. I opened the front door and glanced around. There was what must have been an unmarked police car just past the front of the house. I could see the uniformed officer sitting in the front seat. I waved.

I called, "Asta!"

Not a sound. No small traumatized dog. Back in, I double locked the front door behind me.

I headed for the back. Cracked open the back door a sliver

once again and called, "Asta! Come for a treat." My experience with Walter had taught me that this strategy would often work. But I didn't know Asta and wasn't even sure what word she'd understand. I tried again, calling "cookie" and "biscuit" this time. I listened. Was that a whimper?

CHAPTER TWELVE

You do what you gotta do.
—THE KELLY RULES

THE WHIMPER WAS good news. Asta wasn't too far away. Although by now it was dark, I kept trying and peering around from the roomy back deck into the surrounding garden. There was no way I could go into that dark, sloping backyard with two violent perpetrators on the loose. Especially two who hadn't gotten what they wanted in this house—which I was now in charge of keeping safe, as Officer Martinez had been called to another incident. For all I knew, those perps were out there, holding that dog, waiting for a chance to burst in again. On the other hand, there was no way I could leave a terrified and spoiled little dog alone in the dark. I thought of Walter and how upset he'd be to be locked out of the house. And if these creeps had Asta, what a bargaining chip she'd be!

What to do?

I headed back to the front of the house. I peered out. Sure enough, the police officer was still parked there. Great to be a cop, I thought, parking wherever. Membership does have its privileges.

I looked up and down and behind the bushes. I could see no reason not to knock on the police officer's car window and ask him or her to see if the dog was okay. Or requesting that he accompany me and keep me safe if dog rescue was not in the cards.

Uh-oh! Across the street, I could see Sierra waving frantically. I gave her an apologetic nod and pointed to the police car, parked under the streetlight. She stopped, puzzled, waited.

I knocked on the window and the middle-aged police officer lowered the window. Darn. He was a big guy, pink-faced and pudgy, and looked bored to the point of tears. He wore his cap low on his forehead, a style I always find irritating. I worried he might not feel he had anything to prove by rescuing a dog and earning my undying admiration. Through the window I could see Sierra dodging traffic to cross the street. I just didn't feel up to dealing with her upscale cheerfulness right at that moment.

She came right up and gave me a huge hug. "Are you all right? We saw the police, we didn't know what to think. Then the ambulance and—" She stopped talking and wiped her cheeks. To my astonishment there were tear tracks. "I'm sorry, but I didn't know what to do," she wailed.

"Not your fault at all," I said. "We are all right."

"But someone went in the ambulance."

"Zoya, the housekeeper. She'll be okay. Just a precaution." While we were talking, I kept an eye on the front door. We were feet away from it, but it had been the kind of day, in fact the kind of trip, where anything, no matter how bizarre, could happen.

She shuddered. "Oh good, I mean it's such a nice neighborhood, who would think that—"

"Break-in," I said, not wishing to give her details and send her into hysterics. "They're gone now. But thank you so much for spotting them and calling me."

"Of course, did the police arrest them?"

I touched her arm. "No, but I'm sure they'll want to talk to you."

She turned pale and her hand shot to her throat. "But I had nothing to do with it."

"You saved the day, but they'll need a description. Sorry, Sierra, I need to talk to this officer. Tyler's grandmother's little dog has escaped. She's really upset. We all are." Not exactly true, but I needed Sierra to give me space to talk to the officer.

"Oh no! I didn't know there was a dog. Really? Where do you think it went? This is a busy street."

"Just one moment, Sierra."

"But I was at the window, because I was so worried, and I would have seen if a dog came out. How would it get out the door?"

"Maybe when the paramedics came? Or the police."

"But I think I would have noticed a *dog*."

"I'm just going to ask the officer to help me look in the back. Gram will be so stressed if we don't find Asta."

"In the back of what?"

"The house. She might have run down there and gotten too scared to come out. Maybe you could help, Officer."

He cleared his throat and held the wheel with his pudgy fingers. He did not make eye contact. "Can't leave the vehicle except to go into the house in an emergency."

"Well, it is a type of emergency. Missing dog."

"Need more than that. My captain is not a fan of dogs."

"Really? How is that even possible?" Sierra said. She did outrage well.

I said, "Well then, can you come into the house as it is an emergency."

"Good try," he said.

I couldn't believe this guy. No wonder he had that sloppy beer belly if he wouldn't get out of the car under these circumstances. "No really, if you come in, give me a chance to check on Gram, um, Mrs. Huddy, and then you could legitimately stand in the kitchen by the back door, while I check the back door. You could call for backup if something happened to me."

"Your friend could keep an eye on you."

Seriously? In a way I was glad that Tyler wasn't there. His curly blond hair might have caught fire.

"What? Oh no, I can't go in there." Sierra's eyes widened in a crazy horse eyes kind of way. "Not after what happened."

"But you don't know what happened."

"You said violent! You said traumatized! I have a baby to take care of."

"Where is the baby?" I couldn't believe she'd have left little Harry alone for a minute, let alone for this bizarre conversation.

"He's finally sleeping. He's with my husband."

"Your husband? Maybe he could come with me and—"

"Oh, he'd love that. He adores dangerous situations, but he was up all night with Harry and they're asleep together. I just can't wake him up."

Thanks a bunch, I thought. "Not that dangerous. It's a dog in the backyard. I just need someone to keep an eye on Gram while I look."

"Well," she said, "maybe when he wakes up. I'll send him over. His name is Michael. His code phrase could be Pug."

"What?"

"You know, so you'll be sure he's really Michael and it's all right to let him in."

"How about 'Joe sent me,'" said the cop with a snort.

"But who's Joe?" Sierra's pretty forehead creased in puzzlement.

The cop bit his lower lip. I may have done the same. She meant well and it wouldn't have been nice to laugh.

Uncle Mick used to say about Kev, "Can't help being the way he is," and that seemed to apply to Sierra too. Like Kev, she had some excellent qualities. Brains and bravery weren't among them, but hey.

"Thanks, Sierra. I'll watch for him."

"But only when he's awake."

"Right."

I turned to the cop. "Again, how about joining me inside and just keeping an eye while I check the back?"

He shook his head. "Sorry."

Really really really not sorry. I found myself shaking with anger, not that I wanted to stand next to this miserable sweaty excuse for a police officer.

At that moment, my cell phone vibrated. Smiley!

"Great news," he said. "We're on our way back. Zoya was seen right away and she seems to be all right, although you'd never know it to look at the expression on her face. We'll take a cab to Gram's and see you soon."

"That's great news. The bad news is that Asta, the little pug, has vanished. She's somewhere in back of the house—"

"Jordan, do not go looking for her by yourself. Who knows where those guys are. Do you hear me? Don't—"

"Give me some credit. I wasn't going to take the chance. Officer Martinez had to take a call. I asked the local police officer to help but that was a no go."

"That's second-rate. Never mind. I'll do it. Just take care of Gram and I'll be there soon. Take no chances. Okay?"

I muttered something about being glad Zoya was all right, and disconnected. I supposed there was no reason that poor little Asta couldn't wait ten more minutes.

"Thanks, Sierra," I said. "I'm going in to check on Tyler's grandmother now. I've been out here a bit too long."

She gripped my arm. "Wait! Don't go in until he's back."

I patiently explained that I had been alone in the house and that there were no intruders there. "I just came out to look for the dog."

"What if they have him?"

"You mean the dog? It's a her."

Her voice rose. "What if they hold a gun to its head and force you to open the safe?"

"There's no safe."

"Oh. Shouldn't the officer go with you just to see if it's safe to go back in?"

"No," the officer said. "She's been out here for five minutes and no one has come or gone."

"My fiancé is also a police officer," I said. "He'll be here in a few minutes. We'll look together."

"Should I still send Michael over when he wakes up? I'd like you to meet him."

If he was anything like her, this stressful day wouldn't be the right time to get to know Michael. "We'll be okay."

She smiled and I could see the relief on her face. "Okay. We'll wait to hear. And really, anything we can do. Anything at all."

Right. I knew she meant it, useless as the sentiment was.

Time to reassure Gram. Once through the door, I stopped. What was that noise? I shook it off, but I was sure I heard the thump of footsteps.

"Who's there?" I called, one of the dopiest lines any one of us ever utters. "Gram?"

Gram's voice fluttered down the staircase. I could see her, swaying at the top. "Someone came up the back stairs. I was hoping it was you."

Without thinking, I raced toward the front of the house.

I opened the door and shouted, "There's an intruder in the house! He got back in!"

I heard a clatter on the floor and the sounds of things being knocked over in the dark kitchen. Maybe it wasn't the smartest thing to run toward it, but I was expecting to be followed by the armed officer. As I flicked on the light, a dark figure shot out the back door and into the gloom. In the distant gloom I heard a small *yap*.

There was no sign of that useless cop, But I heard Asta, not too far away.

The garden door leading from the kitchen to the small deck stood open; broken glass lay on the floor surrounding it. It would not be a good idea for Asta to come through that. I rushed to the deck to make sure that didn't happen and picked up the small, shivering pooch before she stepped on the glass. A thrashing and crashing in the hedge separating the two properties told me that our burglar was not all that far away.

"You followed the burglar, didn't you, silly pooch? Not a good idea, but you're home now."

Inside, I shouted, "Please get into bed, Gram. I'm getting the police and Tyler's on his way."

Clutching the shivering dog, I dashed to the front of the house. The police car was gone.

I pulled myself together enough to say, "Good news," to Gram. She was back in the guest bed brandishing her cane with the metal bird's head handle.

"So we're not out of the woods yet," she said.

"Nope. One of the intruders"—well, who else would it have been?—"broke in through the garden door in the kitchen. There's glass everywhere. I found little Asta outside."

Gram beckoned and I deposited Asta beside her. She snuggled up immediately and gave me an irritated bark, on general principles. "Oh, Asta, when will you learn gratitude?"

I said, "Tyler should be back soon."

Of course, the phone was still disabled, but I pulled out my cell phone and tapped 911. I said, "We had a violent break-in here earlier and one of the intruders has just come back and broken in through the kitchen door. You'll have a record of that. We have an elderly woman who has been traumatized and now the officer guarding the house has just driven away. Officer Martinez was here and she was called away. She needs to get back here and I mean now."

"Calm down, ma'am."

I really hate it when someone tells me to calm down. "There's nothing to be calm about. That intruder may come back again the minute he realizes that we are helpless here. You'd better get another car here as soon as possible. What? Fine." I went through the tedious process of repeating everything that had occurred in Gram's house that afternoon and evening. "Yes. Ambulance, police officers, we had the whole enchilada. What? Oh, no, probably just police. We are actually not in need of medical help. One person went to the hospital earlier but we're fine. No, it *is* an emergency because we don't know where the perpetrators are and we are alone here with the back door broken and two dangerous men on the loose. Are they? Are they really on the way?"

Gram said, "I hear sirens. That's a good thing."

"Fine, I will stay on the phone until they get here. Can you tell me why the other officer left us here alone?"

"What? Of course there was an officer here. He was parked right outside the house. I told you that. He was worse than useless because he actually wasted time, but he was there and I was not the only person to have seen him. Oh right, of course you can't give me that information."

When I hung up, Gram said, "Jordan. I'm only getting half of this. What is that about?"

"The cop I talked to in the car outside. The dispatcher couldn't hide her surprise that there was anyone outside. She wouldn't be allowed to tell me that and she tried to cover, but it seemed obvious to me. Something fishy is going on with that guy."

CHAPTER THIRTEEN

No one sees past a uniform.
—THE KELLY RULES

"THAT'S JUST CRAZY."

I thought hard. "He was in an unmarked car. That happens. He had on a uniform, but you know what? He didn't look like a cop. He was flabby and uninterested."

The sirens were getting closer. A good thing, assuming that they belonged to real police officers, something that wasn't one hundred percent certain.

We heard a racket at the front door and the sound of "Police!"

Gram handed me her cane with the metal bird's head. I went downstairs armed. As they say, "Fool me once shame on you, fool me twice shame on me."

Officer Martinez was back with her partner, a pale Scandinavian type called Nordstrom. I did mention the "officer" who'd been parked outside supposedly to watch the house but who did nothing and who, the dispatcher had let slip, might not have been assigned. They exchanged glances but neither one of them offered an opinion about what that had been about.

"Where's the door?" he said.

"Follow me," I said.

"I'll go first," he said. "My partner will keep an eye here."

"Maybe Officer Martinez can guard the elderly lady on the second floor," I said. "She's pretty feisty. Be careful."

Martinez chuckled as she climbed the stairs.

In the kitchen Nordstrom took note of the broken glass and heard my description of the earlier events. He got on his radio.

He stepped outside and shone his flashlight around.

"What did he look like?"

"I didn't see the guy who broke in."

He stepped back in and pointed upstairs. "Did she?"

"I don't think so. I saw this disaster and Mrs. Huddy heard the sound of someone breaking into the house. Lucky I came back in when I did. This was the second time there's been a home invasion here in a few hours, as Officer Martinez may have mentioned."

"She did."

"Was there or was there not a police officer stationed outside the house?"

He shrugged and stepped outside again.

I said, "Well, I think you need a . . . search team." I wasn't sure if that was a phrase used. He didn't respond but made his way around the back garden, talking into his radio. I headed back upstairs. At least I could be of some use to Gram.

She was back in bed in the front room. Asta was sitting on the end of that bed. She jumped up and wagged her stumpy little tail when I entered the room. Here at least I was appreciated.

Officer Martinez had just finished taking the information. Gram seemed to like her and so did Asta.

"So, no one saw anything at all?" she said.

I said, "Hardly that. I saw broken glass all over the kitchen floor, and Mrs. Huddy heard the intruder break the glass and start up the back stairs. And as you know perfectly well, we had been subjected to a violent break-in while she was in bed earlier today, just a few hours ago. Broken glass, blood, the works."

She glanced around and nodded.

I bit my tongue before I went on about how dangerous it could have been. How we could have been badly injured or killed.

Gram said, "But we're all okay."

"Right."

"We fought them off. We acted decisively. That's why I've never been better. I hate feeling old and useless."

So this was definitely weird. It wasn't that I wanted her to feel afraid and have some traumatized reaction; it's just that it *had* been very dangerous and gleefulness didn't seem like the right response. Whatever. I decided it was better for her mental health. My own state of mind was a bit more wobbly.

What the bleep was going on?

There was so much to consider, including things that I hadn't taken so seriously before the home invasion: Being pushed from the cable car. And the Prius that had almost knocked Smiley and me over on our way home from dinner the other night might not have been just a random drunk driver. Speaking of dinner, there was also the bug under the table at Magari. Those all had to be connected.

Who would want to bug our conversation? Why? Did Gram have a secret that was putting all of us in danger? What could it possibly be?

I had not the slightest idea where that danger was coming from. But I couldn't believe it was some old photo album.

I sat on the end of the bed and Asta climbed onto my lap. I missed Walter at that moment more than ever, but this shy little creature had already wormed her way into my heart. Apparently it was mutual. I sure felt loved.

Officer Martinez said, "Well, if you think of anything else, let us know."

I said, "You're not leaving. You can't leave us alone in this house with the back door useless."

She said, "You'll be talking to detectives soon. Another team of evidence techs has just arrived too. Once they're finished, you can get the door fixed. I'll see if my colleague needs help in the search." Her tone implied that Nordstrom would need help. "Sorry I got called away before. I feel bad. We won't leave you until the door is settled. Like I said, if you think of anything else. This time I'll give you my card with my cell and my e-mail so you can get in touch if anything new happens."

Oh sure. Like you could stop an attack with a card.

CHAPTER FOURTEEN

Follow the money.
—THE KELLY RULES

AFTER OFFICER MARTINEZ went off to investigate, I said to Gram, "I don't think you should stay here. It's obviously not safe."

"Don't be silly."

"No, really. You'll be safer with us. We'll take you to our hotel. We have a suite. Tons of room and Asta can come too. If they let Zoya out of the hospital, does she have anywhere to go?"

"Zoya? No. I told you she's alone in the world. Tragic life."

"Right. Well, there will be room for her too." There were two queen-size beds in Tyler's room and a king-size bed in mine, plus the pull-out sofa in the living room area. We could house a convention in that suite.

"Don't be silly. What about my birds? We'll all be more relaxed here."

Relaxed? After the day we'd had? Of course, we'd have no choice but to stay in the house with her. We could hardly leave her alone with her birds unless we hired a security company. Although that was starting to seem like a good idea even if we did stay.

I said, "Well, we'll stay too, of course. But I think we need to improve our defenses."

Tyler would be a good defense. What was taking so long? As he wasn't answering his cell phone, I needed to do something. I hurried downstairs and asked Officer Martinez for the names of reputable alarm companies.

"We're not really allowed to give out—"

"Of course," I said, barely managing not to roll my eyes. "I should have realized. Do you have an alarm system?" She looked like the type who had everything together.

"Yes."

"What kind?"

With the name of her alarm company at hand, I headed back upstairs and I took the liberty of calling to have a system installed. Despite the time of night, I did reach a human being. The alarm company said they would try to get an emergency installation for us first thing in the morning. Fingers crossed.

Next I asked Gram if she had a handyman and was relieved to learn that she did.

"Now why didn't I think of that?" she said. "You must call Gus and the boys."

I called and explained about the back door and the police. Gus earned my gratitude by saying, "I'm coming now. I'll keep an eye on things for Mrs. Jean. What kinda crazy world is this?"

I thanked him profusely. I felt a little bit better about this whole crazy situation thanks to Officer Martinez and Gus. But where was Smiley?

Gram patted her hair. "That Gus," she murmured, "he's such a flirt."

"How about a nice cup of hot chocolate before bed? Or herbal tea?" I said.

She chose the herbal tea.

I had one too. Who knew what else was in store that night?

Gram said, "With Gus on the job, we can all relax. Smart girl, you thinking of calling him."

"Thank you, but really you gave me his name and I just—"

"Smart girl," she repeated.

I was happy to help her out. She didn't seem to need all that much taking care of. I headed downstairs with Asta at my heels. Apparently we were now bonded.

A banging at the front door brought Officer Martinez to the front of the house. She looked down at the wizened little man in the overalls in front of her. The badge sewn on his shirt pocket said, "GUS."

"I'm Gus," he boomed at her. How could such a small man have such a big boom? "You Jordan? How is—"

She arched one perfectly groomed eyebrow. "I'm Officer Martinez."

"*I'm* Jordan," I said, hurrying up behind. "She's pretty good, considering. Thanks for coming, Gus. I know she really appreciates it. I'm not sure when the police are going to be finished with the crime scene. I think they're treating it seriously because of the violent home invasion."

Martinez gave me a dismissive look. "We take all crime seriously."

"No question."

"Who's gonna do such a crazy thing to a nice old lady like Mrs. Jean? Guess I better see the damage," Gus said.

"Won't be long before you can have access," the officer said.

I was glad Gram hadn't heard him call her a nice old lady. It must have been a one-sided flirtation. I said, "It's the garden door in the kitchen. The glass was broken and it looks like it was kicked off the hinges."

Gus said, "Hoh boy," and shook his small bald head. As he was shaking, a pair of crime scene techs headed out. "All yours now," one of them said.

I turned to Martinez. "That was pretty fast."

She said, "They made it a priority because of the age of the victim. And the fact there was an earlier attack with an injury too."

"Oh. I'm glad they could do that." I wondered if some of that priority was because Tyler was also a police officer.

Gus said, "I know that door. I installed it. Thought it was good enough. I'll get a better one, that no tank could get through."

"I'll go with you. Mrs. Huddy wants me to bring her an herbal tea."

Gus laughed. "Oh yeah, usually gotta have her G and T, that one."

And off we went. Gus took some measurements and shook his wizened head. "Gonna be a lot of work. I think we'll just have to board it up tonight and get a new door tomorrow. And a lock. We need it kick-proof. Crazy crazy."

"Do you have to go and get some plywood?" I wasn't happy about being alone here. What if those men were right outside watching until the police left?

"Donchu worry nothin'. My boys will get it. Gus ain't goin nowhere."

That was remarkably reassuring considering he was less than five feet tall and sixty if he was a day. Something told me that Gus had been able to look after himself and others all his life. He bellowed something into his phone before turning to me and grinning. The conversation was all Greek to me.

I waited for the kettle to boil, while Gus paced and muttered. "Who would do this crazy thing?" he said to me. I had the feeling that he might have been talking about payback in his conversation with himself. Maybe the snapping of arms and legs, but that might have been just an impression.

"I stay here. You don worry, Jordan," he said. "My boys is coming soon."

I made my way back to the front stairs and spoke once again to Officer Martinez. "Thank you."

She said, "Someone will be watching the house."

"That was what we thought before. I saw the guy and—"

She looked me in the eye. "You didn't hear it from me, but it looks like you were right. No one was assigned here to look at this house. No car. No officer. Nothing and no one."

"But I saw him."

"Maybe. I don't know what's going on. You were under a lot of stress. Lot of traumatic events."

"But not crazy out of my mind. I wasn't traumatized or injured. I'm pretty tough." Of course, I was wearing a black and white polka dot baby doll dress in not so tough chiffon. "The neighbor across the street was there. She clearly saw that cop too. He was in uniform."

"Huh. It doesn't jive with what I've been told. We need to talk to her anyway about the two guys who broke in. She seems to be out a lot."

"Right. She's always trotting around with her baby, but she'll be back soon. She comes and goes. My point is if he wasn't a cop officially doing a lousy job guarding this house, then he must have been part of the whole thing. Maybe he was disguised as a cop and keeping an eye out for the guy who kicked the door in. Maybe he was the getaway car."

She just had to say "huh" again. "More likely he wanted to get in on the action and prevent more trouble."

I said, "But he didn't prevent anything. Someone kicked in the door! Broke the window!"

"And no one hurt. Nothing taken. You even got the dog back."

"I suppose, but—"

She leaned in and lowered her voice. "I'm telling you that officer was probably just some lazy old hack ten days from retirement, looking to park and relax a bit. Trust me, some of them get like that. I say get out and give some new blood a chance."

I almost said "huh" myself.

She said, "I'll see what else I can find out, who it might have been to put your mind at ease. Meantime, I'm staying around until the detectives show up. For all our sakes, I hope it's before tomorrow."

I was starting to like Officer Martinez. Although her partner seemed to have vanished, I was glad she'd be staying. She was all business, a compact figure, no more than five four. Now that I had time to actually notice her, I liked her sleek black hair in the businesslike bun, glowing skin and those beautifully sculpted eyebrows. She was one tough cookie and yet very appealing.

Her laugh was low and pleasant. "Don't worry about it. You take the Queen Bee her tea and I'll keep an eye on things and that includes this Gus guy."

Just as I was pondering this second surprising side of Officer Martinez, Gus bombed through the front door, leading a charge of three large, burly men who looked just like Gus except about sixty percent bigger. Each of the big guys was carrying a sheet of plywood, which looked to be about three-quarter-inch thick. I knew from the last time that Uncle Mick's place was shot up by the cops that a sheet of three-quarter-inch plywood weighs about seventy-five pounds. None of them was even breathing heavily. In fact, they all gave the impression that bullets would bounce off them. All three gave Officer Martinez the eye. Apparently, I was not their type. Asta expressed her outrage by hiding under the hall console table and yapping insults.

As they marched by, I swear Officer Martinez rolled her eyes, but she also had a vivid red spot on each cheek.

Gus called out, "Gonna be completely safe in ten minutes and then good as new with a special door tomorrow. You tell Mrs. Jean."

"I will." I ascended the stairs thinking Gram's kitchen would be "good as new" if new meant the back of your house was boarded up with three sheets of three-quarter-inch plywood.

"Gus is here," I said, delivering the tea. I thought it might have gotten cool. I was going to have to learn to speed up.

She reached for the cup with a gleam in her eye and said, "Gus is the best."

"It looks like his three sons are here too."

She said, "You mean three of his sons."

"Oh. How many does he have?"

She took a first sip. "No idea. An endless source. Small but mighty, our Gus."

I said, "They're putting up plywood in the back."

"I think I hear that. Whatever you can say about Gus's boys, they're not shy and quiet."

"Well, it should be safe. And Officer Martinez is waiting for the detectives to get here and maybe stay longer. We should be fine until Tyler gets home."

I sat down on the chair by the bed. Asta leapt onto the bed, managed to dodge Gram and climbed onto my lap. She was just like Walter only so much lighter. Walter was a little pudge pot. Asta was a bit too skinny.

"She likes you," Gram said. "That's good."

And she doesn't like you that much, I thought. *Why is that, I wonder?*

"I'm sorry about your house," I said. "It's so beautiful and now all this damage."

She shrugged. "It's only stuff, my dear. You realize that if you've lost two husbands, although that does make me sound remarkably absentminded."

I laughed in spite of myself.

Gram continued, "All kidding aside, at least the birds are safe. And Zoya wasn't killed."

"And Asta's all right."

"What? Oh yes. Right, of course. Poor Asta, quite a bad day for her."

Asta managed a peevish little yip.

"Ridiculous creatures, pugs," Gram said.

"But they're . . ." I paused. I wanted to say beautiful, but of course they weren't beautiful. "Adorable."

"Mmm."

"And we'll fix it all up too," I said. "Tyler's brilliant at cleanup and renos. It's a hobby for him. He's renovating his new house."

"Is he? Well, someday this will all be yours." She gave a grand gesture around the huge bedroom, indicating the elaborate crown molding where the walls met the ceiling, the turret window and the deep bay window with its wooden window seat, and panels of stained glass on the top. I followed her hand, taking in the rich Persian carpet and the oil paintings on the walls.

"What? You mean it will all be Tyler's."

"Aren't you part of the package, pet? You seem perfect for each other."

I smiled. How could she know that? She hadn't seen him since he was a child and she knew nothing at all about me.

Perhaps she read my mind. "Well, you seem to be. Why don't you tell me about yourself?"

I hesitated because, of course, much of me is not public knowledge and I'd like it to stay that way. Still, I could leave out large chunks. She was an old lady and she'd had a rough day. No need to worry.

"I'm from Harrison Falls, New York, which is where I first met Tyler. He was on the police force and I had just started working for Vera Van Alst, a wealthy book collector."

"You never left your hometown?" she asked. It was probably my imagination that her eyes glittered.

"Sure, I went off to college. I still plan to go back to complete grad school. I'm just building up my funds again."

She sipped pensively. "So are you and my boy planning to marry soon?"

CHAPTER FIFTEEN

*You always need friends. You just don't always
know who they are.*
—THE KELLY RULES

W E HAD NEVER talked about getting married. The
fiancée thing was just to give me a bit of status. What
did I know about marriage? "My parents died when I was
very young. My uncles raised me, so it's not like I had a
model of a happy marriage, although I am sure my parents
were very happy." Of course, I had no idea if they had been
or not, and anything my uncles said must be taken with an
entire shaker of salt.

"And you'll want children?" Have I mentioned that her
eyes glittered?

"Maybe someday. I like them, but I still have a lot to do,
finish my education . . ." And figure out if Smiley and I can
make a go of it.

"There's nothing like little ones," she said.

I realized that her eyes weren't glittering. Those were
tears. "First they're beautiful little blond creatures singing
and dancing and blowing kisses, and then in what seems
like no time, they're happy to never see you again."

I stared at her. There was pain in her voice.

She said, "And they'll take people you love with them."

"Tyler?" I said.

"It didn't matter what I said or did, my son couldn't for-give me for getting married again."

I tried diplomacy. "Unfair, but perhaps he was thinking about his father's memory."

Diplomacy didn't get me far.

She snorted and the herbal tea swirled in the china cup. "If he was, it was the first time he ever did. He was thinking of the money, more like it. Money was always so important to him and his wife. But money isn't everything, you know. Do you think it was at all fair to that child to be cut off from me?"

"Do you mean that the reason you couldn't see Tyler was because of money?" I suppose that my tone showed that I found this hard to believe. Which I did.

"That's exactly what I mean. And in case you think I imagined it or attributed motives to Tyler's parents, my son told me that to my face. If I married William, I wouldn't see Tyler again."

I gasped. But I still wondered if it was true. What kind of person would say such a thing?

She said, "He was convinced that William was after my money. Such hogwash. I had my late husband's insurance and the proceeds from the sale of the house and a bit of savings and family heirlooms, that was all. Small potatoes. He said William would clean me out and leave me high and dry. He even asked if I wanted to end up begging on the street. How's that for confidence in your mother?"

"Whoa."

"Whoa indeed. Of course, I didn't believe him for a min-ute. Tyler's father was always a bit of a brat, you know. And Tyler and I were so close that I couldn't believe he'd do that to his son."

"But he did?"

"They did. My daughter-in-law may have been the mo-tivating force, who knows. But my letters were always marked 'Return to sender.' The telephone was never an-swered. Nothing."

"I don't understand how anyone could do that."

"Tell me about it," she said. "I figured they'd get over it, but after a year of nothing, I flew back East because I was missing my boy so much and found their house sold and not one of the neighbors knew where they'd gone. I always re-gretted not going back right away, but . . ."

I said, "But?"

"My son has a powerful personality and I suppose I was afraid he would cause me to change my mind. He's quite the force of nature."

"Would your new husband have come with you?"

"He would have done anything for me. Although if he'd met with my son, that would have added fuel to the fire. He did fly home and helped me pull myself together when I realized that I couldn't find my beautiful boy."

I leaned back and said nothing.

"He insisted on hiring a private detective too."

"No luck?"

"Oh sure. We found them, but they refused contact. When I persisted, my son threatened us with a lawsuit over harass-ment. He actually took out a restraining order." Tears trick-led down her cheeks. "I knew then I'd lost Tyler."

"But you hadn't."

"Wish I'd found him sooner. Think of all the milestones in his life that I missed."

"Why did you wait? Tyler's almost thirty years old. He's been living on his own for a long time now."

"William became very ill. He just wasted away and I nursed him for years. I think I told you that this was his sick room. He liked the bay window so much. We knocked out the adjoining wall so he had two windows, the bay and the turret. He loved watching the street. After a long time, he just faded from life right here. He never lost his sense of humor or his kindness, though. When he went, I didn't have the energy or time or emotion left for a search or for anything else really."

I squeezed her hand. "You loved your husband a lot."

"I did. And I love Tyler a lot. It's hard for me to forgive my son for what he did to end our relationship."

"I get that." I wasn't sure I would have been able to.

"The funny part of it was that William not only didn't plunder my bit of money, he left me comfortably off. Except that I can't get around or look after myself, I don't have a worry in the world. For years I wished I'd had the chance to tell my son and daughter-in-law that face-to-face. But it's too late. I've been cast adrift."

Tyler's parents had cast him adrift too. I was beginning to get an idea of what kind of family he'd come from. No wonder he loved Gram so much.

"That's why I am so glad Tyler found you. He has a chance for happiness."

"I guess so." Tyler had let me down more than once, though. I suppose I had let him down too. And I had chosen my family over our future.

She must have read my mind. "Be patient with him. He's a wonderful boy."

Man, I thought.

"Yet he grew up in that home where there was no place for love or trust or forgiveness," she said.

"They cut him off when he became a police officer."

"He told me before he came out here. I only wish I'd learned that earlier. I would have been able to celebrate that milestone with him."

I realized how lucky I was. My uncles hated the idea of me going straight, especially when the family business was doing so well. And Uncle Mick and Uncle Lucky had never even been arrested. Their hearts were temporarily broken over my legal lifestyle, but they never would have turned me away. Then when I began to see Tyler, I know they felt betrayed. A cop! Close to the family! The shame of it all. But they pulled themselves together and gave me their support. I never doubted their affection.

I reached over and squeezed Gram's hand. I had a feeling she'd be like my uncles.

Tyler could be a challenge all right, and now I had a better idea why. But he also had been willing to step out in opposition to his parents and become a police officer. It was important to him and he didn't let emotional abuse stop him.

I tried to imagine what kind of parents could cut their son out of their lives to make a point about finances or status. You'd need to be strong to stand up to them. Gram and Tyler were both strong. Tyler had stood by me, just like my uncles. So what was wrong with me that I couldn't see past a few slipups? He wasn't perfect. Neither was I.

I leaned forward and gave Gram a huge hug.

"Thank you!"

"Well, don't count your chickens yet," she said, clutching her drink. "There's a few years left in the old girl before it all comes to you. I may run through it before I go."

I laughed. "Make sure you do. It's not about the house. I'm thanking you for being there for Tyler and not giving up."

She sipped what was left of her tea and said, "I suppose I've just been around too many people who were out for what they could get."

"Well, that's not me. And it's not Tyler either."

She put down the cup and squeezed my hand with both of hers. "I know, my dear. I know that."

I asked the question that had been bothering me for a while. "What about Zoya? Is she out for what she can get?"

She closed her eyes and sighed. "Poor hopeless Zoya. She's just trying to survive in a hostile world. She's devoted to me, heaven knows why. We don't need to worry about her being out for what she can get."

"We might need to worry that she's badly hurt."

"Oh, I hope not. I really rely on her every day. I need someone I can count on to be able to manage in this house. I can't really get out for groceries or errands anymore. I need help to get to medical appointments. Zoya does it all. She's a sourpuss, but underneath it all, I think she's good-hearted. If she can't work after this, I'll get help for both of us."

I wasn't convinced about Zoya's good heart, but there was a chance her injuries were from trying to keep Gram safe. I'd give her the benefit of the doubt.

"And Gus? What's he after?"

"Gus? Nothing! He doesn't even charge me for half of what he does. He's a prince."

Let's hope so, I thought.

Shortly after that, Gram dozed off, perhaps a result of the soothing tea. I needed some thinking time anyway. A lot had happened. A lot more could happen. But every event on this trip had taken us by surprise. Some had been good. Gram, for instance. Although I'd heard tales of Grandmother Kelly and her legendary and possibly fictional skill at driving a getaway car, I'd never met her. I'd never had a grandmother. I wanted a share of Gram. She'd been a fabulous surprise. I still worried about what other unexpected thunderbolts the universe was waiting to hurl at us.

After a while, I began to feel stiff sitting in the chair. I dislodged Asta, who looked devastated. I stood up and had a good long stretch. I glanced around the room. Not as fussy as Gram's own grand boudoir, but full of great stuff. I wandered to the desk in the corner and ran my hands along it. I traced my fingers around the lotus flowers on the red and white Ching dynasty ginger jar. That's the problem with stuff.

It makes you covet it. I love old artefacts especially Victorian, Edwardian and Art Deco. Maybe at some point in the future, this would all be Tyler's, but life isn't just about stuff. He was making a new start in Cabot. I should say another new start, because Harrison Falls had been a new start for him too. More important than his new start was Gram. She was a game changer. But what would happen now that they were reunited? Gram was in her mid-eighties. She was fragile. She had this amazing house in San Francisco. San Francisco, which was the place that had taken us twenty-four hours and three separate flights to get to. With the possibility of disrupted travel like we'd experienced, we couldn't just be dashing back and forth whenever. Gram might not have "a worry in the world," but Smiley had just bought a house that needed a lot of work and I was saving everything for grad school. Cross-country commutes would be insanity.

Selfishly, I felt I didn't want to leave my own family, Uncle Mick and Uncle Lucky and even, yes, Uncle Kev, grant me strength. I couldn't just trade them in. And I wasn't sure that Smiley and I would always be together. We had a bit of mending still to do before we were happily ever after or HEA, as I thought of it.

I gave myself a little shake. Our big problem wasn't working out how Smiley (and maybe I) would be managing with Gram for the rest of her life, it was keeping her alive for the immediate future.

That would be considerably easier if Smiley ever returned.

I WAS DOZING in what had been William's leather recliner, apparently drooling, and with Asta parked on my chest. Not a good look for me if the snort from the police officer was any clue.

My eyes snapped open to see Officer Martinez shaking with laughter. From the bed, Gram was snoring musically.

Officer Martinez said, wiping her eyes, "Okay, your guy's back with the Russian sleeper agent, but Gus claims never to have heard of him."

Luckily Gram's eyes popped open. "Did someone say my Tyler's back?"

The cop said, "Lots of elderly people are fooled by fake relatives. How do you know he's really who he says he is?"

I said, "Take a look at the two of them and then ask that."

From the bed, Gram said, "Because *I* found *him* after being estranged for years."

"Why were you estranged?"

"Ask his miserable parents. Now let's get this show on the road." Gram patted her hair and arranged the waves.

Tyler must have taken the steps two at a time because seconds later he practically flew into the room. Zoya was hot on his heels and pale as a hotel sheet. Asta launched herself at Zoya and danced around.

"What happened? Why are the police here?" Smiley pointed at Officer Martinez, who stared at him and then at Gram.

"Yeah, I do see the resemblance," Officer Martinez said.

I answered Smiley. "Break-in number two. Destruction at the back end. Gus the handyman and his lookalikes are boarding up the damaged door."

"But who was it?"

"No idea. He or they came in the back way. Gram heard them, but I was outside talking to the cop watching the house. The only thing is that Officer Martinez here says no one was actually assigned to watch this address, although the cop might have been real."

Out of the corner of my eye, I saw Zoya's knees buckle and it was just by chance that Officer Martinez and I managed to catch her before she hit the floor.

I said, "I think you should go to bed, Zoya." We propped her up on the foot of the bed. I stared at her, worried.

Gram said, "Listen to them, Zoya, and don't be such a

silly goose. You need to let someone take care of you for a change."

Zoya nodded and I couldn't miss two tracks of tears running down her pale cheeks. Were they crocodile tears? No way to tell.

Zoya let herself be led away by me and Officer Martinez and Asta the pug, who managed to scamper in between our legs, just missing being stepped on. I was beginning to miss Asta's shy phase. At the door of her room, Zoya said quite haughtily, "I em fine now. You leaf."

I didn't plan to "leaf." "We don't want you conking your head again. Get changed and into bed and then we'll knock and check that you are all right."

She opened her mouth with a halfhearted attempt to protest. I said, "Accept it. You'll be sleeping with the door open and people will be checking on you during the night. That's what happens after a head injury." I should know. Uncle Kev had had more than enough of them over the years.

I turned and gave Smiley a look that was intended to make his blood run cold. "Nice of you to come by in good time."

He blanched. "Our cab had a fender bender."

"What? Who hit you?"

"No idea. Hit and run. We had to wait for a report and then get another taxi here. I tried calling."

"Oh. I didn't even check my phone. It was chaos here. Is Zoya going to be all right?"

"She wasn't injured in the rear-ender although she did get hysterical. She refused to go back to the ER. At the hospital they said it's probably a mild concussion after the head injury, but we have to watch for nausea and vomiting or changes to her pupils. One was a bit enlarged but it's going back to normal."

"I know the symptoms well. Don't worry, Zoya. You're in safe hands now."

I wished I felt as confident as I sounded. Apparently I hadn't fooled her. She said, "Ve are not safe. Novhere iss safe."

"Tyler's here. He's a police officer. Officer Martinez is here. And Gus."

She snorted. "Gus? You kidding, yes?"

I took her point. "He'll make sure the back entrance won't get opened. Tomorrow, we'll have a new door installed. Maybe without easily breakable windows in it. And we've ordered a security system to be installed in the morning."

"You've been busy," Tyler said.

Zoya flopped onto the bed and curled up into the fetal position, still in her clothes. Asta jumped up and snuggled in. We left them like that. Door open.

In the corridor, with Officer Martinez eavesdropping rather obviously, I said to Smiley, "We can't leave either of them here all night. It's too dangerous."

"Agreed. I'll stay. They're my responsibility."

I glared at him as we walked back to Gram's room.

He said, "You can relax at the hotel. It's your vacation."

"It's your vacation too. And you paid for both of our vacations. On a practical note, do you really think I'm going to relax without you at the hotel where I was attacked? Don't you understand that I'll be worried about what's happening here? I'll decide where to be safe. I agree with Zoya. We're not safe and we don't seem to be safe anywhere. I do think we're better off together."

"That's the spirit," Gram said.

He said, "Stay here then. It will be easier for Gram. And we don't know what other dangers there are at the hotel."

I said, "One of us should stay here and the other one can go to the hotel, pack up and check out. At least we'll have clothes and toiletries. I don't mind—"

Officer Martinez responded to a crackling noise on her radio. She turned away and walked to the hallway for the conversation. When she returned, she said, "Sorry, I'll have to leave you. Orders. Someone else will be coming by shortly."

Smiley said, "Why don't we stay here tonight and go to the hotel in the morning once the security system is set up here? Gus said he's happy to be here whenever. There's no point in you going out in the night alone." He held up his hand before I spoke. "Even though you are capable of taking care of yourself. But we don't really know what's going on."

I nodded. "Safety in numbers."

He said. "Right. The stuff at the hotel is only stuff."

"More important to protect Gram and Zoya."

"Yup. There are lots of mattresses, plenty of towels, and if you want, you could even wash the clothes you're wearing and get the rest in the morning. Or borrow something from Gram or Zoya."

I thought I heard a muffled *"Nyet!"* from down the hallway.

"I guess we could take turns standing guard tonight."

Smiley said, "I'll be standing guard. I brought you to this. You get to sleep. Gram said there are sheets and towels in the linen closet off the upstairs hallway. There's a drawer in the main bathroom with extras, toothbrushes, toothpaste, all that. By the way, Gram says you should sleep in the green room. Out of respect for your Irish roots."

I figured the green room was the one to the rear of the second floor, next to Gram's floral wonder. "How does she know about my Irish roots?"

He shrugged. "We're talking about everything, catching up. Filling in the blanks. I told her all about you."

"*All* about me?"

Again with the grin. "I may have left out specifics about your uncles' line of work."

"Oh, right, the independent businessmen."

"Yep, the gift that keeps on giving."

"And yet, I love them to bits and they're part of the package."

"I'm aware of it. But we'll wait before we spring that part on Gram."

"And when the time comes, we'll lock up the silver and the bank books."

"Leave it with me."

I said, "Oh, wait, as we were talking about valuables, I realized that the home invaders didn't take the sterling silver, just our feelings of security."

"Well, they were after something specific."

"Yeah. But they beaned Zoya with a valuable sterling candelabra and they left it."

"Right. So not the usual MO."

"Sleep on it. Maybe you'll have an insight."

I wish I could say I stayed up to keep Tyler company, like a good little fake fiancée, but as soon as I made up the bed in the green room, I was out like a blown fuse.

I WOKE WITH a shock and had trouble figuring out where I was. Somewhere green. The clock said seven a.m. I heard a familiar voice: Gus bellowing instructions. I made myself respectable and went downstairs and ended up inspecting the repairs.

"Ain't nobody gettin' past this," Gus said, his arms proudly crossing his chest. "Nobody."

I managed not to say, "Oh boy."

What would Gram say when she saw the sheets of ply-wood blocking out the door and window to the backyard? It wasn't pretty, but Gus was right—I couldn't imagine any-one getting past it.

Gus said, "The boys gonna get bars for the windows inna rest of this floor."

Bars? I told myself it didn't matter what it would look like. It might be necessary.

Tyler nodded. He was good with bars on the windows.

I hadn't nodded in agreement at that point. Why did I care so much about the integrity of that old house? Some things were more important than aesthetics.

At that moment, the doorbell rang and we all jerked our heads toward it. In my experience, the doorbell is never a good thing. But lucky us. The alarm company tech had arrived nice and early to install the alarms.

"I took the initiative," I explained to Tyler. "Under the circumstances, it seemed like a sensible decision."

"Good thinking. Gram should have had a service before. Probably never thought she needed it in this area."

"With the bars to keep them out and the security service to sound the alarm and bring first responders, we'll be somewhat ahead. We just need the phone company to repair the phone line and we're good."

I thought of the intruders' weapons. "Yes. I guess."

While the tech installed the sensors on the doors and windows and the monitoring box, Gus supervised "the boys" installing the bars and I hunted down what I needed. After a search through Gram's closet, I borrowed the least flowered dressing gown from a large collection of very bright nightwear. Next I located a pair of velvety pink faux-fur slippers, which still had the tags on. It would be easy to replace the slippers for Gram. I put my clothing in the washing machine. I had a shower and a shampoo in Gram's lavender-scented bathroom, trying to get the previous day out of my system. I put on the dressing gown, wrapped my wet hair in a bright pink towel turban and went downstairs to check on the progress and give Tyler his time to get cleaned up.

When I appeared downstairs in my new outfit, his mouth fell open.

"Not a good look for you," I said, pointing at his open mouth.

"Back atcha," he said with a retaliatory point at the dressing gown. "I don't know if I've ever seen that color before in an article of clothing."

"Fuchsia. Sure you have, on your Gram. And I think you'd better get used to it now that you're part of this family."

"Huh."

"You'll need to strengthen your spine, of course."

"Right. And speaking of building our strength, let's have something to eat. I made my specialty."

"And that is?"

"Grilled cheese sandwiches."

Uncle Mick also calls grilled cheese a specialty. His are made with Wonder Bread and Kraft Slices. I still have fond childhood memories of the worst day being made better with grilled cheese sandwiches and tomato soup.

Smiley's were a variation on the theme: He'd found a twelve-grain rustic loaf of bread, spread it with soft butter, grated a chunk of Monterey Jack and some old cheddar, mixed that with a bit of mustard and a dash of hot sauce. Turned that into sandwiches and cooked them up with a bit of butter in Gram's ancient cast-iron skillet. He'd also squeezed every orange in the house. The results were enough to make you forget all about men with guns.

We ate the first batch and then Smiley did a second batch to take to Gram, who hadn't stirred yet, and for Zoya, who was also sleeping off the trauma of the day before. He got to work and I took the wicker tray to serve Gram breakfast in bed and came back to select a dark wood one for Zoya. William had been an invalid for quite a while; no wonder there were so many choices. I also found two bud vases and clipped a lilac bloom for each.

CHAPTER SIXTEEN

Someone can always take your gun.
—THE KELLY RULES

ZOYA WAS ALSO awake and surprised to get breakfast in bed and accepted it with her usual lack of grace. I smiled at her scowl, left the tray and backed out of her room. I joined Gram and Tyler in the large front bedroom.

"Just what the doctor ordered," Gram said cheerfully after she scarfed down her sandwich in high style. "I was just telling Tyler about my gun."

I stared. "You have a gun?"

Tyler shrugged. He'd already heard, I supposed.

Gram beamed. "William had a pistol. We could use that for protection. If they come back we could shoot them before they shoot us."

Tyler's eyes bulged. "Shoot them?"

"It's them or us."

I preferred if no one was shot. I said, "But do you know how to use it?"

"Me? I'm a little old lady, pet. I only know how to collect marbles and create short circuits. I was hoping you would."

"I don't like guns. No one in my family owns one. I don't

really know much about them." Of course I'd had one
pointed at me more than once—including that very day—
and I'd been forced to fight for control, but I didn't think I'd
be much good at aiming and firing one. The best I could do
was get rid of someone else's weapon. I'd used a statue to
disarm one assailant and the jar of marbles had outgunned
our recent assailants. Could that kind of luck hold? It wasn't
like I had time to train at a gun range. Anyone coming after
us would have a serious advantage.

Tyler said gently, "Maybe that's not the best idea, Gram."

"Come on, pet. We have to do what we can."

I said, "Let's hope we can rely on the police."

Gram said impishly, "Where's your spirit, my dear?"

"My spirit is trying to figure out a way to stay alive, like
the rest of me," I said, perhaps a bit snappily. "Fine. Where
is the stupid thing?"

"It's—oh gosh, I don't remember. Put away in a safe place
so we couldn't have an accident."

I had a feeling that guns needed to be cleaned and perhaps fired every now and then to make sure they didn't jam
or misfire. Whatever a misfire was. So that made this strategy even less viable. On the other hand, what other strategies
did we have? We'd already used the marbles. Aside from
the possibly mythical pistol, this house full of chintz and
china and figurines and birds was an unlikely source of
weaponry.

Smiley was the person who could manage the firearms.
He said, "When you remember where it is, I'll take a look
at it."

"What if it explodes in your hands?" I said.

"Oh, come on, what are the chances that would happen?"
Gram said.

Before Tyler could respond with a likely police statistic
on guns exploding in hands, we had another dog emergency.
I could hear Zoya shrieking "Asta!" If she had been yelling

"cookies" or even "chicken livers," she might have had more success. That was my experience with pugs, but Asta wasn't my dog, it wasn't my house and it really wasn't my business. Okay, maybe it was a little bit my business.

While Zoya was hunting for the little pug, I helped get Gram settled at a large folding table in the bedroom so she could work on a five-thousand-piece puzzle that seemed to consist entirely of sky, with the occasional wispy cloud. I thought it would be quite a while before Gram would be steady on her own. If she was going to continue living here, she'd probably need one of those chair lifts for the stairs. I'd leave it to Tyler to mention that.

We could still hear Zoya's sad wails, "*Aaaassstttttaaaaa!*"

Gram said, "What has gotten into that dog lately? Usually, she's so shy that she just hides under a chair. Why would she keep running away?"

I imagined it was all the violent upheaval, but I said, "She sure has a good life here."

"Yes, and she's good for me too. I got her for Tyler, of course. Did I even mention that?"

"Um, no, you didn't."

"I called her Asta after the dog in *The Thin Man*. You know that Tyler loves Hammett."

"I do know that." I might have felt annoyed with the assumption I knew nothing about my boyfriend, but I realized that Gram was crazy about her grandson and over the moon to have him back in her life. And she also liked to tease a bit.

She chuckled, "His grandfather loved Hammett too. He used to read aloud to me from the Nick and Nora books. He thought I might find the others a bit too gritty. Tyler was very young when he died, but he claims to remember his grandfather's books. It must be in the genes. My second husband never read anything that didn't have to do with science or engineering."

I went back to the previous topic, "So you got him a dog because . . ."

"I suppose it seems silly, but I wanted him to feel at home and he's always loved dogs. He was never allowed to have one when he was growing up." She shook her head and pursed her lips. "Imagine that, a boy with no dog. When we were first back in contact and talking on the phone to catch up, he mentioned a cute little pug belonging to his friend. He seemed really fond of it. I thought the birds would be able to cope. Zoya was slow to get used to Asta, but as you can hear, she's grown quite fond of the little darling."

Zoya's quasi-hysterical shrieks reached our ears from outside. "Asta! Asta!" And then some bizarre Russian commands or possibly threats that apparently didn't work to attract Asta.

"So did you want him to take Asta home with him?" I didn't want to mention that Tyler already had Cobain, a perfectly lovable dog. I could see this new "gift" ending badly, beginning with the plane ride and ending with Smiley and two dogs in the house he was renovating. There was already a pug-in-chief in my life, Walter. How would Walter react to Asta? I also knew who got to look after Cobain when Smiley was out of town or working long shifts. Did I have room on my bed for a third dog?

"No, no, my dear. He'll have his pet here, when he visits, something of an incentive, don't you think? Or if he were to move here, that would be different."

Move here? I couldn't see that happening. Smiley had a life and he had me. He was very happy to reconnect to Gram, but was he likely to drop everything and move across the country to be close to her?

It was a good question. I had serious competition in this foggy city between the adorable and doting grandmother and Hammett's ever-present ghost. But where would a move leave us?

I might have been playing it emotionally cool with Smiley, but I realized that I did not want to be separated from him.

The afternoon got worse when Zoya stomped through the door wailing that Asta must have been kidnapped. Zoya was such a slender creature, and yet she had a knack for storming around dramatically.

"She'll be back, Zoya dear. Don't carry on about it. Who would kidnap a little dog like that?"

"Who vould kidnep? *Who* vould kidnep?" Zoya threw her hands in the air, another thing she had a knack for.

"Well, exactly, Zoya. Who? And why?"

"Maybe Gus? Maybe boys?"

I didn't get involved in this dispute, although I couldn't help worrying about the little dog, now on the loose for the second time. And I wasn't so sure we could trust Gus or the boys, for that matter, but I couldn't see them kidnapping that demanding little pooch.

Gram laughed, a long hearty laugh that seemed to make Zoya's silver eyes pop, rather like the missing Asta's. "Gus and the boys didn't kidnap Asta and you know it. Just keep looking. She'll turn up, I guarantee it."

Zoya muttered, "Sure, sure, *guarantee* it. Huh."

But despite the guarantee, Asta did not turn up.

Smiley did a tour of the neighborhood carrying treats. I joined him. We took turns calling Asta's name. We'd already checked the backyard. We both knew that there was no way that little pug had squeezed out of the fenced yard. So that meant that either someone let her out an open door or someone must have assisted in her getaway.

Gus and the boys were most huffy when asked if they'd let Asta out. Zoya did not have a light touch as an interrogator.

We had plenty to do cleaning up the house now that the drama was over and the police were finished. Much of our effort involved getting Gram's bedroom back to normal, picking up the million spilled marbles and applying bandages to new glass cuts and tidying up the tossed sunroom. We alternated keeping Gram company.

I scrubbed the bloodstain out of the carpet in the dining room. It was a strong reminder that we were not on a carefree vacation.

Still we ordered pizza in for lunch and pretended it was a picnic. We ate outside on Gram's second-floor front porch. It made her giggle to have a picnic looking down on California Street. "I never would have thought of this."

Zoya did not approve. I was sure she muttered, "Peasants!" She did hang around, though, scanning the street for the pug.

Gram took catnaps. Tyler caught up on his sleep. I read a bit more of *The Continental Op* and dozed. It wasn't the vacation I'd expected, but it was what it was.

By late afternoon, there was still no sign of Asta.

In standard vacation terms, it promised to be a glum night at Gram's, what with the missing dog and the fresh memory of the home invasion, our hotel troubles and not knowing who was out to get us. Officer Martinez popped in to see how we were doing. By this time we had all relocated to the sunroom. Gram and Tyler seemed to be having a pretty good time at the sunroom table with a three-thousand-piece puzzle of some vague section showing what could have been the mid-Pacific.

Zoya spent her free time pacing and biting her bright nails. She kept whispering Asta's name. Yes, it was strange, but I understood. I could only imagine the chaos if our Walter had vanished. Or Cobain. There would be hell to pay.

Despite the glumness, we had a great dinner. Zoya and I managed to make Gram's specialty and Tyler's all-time favorite: Buttermilk Fried Chicken. The recipe was handwritten on a yellowed card. Following a very clear sugges-

tion by Gram, we'd located the recipes along with a stock
of blank recipe cards in a kitchen drawer. You could tell by
the grease spots it had sat on the counter many times while
she made this favorite recipe. I strongly discouraged Zoya's
suggestion that we improve it by adding a bit of "wodka."
She tried sulking, but I explained that Tyler would want to
experience the same taste he'd loved as a child, before his
parents separated him from his grandmother.

"People are terrible. *Absolutely* terrible," Zoya said with
a long, tragic glance toward the jigsaw puzzlers.

"Not those two people," I said with a smile, nodding my
head in the direction of Gram and Tyler.

"No," she agreed. "Not Missus and boy, but almost everyone else."

"I'm okay," I said with what is called a hint of asperity.

She shrugged. So, I was not absolutely terrible then.
Maybe better than "boy."

I turned my attention to the chicken. Cooking is not my
best thing and I was wishing that Signora Panetone had
made the trip with us. I could have used her expertise. Our
recipe was complicated by the fact that we didn't have buttermilk and Zoya did not intend to go and get any in case
Asta returned and she wasn't here.

Make do with what you have, my uncles taught me, and
a quick check on the Web told me that there were several
easy substitutes for buttermilk. I decided to use the "vinegar
in milk" version and not to mention it to Smiley. He might
as well enjoy this part of the trip down memory lane.

Dinner took me about five times longer than it should
have. I did my best to follow the recipe exactly. What can I
say? I had no signature dish, not even beans and franks,
which Uncle Mick had taught me. I had no dishes at all. My
talents lay elsewhere. Zoya was not much help, what with
all the sighing and muttering about Asta. I got it, though.
Every now and then I'd give her a sympathetic pat on her

rail-thin arm and she'd give me a dirty look. In her defense, she did cook the potatoes and mashed them to a creamy and delicious texture. She also prepared the peas so that they were just right, not overcooked.

While the chicken was frying (I loved that sizzling sound), she set the table in the dining room so as not to disturb the puzzle. When I stuck my head in the room, she had her arms crossed lightly and was staring into the distance.

"Ve should be looking," she said.

"Right after we eat," I said. I agreed with her that we didn't want the little dog sleeping out on a cool night, frightened and alone, but I felt sure she was curled up in someone else's home.

Dinner was a surprising success.

"This is just the way I remember it, Gram," Smiley said. "Did you teach Zoya?"

Zoya sniffed.

Gram said, "Zoya doesn't touch dead chickens."

Tyler stared at me with . . . astonishment?

"Really," I said, "Is it so *very* hard to believe that I could cook this chicken?"

"No, not at all." That spreading blush put the lie to that. He added, "But I'm proud of you."

I was proud of myself. Of the two of us, Smiley is the cook and a decent one too. Now I would have one dish that I could add to my flair for opening packages of ice cream sandwiches. I could make fried chicken any time I had an extra three and a half hours. I could call it a family heirloom. In my family, Kraft Macaroni and Cheese was the closest we came to a tradition.

Dessert turned out to be a silky lemon pudding cake that had also been one of Smiley's favorites. Zoya had whipped that up using one of Gram's recipe cards because there was no raw chicken in the ingredients. I was pretty sure I couldn't taste vodka in the finished product.

After dinner Zoya and I searched for Asta again. We brought some fried chicken with us to tempt her. We weren't taking all that much of a risk: There were two of us—Smiley was making sure the house was safe—and the young cop who was watching the house promised to keep an eye out for us. Where was that little dog? Terrified and hiding? Or was she holed up being spoiled by a new family who didn't realize they were being used for treats? For Asta's sake, I hoped not hiding and terrified. For everyone's, I prayed she hadn't wandered into traffic.

When we trudged back to Gram's, discouraged and downhearted and with Zoya blowing her nose vigorously, we found Gram and Smiley still working on the puzzle, but there seemed to be more pieces left than at the start. That puzzle was a good metaphor for whatever was going on in our lives.

Too many pieces that looked the same, too many ends that wouldn't fit together, so many bits that didn't add up to a coherent picture. With luck, we'd keep adding small insignificant bits until something began to make sense.

At Gram's suggestion, Zoya went sniffing off to hunt for the possibly mythical pistol. I wandered around the house, checking out the many photos on the walls, on dressers and in the bookcase full of photo albums in the large front bedroom that had been William's. I went through them all, including the box of "extras," many of which had the names and dates written on back. "Howard and Maisy, Feb 14, 1950," or "Jean at the beach—July 1, 1994," in what I figured was William's spidery handwriting. I love old photos, and not just because of the soft graininess and clothes. I love how they preserve moments from the past. We Kellys do not like to keep that kind of record, in case it's used against us. As for the Binghams, your guess is as good as mine. The Huddys and the Dekkers liked a record. As Gram had said, there weren't many of her relatives, but I could spot family traits in Smiley's great-grandfather, like the wavy blond hair and the gap between his teeth. He and his bride stood solemnly in the one shot of them together. Although she took after the father, I thought I recognized some of Gram's fun and sparkle in her mother. There were a few more of the couple with a laughing blond baby, then a toddler. Gram's high school photos were there. I didn't find a record of her as Mrs. Dekker, but there were plenty of Smiley, with Gram and with the man who must have been her first husband. I didn't find any of Tyler's parents, but I could understand that.

I settled into the recliner and smiled at the picture of Gram and her second husband. It must have been a wedding photo. She was rosy-cheeked and pretty in a cream "mermaid" dress with long sheer sleeves. She carried pink roses. I would have enjoyed seeing who was at this wedding, although obviously the Dekker family had boycotted.

I flipped through more photo albums wondering who everyone was. There were photos going back to the early 1900s, if I guessed. Most seemed to be relatives on William's side. I noticed patterns: chubby cheeks here, ski-slope noses there, some were tall and slender, others short and burly. Here and there were photos of bright-eyed toddlers—most likely the cousins—who would probably be in their late twenties now.

It would be fun to ask Gram about everyone when she wasn't so caught up in the puzzle. I wondered if they'd be tall and slender or short and burly. Smiley also rated his own album—the one that caused him such guilt—although it stopped when he was around ten. As I thumbed through the others, Gram kept that one close to her. I was sure glad it hadn't been found when his room was trashed and I was pretty sure he hadn't told her that he thought our burglars might have been looking for it. I couldn't bring myself to believe that, though. Scattered here and there in the other album were occasional newspaper clippings about him. High school graduation. Police academy graduation. A few from the Harrison Falls local paper after some of our joint adventures. I figured William Huddy had had warm feelings toward his step-grandson. I felt sadness for Gram as she'd missed out on the boy she loved and for Tyler too. It was an oddly pleasant evening, considering why we were really there—instead of in our sumptuous downtown hotel suite— to make sure Gram and Zoya were not attacked again, plus we were missing the adorable pug and there was a police officer keeping an eye on the place.

Gram and Tyler enjoyed everything—food, puzzle and each other's company—immensely. I felt I could share in their joy at having found each other. And better than that, still being the people they'd loved. Special.

Zoya slouched off to bed first, after first dishing out Gram's medications. "Iss past your bedtime," she said.

"Don't feel you have to wait for me, Zoya," Gram said. "I'll be fine. It's the first time in many years that I've had such fun." I knew that the fun wasn't the puzzle. It was Tyler. He knew it too.

Zoya glared at Smiley and me as if we were ax murderers just waiting for our big chance.

"It's all right, Zoya," Gram said, looking up with a touch of annoyance. "Stop being such a silly goose."

I understood Zoya's position. We were all vulnerable; no one more so than Gram and none of us understood what was really going on. I smiled at her. "Everything will be fine." Not that I really believed it. Still, it would be a relief to have Zoya not moping, sniffing, blowing her nose and occasionally murmuring Asta's name.

With Zoya gone, I glanced out the window at the officer guarding the house. I checked the reinforced back entrance and rattled the lock in the front door. We might not have known why it happened, but we could reasonably expect to be safe this night. And after all, Tyler was a police officer who knew what he was doing.

I'd already snooped through all the photo albums and framed photos. What now? I decided to be practical and do something. I found a pad of paper and a pen. Sometimes when I'm having trouble sorting things out, it helps to put it on paper.

So many bizarre things had happened in the few short days since we'd arrived. It seemed a good idea to list them. I made myself at home at the dining room table. It was a warm pleasant room with very comfortable upholstered dining chairs. I could hear Gram and Smiley chatting every now and then and periodically a chirp from a bird.

I began to write. I had the situation at Gram's covered with

HOME INVASION.

I also added

MISSING PUG

and

ZOYA'S ATTACK

(although it was probably part of the invasion). That was plenty of weird stuff.

I also listed the hotel happenings.

ROOMS TRASHED

and

JORDAN ATTACKED.

These things had to be connected. I closed my eyes and
thought about what else might have happened that could have
been related. I closed my eyes and mentally worked my way
through our vacation hour by hour. There was the dark sedan
that had nearly clipped us on our walk back to the hotel. There
was the microphone under the table in the restaurant. And there
was whoever had pushed me from the cable car.

I added

BLACK PRIUS

to the list. I had to assume it was part of the crazy package. Too bad we hadn't been able to see anyone in the vehicle. Nor had we noticed an unusual number of dark Priuses
lurking around, if you didn't count the cop cars. Oh. Cop
cars. There was the pudgy faux officer who had been supposedly watching the house after the invasion.

PHONY COP

went on the list.
I also added

RESTAURANT—MIC UNDER TABLE.

Of course,

CABLE CAR

deserved a lot of attention.

At least there I'd seen other people's faces on the cable
car, unlike the masked intruders, the invisible dog thieves,
whoever had trashed our rooms, planted the mic under the
table in Magari and pushed me on the hotel stairs and, of
course, the unseen driver of the dark sedan.

I closed my eyes again and tried to recall the people on the cable car. Who had been there? Some familiar faces. I remembered the squealing schoolgirls with their black asymmetrical haircuts with the weird-colored tips, the shredded jeans and the selfie sticks. Now that I thought about it, we'd seen them around the tourist areas and near our hotel. I decided to start a list.

SUSPECTS

SCHOOLGIRLS

went on the list.

Next, the puffy bickering couple. They'd been at our hotel too.

BICKERING COUPLE!

On the list!

I could hardy forget the hulking guy who'd stood behind me on the cable car: with his large, moon face, tight shirt and general sweatiness. I knew I hadn't seen him since, but perhaps he'd been in the speeding car. That was probably a stretch. Anyway,

SWEATY MOON-FACED GUY

was added.

Perhaps the short, bullet-shaped man with the crisply gelled black hair was a better bet. He'd shouldered his way between me and Smiley. Maybe he'd also given me that sharp push.

BULLET MAN

went on the list.

I mentally scanned the other passengers on the cable car to see if any of them matched up with the many people I'd run into since then. None of them matched anyone else I'd noticed around, either in the hotel or on the street or near Gram's. Of course, the men who invaded Gram's house were masked and "hatted" so how would I ever know?

Unless it was the two sweet silver-haired ladies with the Birkenstock sandals and Tilley hats, I was out of suspects. I laughed at the idea but then thought I could hear a Kelly voice saying, *No one is who you think they are.*

Fine.

BIRKS LADIES

went on the list. I had to chuckle, but you really never know. After all, they were staying in our hotel. They were around in the tourist area and we had seen them in the lobby. They could have overheard Smiley making the dinner plans. They were on the cable car. Could they have pushed me? Yes, but why would they?

Since I was thinking about the hotel, I added another suspect. The

MANAGER

had acted very suspiciously and had insisted on comping us dinner at a restaurant where our conversation was bugged. If that wasn't weird, I didn't know what was.

It seemed like a ridiculous exercise and yet I needed to do something. Doing anything was better than doing nothing. I spent quite a long time trying to come up with more suspects without any success. I wondered whether to add Zoya. She wasn't happy with our presence. How far would that extend?

ZOYA.

Why not?

I paced around after that and checked on the puzzle addicts in the other room. Plenty of Pacific Ocean still to go. I returned with a cup of herbal tea and stared at my list of bad and weird events and my list of suspects, most of them quite unlikely. How were they connected? Or were they? How could I ever untangle any of it? I needed a better arrangement. I needed a white board or a wall that I could write on and stick photos on, like in an incident room. I needed to be able to make links between people and events and draw dramatic sweeping arrows with black markers. I didn't think I could do any of that in Gram's house.

But I did have an idea. I hustled back to the kitchen and helped myself to a stack of recipe file cards from the drawer. Not dramatic, but useful. And you use what you can. I took half blue cards and half white. Gram had no problem with me using them or anything else in the house. She said as much without taking her eye off the puzzle. "If you want anything, take it, my dear. Anything at all."

Excellent.

The home invasion. The disappearance of the dog. The knocking out of Zoya. The use of the fake cop. The tossing of our rooms in the hotel. The attack on me in the staircase. The near hit-and-run. The push from the cable car. The mic in the restaurant. Every item got a card. Every suspect did too. I used blue for the events and white for the suspects. I placed them on the table and tried to figure out which events could be related to which people. I made notes under each heading. I began to see the odd possibility. Maybe I had seen that large man on the cable car. For instance, the moon-faced man on the cable car and the faux cop were both large and sweaty. There had also been the big, finger-snapping waiter at Magari too. Not sweaty, but large. Were they all the same person? I'd only had a glimpse at the moon-faced man because he'd stood behind me and the faux cop had his cap low on his forehead. But it was possible. And if it was possible, it would have to mean that Moon Face and Faux Cop knew who I was and the connection to Gram and her house. I had been the target on the cable car, not Smiley. So what would that be about? Had they merely followed us? Why? Was our every move being shadowed? I shivered. That was creepy enough to be a Sam Spade case. While I tried to think of explanations and relationships, the stress of the past two days caught up with me and I conked out, my head leaning back against the upholstered dining room chair.

CHAPTER SEVENTEEN

Follow the money.
—THE KELLY RULES

I JUMPED WHEN Tyler put his hands on my shoulders.

"That's not the best way to sleep," he said.

"I think you're right. Did you finish your puzzle?" My neck was stiff from dozing on the chair. I rubbed it and grinned.

He shook his head. "It might be a lifetime effort."

"Better you than me. All that ocean."

He grinned back. "To tell the truth, I'm enjoying the puzzles. We're talking about a lot of happy times I'd forgotten. Never thought I'd get such a kick out of spending an entire day in this amazing city doing a puzzle with my grandmother."

"Don't forget the housework," I teased.

But it made sense. I would have loved to have a grandmother to do something with, although maybe not a three-thousand-piece puzzle. Grandmother Kelly's skills had inclined more toward evading police pursuit. My imagined

Grandmother Bingham had endless possibilities, because I knew nothing about her.

"It's nice that you have this chance."

"What have you been up to besides sleeping sitting up?"

I couldn't stop myself from yawning, so my answer wasn't useful.

He said, "Get some real sleep. I'm going to stay up and make sure nothing happens in the night."

"I don't know if I can sleep, there's so much whirling in my head. Do you want to take turns?" I yawned again.

He ruffled my hair and said, "Tomorrow, I'll sleep and you'll watch. How's that for a deal?"

"I thought that's what happened last night."

"My police training is paying off."

I pointed at my list of suspects and troubling events and the cards for each. "Trying to figure out who's after us and why so I can get to the bottom of everything."

"Let me know the minute you figure it out. Once the mystery is solved, then I can get some sleep too."

"I'm on the case."

MY DREAMS HAD been full of shadowy figures, dark sedans, breaking doors. I woke up jumpy. I padded downstairs on sock feet and found Smiley, still staring at the puzzle.

"You made some progress," I said. "There can't be more than ten thousand square miles of ocean to put together."

"I still can't figure out what's going on," he muttered. He wasn't talking about the puzzle.

"Tell me about it."

"First, there's oatmeal for breakfast," he said. "Gram believes in it."

"Hmm. Did she make it?" I grew up on Froot Loops and

Count Chocula and the signora wasn't big on oatmeal, so my first thought was to resist. Resistance turned out to be futile.

"I did, according to her instructions. You'll like it. It's got whipping cream in it and toasted almonds and dried cranberries and maple syrup. Vanilla too."

I did like the oatmeal, which should not come as a surprise. I liked the fresh coffee too.

Gram had taken her breakfast in bed. Zoya was floating through the neighborhood calling for Asta. Smiley was one big yawn machine.

He headed off to crash and I took my place back at the dining room table. I was hoping that the images from my weird night's sleep would lead to some clarity.

They did not.

So many crazy ideas and events were whirling around in my head. Part of the whole Hammett nightmare was the strange randomness of all that had been going on. But still, random or not, I needed to try to sort things out, needed to know what to do next, needed to figure out who to trust and who to run from. I'm a practical girl. As Uncle Mick would say with a wink, "Follow the money." After all, Uncle Mick always did follow money, even if it was usually for the wrong reasons.

So. What money? As far as Smiley and I went, there was little of value. I had the rest of the cash to pay for *Red Harvest*, hardly worth killing for, or even scaring the pants off someone for. There was a photo album but I didn't see that as something worth pushing a girl off a cable car for or breaking into an old lady's home and terrorizing her. Well, attempting to terrorize her. We had nothing else of value in our hotel room and I'd had nothing on my person when I was attacked.

That's if you didn't count the pittance that Tyler and I each had to spend on meals, sightseeing and souvenirs in what was left of our rapidly diminishing holiday.

I bit my lip. Of course, Uncle Mick also would have said, "But there's always money somewhere."

The only possible pot of it that I could imagine was Gram's own equity, whatever amount she had amassed, inherited or earned and socked away.

Did that make sense? Most of that would have been in investment funds and annuities deposited regularly in her bank for her needs. Not the sort of thing you'd break into a home shouting, "Where is it?" because of course, "it" was off being invested.

But the fact was that Gram would be worth a small fortune. The house alone would get my uncles' attention, regardless of the décor. Location. Location. Location.

So who would care about Gram's fortune? Someone who stood to gain?

Presumably Tyler would benefit as she was very fond of him. His horrible parents had cared enough about her money to cut her off from the grandson she loved. Call me crazy but there was no chance he was doing anything sinister to get his hands on his grandmother's wealth. Sometimes, you just have to trust. Smiley's sins had been caring too much about his job, worrying about how things would look, not trusting me and letting me down. In fairness, he hadn't always let me down, and if he owed his life to me, I also owed mine to him. If money was his thing, he would have stayed with the family and not become a small-town cop with a fairly impoverished girlfriend.

So probably not Tyler and he was the only one likely to inherit. I knew that. I assumed he did, but how to know who else would be in the loop?

Still, in the interests of being objective and not ever being blinded by love again (long story for another time), I reluctantly wrote Tyler's name on the list. I'd been fooled before, and even though I felt he was not "about money," I had to keep an open mind.

With a heavy heart, I wrote

SMILEY

on a card, although I realized that was showing my bias toward him. And I moved on quickly. Under his name on the card, I wrote:

Inherit?

Yes, it was silly, but fair's fair. I put my own name there too.

JORDAN.

I had no connection to anything that was going on, except as victim of some close calls. Or at least if I had a connection, I had no idea what that link would be. I liked Gram, and I was not likely to benefit from her in any way, except through Tyler and the fact she made him happy.

I went back to following the money.

His parents might be bitter and possibly vicious, but presumably they weren't in the will. Or were they? However, how would they even know one way or the other?

I put

TYLER'S PARENTS

on the list.

Under the heading I wrote:

Inherit? Not likely, but possible.

I could find no link to Gram's money and any of the other suspects I'd identified. The hotel manager seemed an unlikely heir as did everyone on the cable car. I wrote

No known link

on each of their cards. The black Prius continued to be an unknown. I wrote

Possible link???

on that card.

I stared at my random collection of cards and bit my lip.

What about Zoya? I didn't know for sure but Gram seemed rather fond of Zoya. And so there was a good chance that Zoya would stand to gain if something, say terminal, were to happen to Gram. I'd need to find out about that although I wasn't sure how the conversation would go. If Zoya was favored in the will, say, a share—even a small share of what was probably a large estate—it might be in her interest to hire people to scare the old lady and to scare us off too. She hadn't been so very badly injured in the invasion and being hurt was a good cover. It could throw us off the scent.

There you go,

ZOYA.

You're on the list.
On her card I wrote,

IN WILL? CHECK.

And that was it. Or was it? Hadn't Gram told Tyler, "We'll have to invite your new cousins"?

Who were these cousins? Were they the second husband's grandkids? I had assumed they were the toddlers in the photos.

Whoever and wherever they were, they not only stood to gain if something happened to Gram—say for instance she was scared to death by armed men—but also had something to lose when Smiley showed up to reconnect with Gram. Big time.

It was obvious that Gram cared deeply for Tyler. Did the cousins know this too? Had they been told? Overheard? Maybe Zoya spilled the beans to them?

I sat up straight. I was on to something now. Why hadn't I thought of it before?

The cousins could have hired those home invaders with the idea of shortening Gram's life before any wills could be changed. That was a stretch, because I had no idea who was in Gram's will now. I was pretty sure that Smiley wouldn't have to be aware of being in the will for it to be valid.

So, the cousins, then. Things were looking up. I liked suspecting them much more than Smiley.

COUSINS

went on the list, next to ZOYA and under WILL. I also gave them their own card. It was getting complicated.

I had a few misgivings, though. Did the cousins search our hotel and tear up the room? Maybe they were hunting for that photo album that Gram gave to Tyler. That could make sense if there was something pertaining to them. But why attack me? Unless, it was to scare me away from San Francisco and have him follow me home. After all, they didn't know either of us.

I added

Scare us away?

to the COUSINS card.

For sure, the cousins were looking more plausible.

Not that I had the faintest idea what they actually

looked like. Were they tall men with trench coats and stockings over their faces? Would I have seen them somewhere? Might they have been on that cable car? Or lurking in the hotel hallway? On the elevator? Or brandishing weapons?

I stared at the cards for

HOME INVADERS

and the

HOTEL ATTACKERS.

For the first time I wondered if they could be the same people. I tried to remember what I'd noticed about them. Could they all be the cousins?

Their motive, of course, was money, greed, just like all the others. What other motives for the type of violence we'd experienced were possible?

Face it, the other key motives—jealousy, sex and revenge—didn't seem to work here. There wasn't a political or class aspect that I could see. Drugs and criminal activity lay behind much violence, but I couldn't imagine a connection here.

Still, at the end of my list, I noted some possible motives that I would need to think more about: property disputes, vendettas, someone who hated the family. Old secrets.

Since I was considering unknowns, I went back and added question marks next to

HOTEL MANAGER

I didn't know how he was involved, but there was something weird going on there.

Next, short of the police and Gus and his boys, I was out of people that I could name.

Hmm.

I decided to add Gus and the boys to the list. They had access to the house and would have known how to break in and make it look like outsiders. But on the other side, Gram knew everyone in that family and so did Zoya, so it would be hard to disguise themselves. They did have distinctive silhouettes (three large, one small), but no boys had been our home invaders.

Gram really liked Gus. Might she have earmarked some trinkets or a small amount of money to him? Gus and the boys had a booming repair business and the home invasion plus the hotel rampage would have been very risky. In fact, neither crime had netted the perpetrators a thing, except to scare us all silly. Still, I left Gus and the boys on the list. It didn't cost anything. On the card, I wrote,

Will?

As for the cops, the unknown fool in front of the house may have been involved. I put

STUPID COP

on the list and made a note to ask Officer Martinez to see if she had any more ideas about who he might have been.

My list was getting longer and messier and my cards were getting even worse. I told myself that was why detectives used boards, so they could see connections and draw lines with dry erase markers.

I stalked around the house trying to clear my head. I wandered back upstairs. I was wearing the chiffon dress again. It had lost some of its glamour on day two.

Gram waved to me from her front bedroom. "No smiles today?"

I managed to produce one, by some small miracle.

"Come in, my dear. Where is our boy this lovely sunny day?"

Lovely sunny day? I hadn't even noticed. A quick glance out the window confirmed it. Across the street, Sierra, looking well put together as always, was waving good-bye to her husband and taking the baby for a walk. Her biggest worry would be to walk up the hill to an artisanal coffee roastery or down the hill to an almost identical one. A beautiful day in San Francisco. Perfect for dodging would-be murderers.

I would have liked to join her, but I had stuff to do.

I slid William's recliner over to the vast bed and leaned forward. I said, "That was awesome oatmeal this morning. I'd never had anything like it." I didn't mention the Froot Loops or Count Chocula I grew up with. Gram beamed at me.

I said, "You might not be smiling when this is over, but I need to ask you some questions that may be uncomfortable and even unfair."

"I'm a tough old bird," she said with a chuckle. "What's that they say nowadays? Bring it on?"

I brought it on. "I need to know about your will."

She blinked and the telltale family flush started at her neck and rose higher.

"I realize that it's rude to ask, and I'm sorry, but we need to figure out what is going on with people breaking into your house and threatening you." I left out the missing dog, Zoya's injuries and everything that had happened to us.

"I'm sure it has nothing to do with my financial affairs," she said as the blush spread.

"Maybe not, but let's rule it out then. They do say, 'Follow the money.'"

She looked at me shrewdly. "Fine. What do you need to know?"

"Exactly who stands to benefit."

"Oh. Well, Tyler, of course. He's always been my heir, since my husband died."

"I had assumed that."

"I've never really discussed it with him. Perhaps I should."

"Who else? His parents?"

Her lips pursed. "No way. Most of what I have, and I'm very comfortable, is because William, my second husband, built a successful business. I helped by investing the rather small amount my first husband left me. He made it work for both of us and we never looked back. Tyler's parents cut me off and, worse, cut me off from Tyler, so, no, they won't be getting a cent."

"Right," I said.

"And if you're thinking my first husband should have left some money to his only son, you're right. He should have and he did. My son couldn't stand that I'd use what was rightfully mine and move on with my life."

"Okay then. So not Tyler's parents. Good."

"Why good?"

"Because the more we eliminate, the more likely we are to figure out who is behind these attacks."

"Fair enough."

"What about Zoya?"

"Zoya! Surely you don't think—"

From the door, I heard, "Zoya vat?"

We both whirled. I said, "Surely Zoya will have found out something about this morning."

She squinted suspiciously and waved her arms. "No Asta. Novere. Should call police."

That was bad news. We all wanted Asta back.

Gram rolled her eyes. "By all means, Zoya. See where you get with the police, although they haven't been much help sorting anything else out."

Zoya stomped away and down the stairs. Gram exhaled.

"Yes. She will get a certain amount. Enough to get by on. But she'll lose her home and her meals and everything she has here. She'd definitely need to get another job soon. It might not be as good as this one." Gram glanced at me and pursed her lips.

"I understand her situation," I said. After all, it was much like mine, except that my work was more interesting and my boss was not as nice.

Gram sighed. "I think I am going to have to revise that will to make sure Zoya's looked after better. I'm all she has in the world."

"You might want to wait until we figure out what's going on first."

Gram's blue eyes flashed just a bit. "I'll make that decision."

"Oh course, but before I go, by any chance is there anything for Gus or the boys?"

"In my will?"

"Yes."

"Of course there isn't. Why would there be?"

I used "police talk." "Just eliminating suspects."

"Suspects? Really, my dear. Gus is not a suspect. He's as honest as anyone I've ever met, and his boys are big chips off the little block."

"Well, that's good news, isn't it? There couldn't be any issue with an unpaid bill or something he feels entitled to?"

"There is no issue!"

"Have there ever been any valuables missing from the house?"

"Are you accusing—"

"No. Just eliminating people, as I said."

"Well, except for Gus, you haven't eliminated anyone."

That was true. "What about relatives on your second husband's side? I think you mentioned cousins."

She took a breath. "There are some. I'd been hoping that

Tyler could meet his cousins one of these days, although they're really step-cousins."

"So exactly who are these cousins?"

"First of all, the real relatives are my late husband's nieces, Clara and Janet. They all live in New York State. We weren't close, in any way. Janet has a daughter and Clara has a son. Unless it's the other way around. I did make some small provisions—money and heirlooms—for all four, just as my husband had in his will."

"But they might be upset about the will favoring Tyler?"

"They probably would be, but how would they know? I didn't tell them. As I said, we're not all that close. We're in touch maybe once a year. Nothing's changed. Tyler was always the one. And if something were ever to alter that, the money I'd be leaving to him will go to a foundation to maintain parks. I don't remember the name right off."

"Would they know that?"

"They wouldn't know anything, unless one of them is a mind reader. Now, I think I need to close my eyes. This has been quite upsetting." I noticed she didn't call me "my dear."

"I'm sorry. I had to ask, but that should be the end of it."

I felt like a creep as I tiptoed away. Tyler appeared in his doorway suddenly, stretching. "Nothing like a full hour's sleep to get a guy going."

"Are you staying up?" I asked.

"I think so."

In the middle of our conversation, a text came in, just a bit of silliness from Lance. But after it, I spotted a text I must have missed from Farley Tso: Jordan, I have your item. I felt like dancing. Must have been just a lookalike on the news. Although I'd only met him once, my knees felt weak with relief. Farley was alive and I could collect *Red Harvest* for Vera. "I'll go to the hotel. I'd like to get my clothes and check on everything there."

"I don't like the idea of you going by yourself."

"Well, you're better to defend this place than I am."

"Still, who could you take with you?"

Officer Martinez was long gone. Gus and the boys were hammering away doing something good at least. Zoya was in no shape to do anything. Gram was out of the question.

"I'll be fine. And I'll stay in touch by phone or text."

"Better take a cab and be really careful."

I USED MY phone to book an Uber. There were several drivers in the area and I chose the closest one. Soon I was zooming along in a white Prius with my driver, Steve. Steve was in his late twenties and good-looking in that "short-haired with a large but well-trimmed mustache and suspenders" way. Also he was polite and just friendly enough. I couldn't help noticing that he had a copy of *On the Road* in the passenger seat. I felt a kinship toward him as another reader of classic books. He didn't insist on chatting. That was another point in his favor. We drove down the long hills past elegant row houses. I felt that vacation feeling for a brief moment.

My shoulders sagged thinking about it. San Francisco was so beautiful and charming and scenic, and yet behind the walls of these stately residences and down these whimsical back streets lurked duplicity and danger. We had no idea who was being duplicitous and where the danger was coming from. It was as dark and deadly as a scene from Hammett's own mind. Not the fun-filled Nick and Nora type of adventure, but a Sam Spade or Continental Op in which maybe no one would get out alive. As we neared the area of Farley's Finest, I had a vision of Vera's face. I was awfully glad I wouldn't be going home without *Red Harvest*. Whoever was making this the holiday from hell was not going to give Vera the ammunition to make me miserable at home. As we hurled along the busy streets, I reached into my satchel and fished out the antique handkerchief box that Farley had given me. I'd been too busy staying alive to think much about it. I opened it up. It had a hint of cedar and one crisp white hanky inside. Obviously the hanky was not original, just a sweet touch. I pulled it out to dab the sweat off my lip, elicited by thoughts of Vera. The corner remained in the little box, wedged in a gap along the base. With a slight tug, up came a false bottom. Sitting underneath was a gorgeous Art Deco rhinestone necklace. This was too much! Farley had hidden yet another gift inside and I hadn't even noticed until now. However, considering all that had happened in two days, I suppose I could be excused. I held the necklace up to the light; it was a stunner. Just amazing quality and a nice weight to it. Even as costume jewelry this must have been worth over a thousand dollars. And now that I was considering it, perhaps Mr. Tso had not intended to give me this gift, even if he was a "friend" of Mick's. As gorgeous as it was, and as much as I would have loved to, I decided I would not keep it. It was either a mistake or far too generous a present.

As we approached our destination, I leaned forward and asked Steve, "Can you stop there and wait for me? I just need to pick something up."

"No worries," Steve said.

I settled back and relaxed a bit. The windows were open a bit and I enjoyed the soft touch of the wind on my face. It felt so normal. A touch of normal life would do me good, clear my mind to work on the problem we were facing. Not that Farley's was normal in any way.

When we reached the Dali Mural, Steve found a nearby place to park. "I don't think you can park here."

He said, "No worries," again. A mantra perhaps. "Just message me if I'm not here when you come out and I'll swing back soon as I can." He settled back with his copy of

On the Road, Kerouac still being pretty good company after all these years.

"I shouldn't be long," I said, slipping out of the car. He gave me a businesslike smile, undermined slightly by his suspenders and mustache, and returned to his reading.

On this afternoon there was much less hustle and flow than previously. There was no intoxicating smell of churro nor was there a puppet lady, and when I reached the alley, I was saddened to see that the men on stools were not there either. I put on my "don't mess with me" stride and clicked my heels toward Farley's. The daylight from the street wasn't strong enough to reach the depths of the alley, and steam poured from a low vent.

Well, *that* was totally going to wreck my hair.

Around the corner was a dank empty alcove. Goose bumps pricked my neck and arms. I stepped into the small space; on the ground were a torn business card and a trampled peacock feather. There were scuff marks on the pavement where things had clearly been dragged.

"Farley?" I knocked at the wall. "Mr. Tso?" My voice echoing through the steam was making a creepy situation even creepier. What had happened here? Where did everyone and everything go? There was no door, no "Back in five minutes" sign. You would never have known that a shop bursting with a million curiosities had been here just the day before. This town was starting to give me the creeps.

I took a quick pic of the feather and card on the ground and tried to text it to Uncle Mick. Seeing as he and Farley were friends, on some level, maybe he could shed some light on this weirdness.

Angry voices echoed from behind a doorway, and I thought I heard footsteps slapping the damp cement. My phone chirped about lack of signal and a voice in the back of my head said, *Maybe you should get the heck out of the dark alley where things seem to disappear.* Soon my inner voice was drowned out by the sounds of my boots hitting the pavement as I hightailed it toward the street. I almost dropped my satchel, and wasn't even sure if I would have gone back for it.

When I burst back onto the street, my hair frazzled from steam and impromptu jogging, I could see Steve parked across the way. He seemed to have put down his book and picked up some knitting. Relieved to be back in the sunlight, and to have a signal, I made sure to send the picture of the naked alcove to Uncle Mick, emphasizing that I was counting on his contact to get Vera's item and could he get back to me ASAP, adding that I had given Farley Tso six hundred dollars of Vera's money. I had been hoping to get some shopping done in a few of the amazing vintage stores San Francisco has in droves. And I was also looking forward to taking some pix in Delores Park. Cheesy as it was, I wanted a shot of the Painted Ladies to send to Lance and Tiff, because, let's face it, all us people of "a certain age" watched *Full House.* Don't judge us, there was little else on. Looked like the shopping and photo-snapping items on my bucket list would have to wait for another time. Farley Tso was possibly dead. The shop was gone and so was the cash. It made me really sad and it meant I needed to put some distance between me and this place.

Although I didn't want to involve myself in whatever happened to Farley, I took time in the cab to enter Officer Martinez's information into my phone. Because you just never know.

CHAPTER EIGHTEEN

Look up and sideways, but never look down.
—THE KELLY RULES

THE SCHOOLGIRLS WERE heading out from the hotel, and the Tilley hat ladies seemed to have arrived just when I did. The ladies waved extravagantly. I waved back and grinned. The beautifully exotic students didn't take their eyes off their screens. The bickering couple had just left in a taxi.

I stepped out of the cab, walked across the street and took a picture of the hotel with my phone. For fun, I captured the Tilley hat ladies fussing with a map and what looked like a guidebook. I'd find a way to send them the pix afterward. The students were still there, both fascinated by their phones. Click. For good measure, I took a photo of the doorman and one of Steve the Uber guy with his book. I could send that to him later. The doorman seemed to have an issue with Steve. Steve in turn pointed to me. I waved and hurried back over. "He's helping me and I asked him to wait."

With all these cabs and unexpected activities, I was going to have to dip into Vera's cash. I'd be replacing that along with the chunk of change that had vanished with Farley Tso. Poor little college fund would take another blow.

I swept through the lobby, phone to my ear, pausing to take discreet photos as I waited for the elevator. I got the registration desk, the bellman, the concierge, and just as the elevator opened, I thought that I should really get a shot of the manager. I pivoted and made my way to the front desk. I spoke to the nice young man and asked to see the manager.

If asked, I would have had to classify the look on his face as furtive.

I smiled and waited.

"Um, he's not here." He was looking a bit paler by the minute.

"Oh. When will he be back?"

He glanced around nervously. "I don't think he's coming back." He blurted out, "Apparently there was a serious mistake made."

"Is there someone in charge?"

"Um, yes, she's in the office."

"Can you tell her I'd like to speak to her?"

"We have orders not to disturb her, at least for now."

"Well then, I'll try later."

He leaned forward. "It's just that you weren't supposed to have that upgrade. He wasn't authorized to give you that suite or do anything that he did."

I said, "But what will that mean for us?"

He shrugged. "Don't quote me, but I think they'll have to honor his commitment. But he's out of a job."

I HEADED UP to the suite and slipped through the doors, I flicked the safety latch. This time there had not been a mauling of the contents and our possessions. But there were subtle signs that someone had been there. My raincoat was not quite where I had left it. A small writing pad had been moved from the desk.

I took out my phone to call Smiley. This wasn't quite as straightforward a visit as I'd thought. Should I take the video devices with me? Should I call him? I should really decide what to do before calling him and having him make the decision. Not my style.

I changed into skinny jeans and a clean tee while I decided. The best thing would be to take the device from the living room and at least find out who'd been there. At least it would still be recording if there were more "visitors."

I was reaching for the phone to tell Smiley all was well when I thought I heard voices from the hallway. A knock on the door followed, then a man's voice. "Miss Bingham? This is"—a muffled name—"the manager. I need to speak to you."

"One moment." The manager? But I'd just been told the manager was a woman and this was definitely a man's voice. I scrambled to pick up my camera and stuffed it in my deep orange satchel. "Just need to get changed. Can you give me a bit of time?"

"I'm afraid I need to speak to you now. You are not authorized to be in this suite and we need you to vacate it now."

"No problem with that," I shouted. "But how do I know you are who you say you are? I'm calling the police." I put a little shake in my voice. I tiptoed to the door and held my phone up to the peephole in the door. I was able to see a distorted image of two large men in the hall. Even though they were wearing suits, I doubted that they were hotel officials. The former manager was a small man and this definitely wasn't him. I snapped a couple of shots and stepped back. From their heights and builds, there was a good chance they were the two who had terrorized us at Gram's house. They weren't wearing masks now, probably because that

would be highly suspicious in a hotel corridor. I was relieved
that I'd been able to get pictures of them. Maybe they'd be
good enough to identify despite the distortion of the peephole. I tried not to add in the thought "if my body was
found." My hands were shaking as I sent the photos to Smiley and for good measure to Lance and Uncle Mick. I
couldn't really think of anyone else until I remembered
Officer Martinez. My hands were shaking as I sent them to
her as well, with the note:

> I think these are the intruders. Now on ninth floor
> of La Perla Hotel.

"You have two minutes," the voice said.
"Perfect," I trilled. "That's all I need. Oh, maybe make
it three, please. I need to use the bathroom."
I grabbed the portable telephone receiver and dashed
toward the bedroom and the balcony door. Out on the balcony, I closed the door firmly behind me. I told myself not
to think about the fact it was the ninth floor. Of course, that
instruction had the opposite effect. I didn't know for sure
the two guys in the hall were our home invaders, but it
seemed like a pretty good bet. And they were at least as
scary as the drop from the balcony. With my orange bag
slung by its strap around my neck, I climbed over to the
adjoining balcony. The noise from the seagulls was drowned
out by the pounding of my heart. I landed with a thud on
the cement floor. I jumped to my feet and tried the door to
the next room. Ours had been the corner suite. My guessti-
mate told me that this one should be a standard room.
The door was locked.
With my breath still ragged, I prayed that my room phone
would work from that distance. I called the front desk. It
did. "There are men with guns on the ninth floor. Please
send security and call 911."

"Is that you, Miss Bingham?"

"Please, they're trying to break down my door. You know I've been attacked before. Security and 911. Now, or it's on you."

Time to take my life in my hands again. I probably had seconds left before they realized that I had escaped through the balcony door and followed. If they caught up with me out here, it would be a long way down. I went over to the next balcony. At least there was one of those large square concrete planters to hide behind. If this door didn't open, I would have to keep going. The good news was because of the stories about Uncle Seamus's exploits, I knew it could be done. The bad news was that after this, there was only one more balcony before a blank wall projected. Behind me I could hear shouting and footsteps. Unless I was going to try an Uncle Seamus and go down, I had to get in this door.

By a miracle, it opened. Who besides me worries about locking the door on the ninth floor?

I saw a shadow move behind me and barely stifled a scream. A woman stood in the bathroom door, her mouth open in an "O." She wore a towel and a look of terror. And she wanted to scream too.

I put my fingers to my lips first and then whispered, "Help me until security gets here." I turned and locked the balcony door.

"What—"

"It's the second time I've been attacked in this hotel. I climbed over the balconies. I need to hide. Don't let anyone in. Call the desk and say you hear sounds of a violent struggle. I need to hide."

Her hands shook as she called. Her voice warbled with fear. She was good. No doubt the desk clerk believed *her*.

I began to pull the cord to close the blinds. My new roommate's eyes opened wide and she turned toward the balcony and screamed, long and loud. She was a world-class screamer. She wasn't faking it. I was frantically searching for something that could be used as a weapon. Somehow the floor lamp wasn't going to do the trick.

"Is it a big man in a suit?" I whispered.

She nodded and went back to screaming. She stopped as suddenly as she'd started and said, "He kept going."

"Did he see you?" My knees felt like melting wax. I struggled to fake being calm.

She swiveled, horror written on her face. "Oh. My. God."

"No no, it's good. He knows what I look like and he knows you're not me. They want me. I don't know why."

She said in her shaky voice, "He tried the balcony door. I don't know why he didn't come in."

"It was open when I got here, but I locked it behind me."

"He could have shot at it and shattered the glass," she said practically.

"Let's just be glad he didn't. He's looking for me. I'm sure he doesn't want to kill half the hotel."

"But what does he want with you?"

"Wouldn't I like to know that."

This conversation was conducted in the lowest of whispers. We both knew they were out there. One was on the balconies. What if the other one was in the corridor? They'd probably ruled out this room as my refuge as there was a hysterical woman who was clearly not me in it.

I thought I heard the splintering of a glass in the room next to us. They'd be in there searching for me. If help didn't arrive soon, they'd invade the room on the other side and then they'd be back. They'd know I couldn't get far. Security should be here any minute, if they weren't in on the whole thing. The police would still need a couple of minutes. As long as the desk had really called the police.

I could tell that the woman whose life I had crashed in on had the same reaction. We didn't have much time and we had a lot to lose.

Sure enough, there was a bang at the door. "Let's go," I whispered, grabbing another towel. She clutched hers closer and shook her head.

I took her hand. "No choice." We hurried to the balcony door, opened it, closed it behind us. Even with the door closed, we could still hear the sounds of the door being battered in. What were they using?

"Don't look down," I said. "Look ahead to safety." We climbed over to the balcony on the right and then into the room next to our suite, the one they'd already checked. Unlike me, they didn't lock doors behind them. They'd ripped the shower curtain and the bedspreads off looking for me. Tossed over the chair and broken the television, just for fun, I suppose. Or maybe it was as an outlet for their frustration.

I figured they'd go through them all and then check again because they knew about the balconies as an escape route. Most likely they would return to this one once they found my new friend's room empty. I peered into the hallway. It was now or never. "We have to run for it. It's just a few feet until the turn in the corridor." And run we did. We raced around the corner and along to the staircase exit. She was sobbing behind me as we clattered down the stairs and onto the eighth floor. Would we be safe there? Who knew? A siren shrieked nearby and then we heard a few whoops. Police, at last.

A maid looked startled at our panicked appearance, especially my nameless, weeping friend in her not-roomy-enough towel. Uncle Seamus always spoke highly of hotel staff. I recognized her as the friendly person who'd delivered our towels, back when I thought the suite was a luxurious and happy solution. "Don't scream," I said, "there's a man with a gun. Let us into a room and you stay too. Put your housekeeping cart in with us. We'll all be safe there."

"I could lose my job. We don't put the carts in the rooms."

"You could lose your life if they find us. Please, let's go."

We scurried into the closest room on the opposite side from where our rooms had been, the street side. I made my way to the window—no balconies on this side—and looked down. A trio of police cars were parked randomly in front of the building. My new friend sat on the bed and burst into tears.

I said, "I'm pretty sure we'll be safe here on this floor. We just have to wait it out."

The maid said, "And hope that the people do not come back while we are here." That would be the worst thing.

My towel friend gasped. "We'll be arrested. I'll go to the police station in a towel. I can't think of anything worse than that."

I thought that being shot or taken away by the men who were trashing the ninth floor in search of me would be considerably worse, but I knew better than to say so. My companions were already pretty stressed out. That got worse when we heard banging and shouting in the hallway.

"Police!" I motioned the others to hide in the closet. I put my eye to the door again and spotted two armed police officers. I decided that my pursuers didn't have uniforms or they would have pulled the stunt before.

"What is it?" I said. "What's going on, Officer?"

"Open up."

I did as I was told with my heart thundering. The shake in my hands was real as the officer pulled me from the room. "What's happening?"

"Have you seen any males with weapons?"

I said, "Yes. We were on the ninth floor. We ran here to hide."

"Who else is in the room?"

I hesitated. "I'm with two women. One terrified guest from the ninth floor and a chambermaid. They have nothing to do with this. But I can tell you what the—"

"Get them out because we're going in."

"But I saw the armed men. They were on the ninth floor. They broke into my room and I saw them—"

My pathetic attempt to describe the would-be killers got me nowhere. I found myself staring at the officers' drawn weapons and decided to cut my losses. These guys were the foot soldiers, not detectives. Just as I was about to call the other two women, the crackle of voices came over the radio. The officers backed away and lumbered toward the stairs. At least my new companion wouldn't have to go to the police station in a towel. I wasn't sure if she'd be able to go back to her room yet, though. Back in this room, the maid was shaking even worse than I had been.

I felt a wave of guilt. I'd brought this poor woman into this. Who knows what a group of armed men meant to her. On the other hand, she'd have still been standing in the hallway with her cart when the armed cops arrived and that would have been awful. At least with me and my towel friend, she had company and support, such as it was on this bizarre day.

"My name is Elaine," the woman in the towel said.

"I'm Jordan."

"Ana Maria," said the chambermaid.

I was glad we at least knew one another's names.

"They're gone," I said inanely.

"Gone where?"

"I don't know. To the stairs. I think to the ninth floor."

"We need to find out where they've gone and go the opposite way," Elaine said. "Well, as long as that's back to the ninth floor."

"I don't plan to stick my head into that stairwell until we

know that they've cleared the building. It can't be that long. We're as safe here as anywhere."

"What if someone's ransacking our rooms right now?"

Ana Maria was shaking. I put my arms around her and led her to the king-size bed. "Just sit. Take a deep breath. We'll be all right. You'll be all right."

"I cannot do this. I will lose my job!"

"You won't. It's not your fault."

"But I am hiding in a guest's room! I am sitting on the bed. It is wrong. Very wrong."

"Well, that's true enough," Elaine said. "But still not your fault. And it's not my fault either." She pointed at me. "Some of it *may* be her fault."

"I was fleeing for my life," I said defensively.

"Sure, but you climbed onto *my* balcony and opened *my* door and now we're in the soup."

"What do you think would have happened if I hadn't come to your balcony door and you'd stayed on the ninth floor and those guys had barged into your room? At least I was company." As arguments went, it was pretty lame.

She bit her lip and looked understandably peevish. "Good point. Now what?"

"Now we wait until they clear the building."

I wish I could say that the long wait until the announcement that the coast was clear was filled with brave banter, but all that occurred was sulky silence from Elaine and worried sighs from Ana Maria. As for me, I hunkered down and pondered how my lovely world of golden age mysteries, priceless first editions and days surrounded by family and friends (and Vera, of course) had morphed into a nightmare with guns and fear. I was well out of my comfort zone. That's what Hammett had brought me. It was the opposite of everything I loved about mysteries. Christie and Sayers and Ngaio Marsh had their dangers in those remote grand houses, for sure—a swig of poison, a slippery grand staircase, someone who is up to no good and everything talked out in a game of wits at the end, most of the sparring verbal.

I had encountered and lived through some scary stuff in trying to help Vera build or retrieve those collections. Nero Wolfe had his dark side too, but really, most of the sleuthing and discussion took place in the elegant confines of his New York study. I, on the other hand, was used to knowing my town, being comfortable in my environment and having a pretty good idea on how to proceed when faced with what my uncles would call "a sticky situation."

But disappearing bookshops with murdered owners, people breaking into homes with fragile seniors, a rampage through a hotel in the heart of San Francisco? This was beyond my imagination. The Uncle Seamus stories were full of fun and daring, like a high-wire act. People didn't die in them. Presumably those who lost jewels or money were unhappy but they never got a voice in the story. This situation was more like Hammett's world. If you leave out the fun and games of Nick and Nora Charles, a high percentage of characters didn't survive in his books. No one could be trusted. No one. Not the sweet little lady who answers the door, not the housekeeper, not the police and not the love interest. You could barely trust the protagonist, and even then, not always. Still, I was the lead in this disaster and I knew I could trust myself.

That was one of Uncle Seamus's rules: Trust yourself. No one else will. Words to live by. Of course, my favorite had always been, "If you can't be yourself, then be somebody else."

At the moment Jordan Kelly Bingham was probably a prime target, the minute she exited the hotel. I wouldn't even know who to watch out for. Therefore, I wouldn't be going anywhere. Instead, I was going to be someone else. Confession time: I've always loved disguises, but this time there was no fun in it, just survival. In case it didn't go well, I wanted time to say good-bye to Smiley. I dug for my phone. Where was it?

CHAPTER NINETEEN

If you can't be yourself, then be somebody else.
—THE KELLY RULES

PANICKED, I RIFFLED through my orange bag. Had I dropped the phone in our frantic escape? Well, there was no going back for it.

I ducked into the bathroom to do a better job of checking my purse. I still had my camera but no phone. I did spot a tin of talcum powder on the vanity. Just what the doctor ordered. I dropped it in my satchel and slipped a fiver on the counter to keep things honest.

Things had gotten quiet on our floor. Elaine knocked on the bathroom door and suggested that I not hog the facilities. Perfect. Elaine closed the bathroom door behind her and said she was not going anywhere else with me. I really couldn't blame her. I beckoned Ana Maria out of the room. She pushed her cart and followed me along the hall to the cupboard where they keep the housekeeping carts. I didn't want Elaine to hear. I stepped into the empty room before she did and waved her in. She hesitated. Who could blame her? I reached into my purse and pulled out two twenties.

She inched into the closet-sized room with the cart ahead of her and in front of me. Good survival instinct.

I said, "I just want your scarf and your uniform."

She shook her head. "No. I will lose my job if I'm not wearing it."

"If anyone asks, tell them you had to change clothes because you got cut on broken glass and there was blood on your uniform. Believe me, all the staff will know that there's been an uproar, even if they try to keep it a secret."

She gasped.

I reached into my purse and pulled out three more twenties. "It's a hundred dollars and I guarantee you won't lose your job. There have been armed men here. No one will pay attention to you. You are a known staff member. Do you have another uniform in your locker? Do you have a locker?"

"I have another uniform at home. But if I lose one, they will dock my wages for the cost."

"Are you allowed to wear it when you leave for home?"

"They wash them here, but we can wear them home. Sometimes I do. If I have to go somewhere, no."

"Do you have an extra scarf in your locker?"

She shook her head.

"Do you always wear a scarf?"

"No. It was what you call a bad hair day."

"I'm having a bad life day. So let's switch clothing."

"I need my badge and my ID card!" I swear there were tears in her eyes. "If you keep it, they will think I was involved."

"Fair enough. You keep your badge and your card. I'll head out in the uniform. Just show me the exit you use."

She was still not convinced.

I said, "I am sorry about all of this. The men who shot up the floor are trying to kill me. They have no interest in you. They may have seen what I am wearing but it's pretty ordinary, so they won't make the connection between me and you."

She was biting her lower lip. "I don't know. I can't lose my job."

I said, "You will save my life. It's the right thing to do." I sprinkled talcum powder onto my dark curls, worked it through, parted my hair in the middle and tucked it back under her scarf, a style that doesn't look good on most people and is particularly unflattering on me. I slipped my long dangling earrings into my pocket along with the talcum powder.

I waited for the decision about the uniform, wondering if I'd have to up the ante. After what seemed like an eternity, Ana Maria nodded finally. She turned her back and unzipped the pink and white uniform. I pulled off my T-shirt and stepped out of my skinny jeans.

She was my height, but quite a bit curvier. My skinny jeans had a bit of stretch and they looked great on her. My T-shirt was given a workout too. She also looked fine without the scarf. She produced a brush and twisted her long dark hair into a bun. I knew people who would kill for a bad hair day like that.

I figured that no one would be watching the maids leave, and I hoped I was right. I did not fill out the uniform like she had and it left me feeling dumpy, which under these circumstances was a good thing. She said, "You do not look . . ."

I said, "Human?"

"As pretty that way. Also you look much older."

"Good! In fact, excellent. One of my ambitions is to actually *get* older as opposed to deader. When is your shift over?"

"Not until four, but I can take a break when I need to if my rooms are done."

"You can't be expected to clean up now. And where do you leave the building?"

"There's an employee entrance in the basement at the back of the building. The stairs go up and out onto the street."

"You go the way you usually do and I'll meet you there. I'll find a way to return your uniform without causing trouble." I grinned. "If I'm still alive."

"I cannot take all your money."

"Yes. You take it. I'm taking your uniform. If something happens, you will have to replace it. I want to pay for it."

"Then I will just accept the cost of the uniform. I do not wish to take advantage of you. You are a good person." She peeled off three twenties and thrust the other two back into my hand.

"You don't actually know that I'm a good person," I said with a grin. "But I am glad you think so."

"I know you are honest and kind. You left a tip for me on the pillow in your room. You are not the kind of person to cheat."

Before I could respond, she added, "And I will return your jeans. I think they are very expensive."

They'd come from my favorite outlet, but Ana Maria was saving my bacon. "You can keep them. They look better on you anyway. I'll return your uniform, though. Just give me your telephone number." I found a scrap of paper and a pen in the orange bag. It rarely fails me, except this time with my phone. Ana Maria carefully wrote out her number and I stuffed it into the uniform pocket. "Should I take the cart?" I thought it would add to my disguise.

"The cart has to stay on the floor we're cleaning. None of the maids will have carts downstairs."

"Okay."

"And I cannot give you the housekeeping key. Even if you try to pay me more, I will not do that. It would not be right."

I didn't bother to say that I could probably get into most rooms without a key, that being my distinguished heritage.

"Fair enough. If you are questioned about your uniform, just cry and shake and blame me."

She smiled for the first time since her ordeal started. "I think I can do that."

"It's a white lie as we say in my family, but if anyone, a guest, a manager, anyone at all, asks if you saw someone of my description, say I went back to my room. For one thing, they'll race off and leave you alone. Can you do that?"

Apparently she could.

I stuck my gray and scarfed head out the door and noted that the coast was clear.

We headed to the service elevators, which were through a set of double doors and a labyrinth of storage spaces: extra tables, cots, stacking chairs. What a thrill that the service elevator seemed to be working. We stepped in and held our breath until we got to the basement floor. Things were looking great until a uniformed officer came around the corner. He was young, tall and skinny with red hair and freckles and I didn't want to see him.

Now what? I didn't want to be stopped by police, even though I preferred them to armed assassins. I needed to get away and not be identified. Whoever was after me could just as easily shoot me if I was escorted by police. I had places to go. And something told me that this young police officer would not believe this crazy story.

I said with my heaviest faux-Spanish accent, "Take care of my friend, please. She is very upset and scared. All the shooting! I will tell the boss that we are safe."

Ana Maria lurched toward him, shaking and, amazingly, crying. She spoke rapidly in Spanish and English and pointed upstairs, wiping her tearstained cheeks as she went.

I left my new accomplice and barreled on to safety. The basement was a rabbit warren of equipment, carts, AV gear, what had to be the staff cafeteria and a hot and steamy laundry room with mountains of sheets and towels. Staff was scurrying here and there. No one paid attention to me.

Ten minutes later, as I made one wrong turn after another in the back rooms of the hotel workers area, searching for the stairs to the employees' exit, someone grabbed my elbow. I shrieked and jumped. Ana Maria said, "Sorry. He was so nice and I feel bad about lying to him."

"It was necessary. How do I get out of here?"

"Through here."

As we walked, I asked, "What did the cop want?"

"Just to know that we were all right and what we saw."

"Did he ask about me?"

"He asked about the older maid who was with me. I said she was very tough and not to worry. But he was more interested in me."

"Can't say I blame him. Did you give him your name?"

She shrugged. "I think I had to. *Sí?*"

I nodded as we pushed open the last door into a rear courtyard. "Don't be surprised if you see him again."

She grinned. "I will not be surprised. This is the best way out. Some maids are leaving for a break in the little park. Let us walk with them. I will go back later and get my things."

To my astonishment, we got away with it. I hugged Ana Maria and got the hell out of there.

I didn't call Steve, just in case he was being observed, or part of the plot. Half an hour later, a tired, stooped, gray-haired maid in a pink and white uniform trudged up yet another hill, dragging a pair of cheap plastic bags with purchases acquired from a narrow, dingy shop. One of the bags hid my oversize orange handbag, which was identifiable. I'd purchased a gray T-shirt with a bad sketch of the Golden Gate Bridge, an A's ball cap with a yellow brim, and a pair of navy cotton jersey shorts. They were in one of the plastic bags. I knew they'd come in handy. I'd also picked up a pair of oversized sunglasses. Finally, I'd borrowed some more of Vera's remaining *Red Harvest* money to get the cheapest smart phone and loaded up some minutes.

CHAPTER TWENTY

Always eat when you get a chance.
—THE KELLY RULES

I DUCKED DOWN alleys and up side streets, trying to stay in character while getting away from anyone who might have identified me. I did manage to pop up to the window of a tiny taco shop and pick up a bite to eat. Uncle Seamus's words echoed in my head, and whatever else I could say, Uncle Seamus and his—possibly mythical—advice were the only reason I was still alive. Of course, I hadn't thought about food during the drama at the hotel, but now it was almost all I could concentrate on. I got two extra tacos to bring with me, one was part of a planned "hostess gift." There was method in my madness.

Of course, I couldn't go to Gram's. For one thing, there was a good chance the house was being watched. And if it wasn't being watched, I wasn't sure whom in that household I could trust, aside from Smiley. I needed a place to hide and a place to observe. I needed someone who wasn't involved at all and who could be trusted. I was pretty sure that my new friend Sierra would help me. The two extra tacos were part of my plan to seek refuge with her, claiming to bring lunch, until I got things sorted out. I could easily eat another one.

I trudged up and along the street, looking and feeling like the exhausted maid. I reached Sierra's front door without seeing anyone too suspicious. I rang the doorbell and waited. And waited. Nothing. No one. I imagined her out on those endless walks with the child that never slept. Unless he was actually sleeping at that moment and I was going to wake him up. Oh well, it couldn't be helped. I rang yet again and knocked.

Nothing.

My new strategy was to find access to the rear of the building and find a way in. Sierra was friendly and even naïve. She'd most likely forgive me for getting in the back door given my life was in peril. Or maybe she wouldn't appreciate me bringing danger to her home. Still, I thought she'd enjoyed the sense of adventure I had brought to her life. Because surely she was bored.

As I trudged down Sierra's front steps, still in character, a plump woman who looked to be in her sixties called out to me in a sympathetic voice, "There's no one there, dear."

"Yes, they are out. I will wait." I'd adopted a vague and unidentifiable accent.

She raised her voice a bit and spoke slowly. "No. No. Nobody lives there."

I blinked. "What?"

"The house is empty."

"Empty?" I was so surprised that I thought for a minute that my accent had slipped.

"Yes. Unoccupied."

"But I met the lady. She said she needs help. I must have another job and she said—"

She shook her head kindly. "You must have the houses mixed up. This one has been empty since the man who owned it died."

"He died?"

I must have sounded panicked, because she chattered on soothingly, "Yes, Mr. Himmelfarb was ninety-five. He was a lovely man. It was sad, of course, but he'd been failing since Alice died five years ago. Alice was his wife. She was lovely too. You know they'd been in this house since 1962. Can you imagine? I miss them both very much."

"But this woman, she was here yesterday. I saw her this morning."

"Couldn't have been. The house is definitely empty."

I glanced at the door where the number was clearly the right one. The same one that Sierra had dragged her stroller into to see her husband, Michael. Was I losing it? That was entirely possible, but no, the number was exactly as I'd seen it earlier.

I said, "Lady, I am not mistaken. It was a young woman. I am sure she lived there. There was a baby and a husband sleeping inside . . ."

My voice trailed off as I recalled yet another of Uncle Seamus's guidelines, something about making sure they believe what you want them to. After all, I had never actually seen the husband. He had just seemed very real and very tired with a baby up all night. Come to think of it, I'd never actually seen the baby that was at the root of all the young couple's supposed stress and fatigue. I'd never even heard him cry. I was trying to deceive this kind woman and here I'd been fooled myself.

She smiled again. "Probably it was one of the real estate ladies. They're very keen about getting the listing for the place."

I said, "Okay, maybe that is it."

"Did she want you to do some work for her?"

I blinked and realized that I looked pretty down at heel. "We were talking about it, but she had to leave. She was very pretty. About this tall." I indicated Sierra's height. "She had a ponytail with what do you say? Highlights? And she loved to run. Oh, and she had a baby stroller."

My source shrugged. "She does sound like one of the real estate gals. One of them had a stroller with her. Not very professional if you ask me."

"How long has she been coming to this—"

"Sorry, dear, but you'll have to excuse me. My taxi's here now. Oh, my name is Gloria Zeller. I live next door. Come and see me and give me your name next time. Some of my friends may have a few hours for you." She eased herself into the cab and closed the door.

I watched her pull away and thought hard. Was this actually true? Or was the deceiver the woman who'd just let me down? The nightmarish aspect of this day continued on. I spoke to a man entering a house two doors down, but he knew nothing and no one and didn't want to know me either.

I trudged down the hill a bit until I found a side passage that might let me get to the back of the Himmelfarb house, without appearing to be heading for it. Sure enough, some furtive scurrying through backyards got me to the rear of the house. I didn't dare go back to Gram's place until I had a better idea of what was going on. I needed to think and I needed a quiet place to do that. Sierra's alleged house seemed as good a place as any. I glanced around to see if I was being observed and didn't spot anyone. I waved elaborately to a nonexistent neighbor. And did what I thought was a very good pantomime of a person being invited into a home and accepting. I try not to break and enter, I want to be clear about that. I'm quite serious about living an honest and honorable life, but sometimes you gotta do what you gotta do. This was one of those times. In fact, this entire day had been a series of those times.

The security was nonexistent. My bank card was all it took to open the door. I made a big production of pretending to offer the bag from the taco shop to the nonexistent person on the inside and then stepped in, locking the door behind myself. You can never be too careful, as I kept finding out.

On the inside, the house had that empty and echoing quality of an uninhabited home. So far it looked like my source, Gloria Zeller, had been right. From the style of the cupboards, backsplash and counter tops, the kitchen had been renovated not long ago with dark traditional cupboards and materials and appliances that matched the fine quality of the old house. It was spotless and the fridge was empty. Yes, I checked. The cupboards were quite empty too, although there were still dishes, pots, pans and utensils to give a sense of life to the place, I figured. There was no sign of an elderly man who'd lived alone for a few years. All that remained was the faint odor of a pet, probably also long gone.

The clock on the fairly new stainless steel microwave was working. Nearly four p.m.

I walked through the dining room and toward the living room, hugging the walls and making sure I wasn't visible to anyone on the outside, not that many people in the area would care. I wasn't worried about the neighbors, but I didn't know whom I *was* worried about. Any respectable Hammett character would be taking no chances in this no-man's-land. This house was very nice and beautifully preserved with some stained glass windows and mahogany floors and crown moldings. Everything looked original, something I value. It was considerably smaller than Gram's rambling Victorian, so I figured I could check it out quickly enough.

I got down on all fours and scuttled over to the living room bay window with the lace curtains. Sure enough, there was a perfect view of Gram's house and anyone coming and going from it. Now I knew what Sierra had been doing here.

I just didn't know why she'd been doing it. It didn't look like I'd learn anything more about that either. Up close, there were no indications of anyone having been there. No stroller. No baby toys. Nothing.

I crawled backward to the hallway, turned and headed up the stairs. Upstairs, the front bedroom was a mirror of the living room with that matching bay window I'd admired. Still pressed against the walls, I edged over. For all I knew, someone in Gram's house (Zoya? Gus and his boys?) was in touch with Sierra and whomever Sierra was working with or for.

This bedroom was crowded with antique mahogany furniture. Normally, I'd be very impressed with the heavy sleigh bed, the massive dressers and the two bedside tables with serious scale. But not today. A solid leather club chair was positioned by the window, and to judge by the darker spot on the carpet, where it had obviously been for years, it had been relocated. What a cozy spot to watch Gram's house.

Apparently Himmelfarb had been liked, so perhaps he wouldn't have minded. I did have goose bumps by this point. Over by the window, I had an even better view of the goings-on at Gram's. From the gap in the curtain I watched as Smiley hurried up the street, took the stairs two at a time and opened the door. It looked as though Zoya did her best to stop him getting in, but that may have been my imagination. A minute later, I saw his shadow in the bay window of Gram's new room upstairs. The shorter shadow must have been Gram herself.

Our watchers had ringside seats for sure. I glanced down at the window ledge and spotted the first sign of the spies, two Starbucks cups, off to the left, behind the heavy drapes. I bent down and took a look at the cups. One had a smear of glossy pale coral lipstick, easily recognizable as Sierra's. The other had none. I'd never seen Sierra without full and glossy lip color. It was a safe bet that she had an accomplice, or maybe she was the accomplice. It was pretty brazen as it seemed they had no business being in this house.

I hesitated. If I took the cups and stuffed them into the plastic bag for the tacos, I might have a way to get them to Officer Martinez. She could keep them as evidence. Although I knew from talking to Smiley that the chain of evidence would be broken if I, not the police, produced it. The cops are picky about these details. I stuffed them into the bag. I could always return them later if I came up with a good plan.

I was desperate to call Smiley, but I could not remember his new cell number. I'd been relying on my phone a bit too much. Technology's great except when it isn't.

Since other people hadn't been too careful, I took advantage of the quiet and comfort to eat my taco in peace. When I say eat, I mean wolf. I inhaled the first taco and then I gobbled the one I'd bought for Sierra too. I washed them down with a can of cola. I leaned back, feeling a bit better, and closed my eyes. I needed peace to try to figure out what to do next. Who was the enemy? Who was Sierra? Who was Michael? Was there a Michael? Was he one of the men at the hotel and in the home invasion? What did they want? How were they involved with me, with Gram, with Zoya, with Tyler? And why would Sierra have warned me about the home invasion? Had she wanted me to be caught by the masked men?

We'd come to San Francisco to have a wonderful vacation and it had turned into a nightmare. For all unknown reasons, I felt myself dragged down into a dangerous world that Hammett himself might have invented. Sure there weren't "down and outers" and people with known criminal connections and there were a limited number of dark alleys, but we'd found villains willing to knock out Zoya, to threaten Gram with guns, to pose as a police officer in front of Gram's house, to shoot up a hotel room, steal beloved dogs and take serious chances chasing me across the ninth-floor balconies, and to spy on us from an unoccupied house across the street. Whatever their reasons, they must have been powerful. And worst of all, there appeared to be so many of them.

I figured I'd have more information when I had a chance to look at the cameras we'd hidden in the hotel suite, unless the police found them as they sealed off the room as a crime scene, assuming that they'd done that. To be fair, the entire hotel was in an uproar, and it would have been very hard for the authorities to figure out what exactly had gone down and in what order.

I leaned back in the club chair and closed my eyes. It will sound weird, but for the first time in days, I actually felt relaxed. This house had a serenity about it, despite the gloom and the fact that at least two deceitful people had been spying on us from it. I felt grateful to Mr. Himmelfarb. I wished that I'd known him.

Never mind, it felt good to let my body relax and my mind stop whirring. I yawned and gave myself a little shake. No time for napping. I may not have had places to go, people to see, things to do, but I did have a lot of thinking to catch up with.

Wait a minute! My eyes snapped open. The seat of that chair had been warm when I sat on it. Warm! And yet the sun from the window didn't reach there. Was there someone still in the house? My mouth went dry and goose bumps rose on my arms. As I heaved myself out of the chair, I noticed something else: a few brightly covered candy wrappers. Not that I wanted to be noticing things when I was in danger of being discovered by whomever it was that had been sitting there.

I was bending over to check the wrappers when I heard voices from the first floor and what sounded like a door closing. It was way past time to get moving. I picked up the wrappers, grabbed my taco bag and the bag with the other debris and tried to figure out where to hide. If it was Sierra and whoever her accomplice was—or even if she was the accomplice—this room would probably be where they'd head, if those coffee cups were anything to go by. I hesitated. Should I put them back? But too late for that. They were already in the bag. The voices were coming closer.

On the other hand, if it was a real estate person or a member of the family, they could go anywhere. In case it was the spies, I hightailed it out of the master bedroom and into the next room. There wasn't much choice as I could hear footsteps on the stairs. What now? This room had a large four-poster bed, a bit more feminine with a blue bedspread, blue and white curtains and a lot of lace. This must have been Alice's room. Perhaps in later years, they'd each had their own. There would be room for me under the bed, but my experience with hiding under beds had not been good in recent months.

That left the closet and behind the drapes. The blue and white drapes didn't quite reach the floor and my desert boots would have been hard to miss if anyone checked out the room. I prayed that the closet hinges wouldn't squeak.

The closet didn't have the original heavy doors, but more modern louvered ones. I was glad because that allowed me to hear. I sank to the floor and wormed my way behind what I took to be a collection of long dressing gowns with a fading scent of lily of the valley. I supposed they were also to give a lived in look, or maybe the relatives hadn't been able to clear things out. They took my mind off my hammering heart for a second, although you would think I'd have gotten used to scary situations by this time. The voices were coming closer. A man and a woman. I recognized Sierra, sounding a lot more in charge than when she'd been talking to me.

Was that who'd been sitting in the club chair? But if it was Sierra, why was she just arriving? How could that be? And more to the point, what did she have to do with what

I'd noticed just before fleeing to the closet? I'd spotted a cluster of dog hair on the carpet in Alice's room. Where there's dog hair, there's a dog. But why would there be a dog in an empty house? Especially a dog the same familiar color as our missing pug. It was a shade I knew well. There was no mistaking the signs of that little Asta. The answers would be on the other side of the closet door, so I wouldn't be getting them instantly.

I listened intently to footsteps reaching the top of the stairs and the slight sounds of squabbling about who should do what about something that I didn't quite catch. The squabbling got louder. The man's voice was not what I'd expected. I'd imagined Sierra's husband—Michael?—as a business type, stylish in that hip San Francisco way, sophisticated and yet indulgent of his young wife and child. Instead he sounded like a peevish teenager.

I shook my head. The thing that was most surprising was that my "friend" was not at all who she said she was, or at least she didn't live where she said she lived. You understand, I had nothing to do but speculate and listen. I could hear them bickering in the bedroom. What was going on?

It was possible that they were here for reasons that had nothing to do with us and with Gram's house, but that was highly unlikely. Looking back, I realized that she had struck up a conversation with me and instigated the relationship. Why else would she do that unless she wanted to find out more about us or about the inhabitants of Gram's house? I just hope that didn't include finding me in the closet.

"What's that smell?" Sierra snapped.

"What smell?"

"I'm asking you. It smells like Tex-Mex or something."

"Oh yeah. Now I'm kind of hungry."

"Don't be an idiot."

"Come on, Jessica, why do you always talk to me like that? A guy can be hungry."

So Sierra's real name was Jessica. Good to know.

She said, "A guy can do the job he's supposed to and not be such a big baby all the time."

Whoever they were, they didn't sound like criminal masterminds.

"Tacos, for sure."

"Did you bring tacos in here?"

"No. I didn't bring in any food. You said that was a rule, but then you brought coffee in—"

"That was part of my cover, you dimwit. You know that and you shouldn't have left the empty cups there. I don't ask that much of you. We are so close to getting rid of them. They're starting to panic. So let's not screw up."

Their voices dimmed as they entered the front bedroom. I strained to hear.

He said, "Well, they're gone now anyways."

"What do you mean, they're gone?"

"They're gone. Someone must have cleaned them up."

"Oh, the cups. I thought you meant the so-called grandson and his nasty little girlfriend. That's dumb even for you, Josh. Who the hell do you think breaks into a house and cleans it up? I don't know what to do with you sometimes."

I sat up straight. So-called grandson? Nasty little girlfriend? What a pair of jerks these two were.

"Blah blah. All I know is that the stupid cups are gone and I didn't throw them out. Maybe the real estate people?"

"Let's hope not. We don't want them knowing we're here. Especially when we're getting close to success with the old lady."

"Well, duh."

Jessica and Josh. Who were these peevish creeps and how were they connected to the people who had attacked me so far? I couldn't figure out any link at all, except me, Gram and Tyler—or possibly Zoya—and while they sounded like squabbling adolescents, I was under no illusion that they were innocent or harmless.

The closet was dusty, not surprising as Alice Himmelfarb had been dead for five years. My nose twitched and I pinched it to keep myself from sneezing.

What? Had I missed something? Voices were raised in the next room. "Oh my God!"

"What now? Do you have to be so hysterical about every little thing?"

"I am not hysterical about every little thing, but here's a little thing to be hysterical over: Where's the stupid dog?"

"What?"

"Not 'what,' Josh, you moron. Where! Where is it?"

"Well, it must be hiding."

"Why would it be hiding?"

"Duh, because it hates you?"

"It doesn't really hate me, Josh."

"It does. And we have to find it. Right now."

CHAPTER TWENTY-ONE

*Nobody looks dangerous drinking
fancy coffee.*
—THE KELLY RULES

"FINE. GO FIND the stupid dog, Josh. Like anybody cares."

I cared. I didn't want to come nose to nose with Josh as I crouched in a closet I had no business being in. My heart was thundering as I considered what weapons were at my disposal among the clothing of a dead octogenarian. Dressing gowns to drop over someone's head enough to get a head start? Hangers? Hatboxes? Nothing seemed promising. Shoes could make good emergency hammers, but they weren't that good in a fight, especially if it was two to one. Where was Asta? Had they mistreated the little pooch? Or was Asta just so stressed that under a bed seemed like the best solution? We already knew she liked to keep a low profile, convenient or not.

But why would Josh open the closet door to search for the dog? That was just dopey. However, they both did appear to be perfectly dopey. I picked up a pair of shoes, one in each hand.

Josh said, "Maybe the real estate people took the dog."

"Why would they do that?"

"Because a dog left alone in a house would not make it easier to sell. You know that little sucker had some accidents."

"It's bad news if they found the dog. For one thing, they'll watch the house to see how it got here, and for another, we need that stupid thing. What's that?"

"What?"

"There's someone coming!"

"Chill out."

"I am chill."

He said, "You're not chill. You're never chill. Stop screaming. No one knows we're here unless they heard you."

"The person who picked up those cups knows we were here. The person who stole the dog knows we're here."

"No. We stole the dog, remember? That person might know that someone was here, but most likely they won't think anything of it."

"Right, sure."

"They'll figure it's one of the stagers, or whatever you call them."

"That is so dumb. First of all, real estate people don't leave messes or steal dogs and neither do stagers."

"And second of all, Jessica?"

"What?"

"You said first of all, what's second of all?"

"Josh, stop being an idiot. Oh my God. They're coming up to the front door."

"Okay, move it, down the back stairs."

"Don't leave anything, stupid."

"If you run into them, just say that we're former neighbors and we had a key. They can't prove that's—"

"Get moving!"

There was a scramble and I took a chance to open the louvered door an inch and peek. I had to see if I could get a look at the so-called husband. I opened the closet door a crack and watched as Sierra raced in a panic along the upstairs hall and "Michael" actually passed her running. I couldn't see his hair, but aside from that missing bit of data, he looked and sounded just like a male version of Sierra, now Jessica. They must have crept down the stairs, because the racket stopped, just as the doorbell started to ring.

That perhaps was good news for me. I rushed to the back of the house in time to see Sierra and "Michael" race into the backyard and vanish through the neighbor's hedge. Of course, with those high hedges, no one was likely to see them.

The doorbell rang again. And now someone was banging on the door. Was that person yelling? Who would they be yelling at? I took my chances and hightailed it down the back stairs too. I nearly tripped over the stroller, abandoned in the kitchen by the door. Was that the baby? I had stopped thinking about that baby. I stopped just long enough to check the sleeping figure in the blankets. A large and lifelike doll. Figured. I flicked the lock and pulled the door closed after me. I hoped that no one spotted me leaving the empty house.

Now what?

I zipped through the narrow side yard in time to spot Sierra and Michael heading up the hill. What to do? Follow them? Or wait and see if anyone else approached Gram's house? On the sidewalk, I turned back. No one was standing at the entrance to the late Mr. Himmelfarb's house. No one was ringing the doorbell or banging. Perhaps they had gone around to the back? I could have taken my chances, but I had no desire to be caught in back without any witnesses.

Uncle Mick would have said, "Better a bird in the hand," by which he would have meant a pair of Georgian candlesticks. I would have to settle for two new suspects.

Fine. That meant forgetting about the off chance that someone tried to get into Gram's house. After all, Tyler and Zoya along with Gus and the boys could take care of things. I darted back into the side yard, ducked down behind the garbage cans and took a few seconds to stuff the maid's dress in one of my collection of plastic bags, slipped into the baggy navy cotton shorts, the T-shirt with the badly drawn Golden Gate Bridge and the A's cap with the yellow brim. I tucked my hair under and slipped on my oversized sunglasses. My purchases were paying off. Back on the sidewalk, I looked both ways and spotted Michael and Sierra quite far up the hill. I hoofed it up the steep slope after the two of them. I thought my lungs would explode after running to get within clear sight of them. I was glad I'd changed. It made more sense to be running in shorts than in my maid's uniform. When I got within hearing distance, I slowed and caught my breath. They had no interest in anyone else but themselves. They were stomping along, sulking and shouting at each other.

I realized that I was in prime Hammett mode, doing a variant of the Pinkerton's specialty of shadowing a suspect. Of course. I wasn't sure what Sierra and Michael were up to, but they were up to something. Sierra hadn't even been on my list although it was obvious now that she should have been.

For sure, as an unfashionable pedestrian, I wouldn't even register on their self-absorbed brains. I was counting on it. As the hill flattened out—thank heavens—I found it easier to keep up. How could anyone live in this city with all these hills? I was ready to crash, but then I did seem to be the only person actually running up that slope in desert boots. If Smiley had been there, he probably would have been unable to resist saying that if Dashiell Hammett could work in the damp, foggy city while coping with lung disease, then I could climb this hill. In the middle of a real case, Hammett sometimes didn't know what was going on, and now there I was with no clue either.

Still I pulled myself together and did my best to keep up without giving myself away. I didn't have much to worry about. The two of them didn't turn around. They were pretty lousy criminals actually. No sense of self-preservation. Uncle Seamus would have set them straight with one of his rules, say, for instance, only a jackass draws attention to himself. I added "or herself" to reflect Sierra's contribution.

As if they were thinking with a single brain, the squabbling pair turned abruptly into Down by the Bean, one of many local coffee shops that promised their own roasted beans.

I soon followed them in without seeming to notice them at all. They took their organic Fair Trade pour-overs to a small table in the window and continued to snarl at each other.

I got myself an Americano to go from the good-looking guy behind the counter and slumped at a nearby table, pulling out the new smart phone and pretending to be immersed in the world of social media. I was glad I remembered my Facebook password: PUGLIFE. I was really annoyed that Tyler refused to have a Facebook account or I could have contacted him. I scrolled randomly through my timeline, "liking" and "sharing" mindlessly. I knew this would come back to haunt me as The Church of the Flying Spaghetti Monster wasn't exactly my kind of group, nor was the article on Optimizing Your Fit-Bit Workout.

A Facebook message bubble from Lance popped up.

Are you having some sort of psychotic break?
LOL

I lied nonchalantly.

Just bored waiting for Tyler to get ready.

I didn't need Lance freaking and calling out the cavalry.

Lance replied with an engagement ring emoji and eighteen question marks.

I replied:

Oops, used all my data. Gotta run.

I went up to the barista, handed him my phone and lowered my voice. "I'm just visiting the city and I'd love to get a picture of your coffee house. It's so unique. I love everything about it. Would you mind taking the shot?" It wasn't such an unusual request apparently. I pulled my baseball cap low on my forehead and hammed it up a bit with a duck face and peace signs making sure my two new suspects were in the background on most of the shots.

When he handed the phone back to me, I checked the shots. I looked like a first-class dweeb but my targets were nice and clear. Unfortunately, they were also getting up to leave. Didn't anybody linger over coffee anymore?

I thanked my barista and said I had to rush to meet a friend. He said, "Come again. Anytime."

I headed out, sloshing my Americano and hustled after them, now back on the sidewalk and heading somewhere even farther up. Unlike them, I turned around regularly to make sure no one was following me. The third time I turned around, I thought I saw a flash of red hair and something else. Something fawn? Was that possible? Was I hallucinating out of stress?

Someone was following me and I was following someone

else. Whatever I turned my attention to, I didn't want to lose track of the other thing that needed watching—in this case, it was the redheaded man or Sierra and Michael. Tricky situation. I decided to keep on their trail while keeping my own back and checking for the flash of ginger again. It was not the first creepy thing that had happened, and part of the creepiness was that I'd read that Hammett had also had red hair, back in the early days. I shivered and kept going, doing my best to look casual and inconspicuous while running up a hill with a cup of coffee.

I had to do a bit of fancy footwork when my targets turned and entered a multiunit dwelling. It was a snazzy-looking place with an Art Deco vibe. I kept going without appearing to notice them. I circled round when they didn't come right out. The foyer was empty. They were gone.

I stood on the sidewalk and stared up at the windows, hoping I'd figure out where they had gone. Nothing happened. But there was that little flash of red hair, near an alley I'd just passed.

It was a good bet they wouldn't be emerging within a minute or two. I whirled and ran to the alley. Sure enough, there was my trembling quarry, startlingly blue eyes wide and terrified, mouth open in protest, hands held up in defense mode. I grabbed him by the collar and screamed in his face.

"Uncle Kev, don't make me kill you!"

A small emotional pug told me what she thought of my outburst. *Yap yap yap!*

As for Uncle Kev, I swear he had tears in his eyes. Of course, all the Kelly men can turn the waterworks on anytime they need to.

"Aw, Jordie, don't be mad."

"Don't be mad? Don't be *mad*? Are you insane? What are you doing with Asta?"

"Who?"

Nothing ever changes with Uncle Kev. "Asta. The little pug."

"Well, I saved him, didn't I? You should be happy, Jordie."

"Her, you saved her."

"Right, whatever."

"And by 'saved,' you mean you stole her from Tyler's grandmother's house?"

"No. I stole him from the people who must have stolen him from the grandmother's house. They are not nice. They left him alone in that empty house. It was no way to treat a dog."

Asta agreed, completely. She spun around and looked adoringly at Uncle Kev.

I needed information on the spot. I could deal with Uncle Kev's other issues, such as Asta's gender, later. "And who are they?"

He blinked, his startlingly blue eyes even more vacant than usual.

"I don't know. You're the one who talks to her all the time but she's not your friend. They spied on you. And I overheard them say something about 'needing to get rid of you.' That's why I was watching them. I was careful. How'd you find me, Jordie?"

Just blind luck actually and, of course, the clue of the Jolly Rancher wrappers. "Never mind. Did they see you?"

"No way, Jordie."

Maybe accurate, maybe not. I decided to go with it.

"Come on, we'll be a team. I see you have a backpack. Is there anything in it to disguise yourself with?"

"I got a hoodie I could put on. I got two actually. A blue and green. What color do you want, Jordie? And this bandanna for the pooch." I knew better than to ask Uncle Kev why he'd bought any of it. Or more likely lifted as the tags were still on. I could always make a donation to a charity later on to soothe my conscience.

When we stepped out of the narrow space between two buildings, we looked different enough that I thought we just might fool the two self-absorbed crooks we were looking for. If we could track them down, they wouldn't recognize me as the woman from the coffee shop.

I tied the little bandanna on Asta. Jaunty. I picked her up, not sure why, but I was awfully glad we had the cuddly, snuffling little creature. We headed into the apartment building pretending to chat in a friendly fashion. An attractive dark-haired woman with a teacup poodle in her arms was just emerging. I gave her my best smile from the Kelly family collection of "fool some of the people some of the time."

"What an adorable little poochie!" I squealed. Uncle Kev said, "A beauty."

Her hand went to her hair and her eyes were drawn to Kev's ridiculously blue ones. As they stared at each other, I tried to avoid rolling mine. I said, "We were trying to find a couple of people who just came into this building. I don't know their names, but she dropped this cell phone." I pulled my own phone out of my orange handbag, still disguised in a plastic sac.

"What's her name?" The woman didn't turn her gaze to me.

Kev beamed at her. *Please, don't open your mouth and ruin everything, Kev*, I thought.

"I don't know but she's about this high . . ."

She turned to note that.

"And pretty with honey-brown hair in a ponytail and some nice highlights. She looks quite athletic and—"

"I don't know their names. I'm new here."

Kev said, "Too bad, eh."

I shot him a shut-up glance.

She said, "But I think they're on the third floor."

"Great. I'll call up to them." I turned to the panel with the codes for each apartment. I considering ringing bell by

bell until someone let me in. Of course, my plan wasn't
going to work with a witness.

The board had a list of occupants' names. None of them
looked familiar. Meanwhile Kev made small—and I do
mean small—talk with his new friend and her dog. Asta
seemed quite happy to be part of it. "Oh well," I said.
"They're not answering. Maybe they went looking for the
wallet. Is there another exit?"

"Well, garage and the back door. Both are actually on
the side street." She pointed.

"We should just get a coffee and then try later. Maybe
the doggies would like a stroll together," Kev said. She was
quite mesmerized by him or she might have noticed that I
already had a coffee.

She said, "I can tell them if I see them."

Before Kev could agree, I said, "You know, it would be
fun to surprise her. She must be very worried about it. What
if we let you know when we find them, if you want to be in
on the surprise? When are you going home again?"

She glanced at her watch. "Oh. I'm supposed to meet my
friend. Here, let me give you my number." She wrote it
quickly on a piece of paper and handed it to Kev.

We both smiled and waved good-bye to her. Kev took
great care with the number. That was fine. *We might actually
need it*, I thought.

I pointed at one of the names I'd written down. "Kev, I've
seen this somewhere."

Kev was still watching his new flame hurry away.

"Kev!"

"I have to go back to Tyler's grandmother's house. I have
to figure out a way. Can you watch the place and let me know
if they leave?"

"Course I can, Jordie."

Right.

"And can you stay in touch with me?"

"Say what?"

"Can you call me if you see them come out? Can you follow them?"

"Follow them?"

I rubbed my temple. "That's correct. Like you were following me. Do you have a phone?"

He beamed and dug in his pocket. "Sure, I have a burner."

I put his number into my new phone and gave him mine. I watched him enter it in his burner. The next minute, he keyed in the number of his new friend. Oh well, she was an adult and I had more than enough people and dogs already to worry about.

"Can I trust you, Uncle Kev?" I raised my hand to hail a cab and was pleased to see one pull in almost immediately. I hopped in with Asta.

"Sure you can, Jordie. Why wouldn't you be able to?"

Such a long list.

As the taxi pulled away, Uncle Kev said, "That reminds me. There's something I have to tell you."

"That will have to be for later," I shouted as the cab shot into the traffic.

CHAPTER TWENTY-TWO

No one is who you think they are.
—THE KELLY RULES

GRAM'S PLACE WASN'T far, maybe a mile down the hill, but timing is everything.

In the cab, I asked myself, belatedly, why Kev would have been in San Francisco and following me. How could he afford a ticket? Who had paid for it? What had he wanted to say? I considered asking the driver to turn around so I could ask him, but by then we'd arrived.

Tyler answered the bell and, after a stunned glance at my "sporty" new outfit, wrapped us in a bear hug. Gram and Zoya responded to my "hello" from the sunroom. Asta did a happy little dance to see Zoya and greeted Gram cordially. She gave Tyler suspicious bug-eyed looks. Maybe because of the hug.

Tyler said, "What is going on? I've been half crazy with worry. There was a shooting at the hotel. No one knew where you were. I've been back to the hotel twice and I still can't get to our suite."

I leaned into the latest hug and let myself just go limp. "You won't believe the stuff that's happened."

This time he didn't let me go. I was afraid my ribs would crack. But in a good way.

"I thought something happened to you."

"I can't breathe."

He loosened his hold on me but not much. "Why didn't you call me?"

"Sorry," I said. "I sent you a picture from the hotel, before the shooting started."

"Yeah. I got that. That scared me too. Were those the guys who did the shooting?"

"Yes. They were after me. I sent that photo to Officer Martinez as well."

"She told me. She also filled me in on some of what happened. They'll want to talk to you. The cops don't know if you're dead or alive. And like I said, no call."

"I lost my phone somewhere in the hotel when I was trying to get away. I was in a panic. I picked up this little, um, inexpensive phone when I got away from the hotel. I couldn't remember your new number."

"I was going crazy. I've been to the police and to the hotel and back here and—"

"I knew you'd be worried and . . . a lot has happened, including finding Asta."

"And where were you hiding, you wicked little creature?" Gram said.

Zoya gasped. "Not vicked!"

I said, "Right, Zoya, not wicked at all, abducted."

Tyler said, "What?"

Gram said, "Oh, come now."

Zoya sniffed. "I knew. Not vicked. Kidnepped."

I said, "She was being held not far from here."

Tyler said, "Abducted? Held? Don't leave it like that."

"I'll fill you in but I have to check something out upstairs."

"Check what?" Gram said.

"A clue. Please just give me a minute, and I think I can explain everything."

Not everything, of course. There was still the business of Uncle Kev following me. I wasn't sure if I wanted to tell Tyler he was here, not until I found out what he was up to. Tyler was still a cop, after all. And a Kelly is a Kelly, i.e. usually up to no good.

IN THE LARGE front bedroom with Tyler standing behind me breathing hard, I looked up from the photos in the box.

He said, "What is going on, Jordan? Why are you pawing through photos at a time like this? It doesn't make—"

"We need to find out a little more about your new step-relatives. Something very weird is going on."

He practically crackled with impatience. "I know that. Tell me what you're talking about and stop being vague."

"I think they're behind what's been going on."

"Are you kidding me?"

"No. But I just need a bit of proof."

"Yeah, you do. That's a serious allegation."

"So it's worth a couple more minutes for me to sort it out. You wouldn't want me to make a mistake."

"Do it fast. This is making me buggy. I'm calling Martinez to tell her you're alive."

"Yeah, that's good."

Sure enough, in the photos I found some familiar features if not faces. I tried to calm myself long enough to think clearly. Sure enough, that tall fair man looked familiar although he was probably long gone. William's brother, Howard, his name on the back. There was enough of a resemblance to the photo of Gram's husband. I plucked that photo and the one with the toddlers and put them on top of the box. I checked the writing on the back of some the loose photos, but didn't find the name I was looking for.

When Smiley finished leaving a message for Martinez, I said, "Bear with me just a bit longer. We need to talk to Gram again."

Back in the sunroom, there was much partying going on with Asta being alternately cuddled and fed treats. Gram was fussing as much as Zoya. The birds chirped their disapproval. Smiley plunked the photo box on the ottoman closest to Gram.

I said, "We need a bit of help with names, Gram."

"Of course, my dear," she said, dropping a liver crisp into Asta's open mouth.

"These children," I said, pointing to the picture of the two toddlers. "Who are they?"

"My late husband's great-niece and -nephew," she said. "They were so cute. The children of his nieces."

"So their name would not be Huddy."

"No, my dear. There aren't any Huddys left except me."

She shook her pale curls and closed her eyes. "Oh, I really can't remember. They were the children of William's nieces. The nieces were Clara and Janet Huddy, pretty girls, good-looking like Howard. I remember their husbands before they divorced, but just now I can't recall their married names. They were grown up and married before I even met William."

I said, "Okay. And this man?" I pointed to a tall, slender, fair-haired man.

"That was my husband's older brother, Howard. Wasn't he handsome? A lovely man too. He's long gone, dear."

"Was he the father of the nieces?"

"He was. Once William and I married and came out here, they visited a couple of times and then we drifted apart after Howard died, except for the odd letter and card. I think they might have been a bit miffed about something. Probably money, if my family is anything to go by."

Cards? Cards meant envelopes. "Would you have any cards or envelopes?"

"No dear. I got rid of a lot of that when William passed. I didn't get around to clearing out the photos. He was sentimental about them. He would have kept any envelopes. I'm not really keen on that kind of, well, junk. William wrote names on the backs of lots of photos. Why is this important?"

Tyler gave me a suspicious look.

I didn't answer but instead asked, "So you haven't heard from them in years?"

"It's funny you should ask. I *hadn't* heard from any of them for ages, then a few months ago, I got a call from Clara. Or maybe it was Janet. No, it was Clara. She's the friendlier of the two. One of the kids—can't remember which one—was thinking of a vacation in California in the fall and wondered if they could visit me. We had a nice long chat. It was very pleasant. I'd like to see them. But not as much as I'm enjoying your visit. You know, now that you're back and the sun is definitely over the yardarm, I think a G and T would be just the ticket."

Zoya said glumly, "I vill fix."

"The kids' names?"

"Oh. Good question. But silly me, I'd need to think, my dear. You can't believe what doesn't stick in your brain once you pass a certain age. Oh, thank you, Zoya. Tyler and Jordan, I'm so sorry. I should have offered you one. Anything you want. Zoya will be happy to mix you a cocktail."

Tyler and I glanced at Zoya's thunderous expression and then both looked away. I made sure not to make eye contact with him in case we both laughed our heads off. Neither Gram nor Zoya would appreciate that.

"Thanks, but I need a clear head for a bit," I said.

Smiley grinned. "Maybe later, Gram."

* * *

TYLER AND I left Gram and Zoya and Asta with the birds and went off to talk again. I had been holding back on him and he was running out of patience. I hadn't figured out a way to tell him about Uncle Kev. And I preferred not to mention that I'd made what the boys in blue call an "unauthorized entry" into the Himmelfarb house.

I smiled and changed the subject. "I always wanted cousins."

Tyler said, "And I always wanted answers. This would be a good time to get some."

"Now I don't want cousins. I think your cousins are behind the bizarre stuff that's been going on."

"Step-cousins. Okay, but why?"

"I'll look on the backs of the photos for clues to who's who. If I can get their names, I may be able to find out where they are. Don't ask me how just yet."

"Before we do any of that, let's get the right telephone numbers keyed into this phone."

"Good thinking. I hope I'm not in that situation again."

He glowered as he keyed in the numbers. "You won't be. I'll be with you the next time. You won't be off on your own taking your life into your hands. After this, I won't let you down."

I put my arms around him. "You didn't let me down. You were up all night guarding the house so that I could sleep and you stayed here where you were needed."

"Doesn't matter. Anything could have happened. I should have been at that hotel with you. I should have found a way to be there."

"And I should have realized that if I'd been attacked at the hotel once, it could happen again. Maybe we should just give each other a hall pass on this."

He grinned. "A hall pass. Just this once. And that reminds

me, while you are at the hotel, did you have a chance to grab any of the cameras?"

"Everything happened too fast. We'll have to go back and get them."

"We'll go together and we'll get Officer Martinez to come with us. I don't know who those two guys were, but they looked like they meant business."

"They did not intend to leave me alive. I can't figure out how they can be connected to—"

"They look like professional thugs. A simple thief has no interest in shooting up a hotel room and terrorizing guests. These are seriously dangerous people."

"I know that." And they may be more of your new relatives.

"We'll find out who they are. Officer Martinez is looking into it. She's pretty sharp and she feels connected to this case."

"That's good."

Tyler said, "We have Howard's name. I'll see what I can find out online about him and his relatives. New York State. That will be a start to give us names. And Jordan?"

"Mmm?"

"I hope you're going to get it off your chest sooner rather than later. Not only about why you think it's the cousins, but also whatever else it is."

Of course, he could tell I was keeping something else from him. I just needed a bit more information before I dropped the Uncle Kev bombshell.

I said, "Don't worry. There is something, but it's not related to this and I'll come clean soon. In the meantime, how about I fill you in on everything that happened at the hotel?"

He settled back and folded his arms and I went through the events from the first knock on the door of the suite. I stopped just before I got to the Himmelfarb section. I did put in the part about changing into the shorts, T-shirt and

A's cap in an alley behind a garbage can. I just didn't mention which alley.

Tyler cracked up at that image of me getting changed outside in broad daylight.

I had to laugh too. "I'm glad you see the humor in my changing in an alley."

"It's just that you always look so—I'm sorry I missed you in the chambermaid's uniform too. You'll have to model it for me." It lightened the mood between us a bit.

But I fought back a moment's panic. Where was that uniform? Did I have it with me when I got to Gram's? And where was the "evidence" from the Himmelfarb house? "Hang on!"

I headed back to the front door. I found one plastic bag with my orange satchel in it. No uniform. No Starbucks cups and Jolly Rancher wrappers.

"Now that you say that, I seem to have lost it. I stuffed it into one of the plastic bags from the store where I bought my snazzy new outfit."

The uniform bag was probably sitting behind the Himmelfarb garbage can. Had I left the evidence in the closet?

"Maybe you dropped it when you were 'changing'?" He made a big deal out of the air quotes.

My mind was still whirling on the location of that bag. Had I dropped one when I surprised Uncle Kev in the alley? That would be the best thing. And easy enough to verify as Uncle Kev was supposed to be watching the Art Deco apartment for signs of Jessica and Josh.

I said, "I'm just going to search the house and see if I can find it. I was pretty stressed and I could have dropped it anywhere."

I even checked back in the sunroom. "I'm just looking for a plastic shopping bag I misplaced. Did you notice it, Zoya?"

I figured the sniff meant "no."

Gram sipped her drink and said, "Don't be long, my dear. Tyler, sit for a minute. We should have a nice dinner tonight. Zoya does a wonderful stroganoff. Don't you, Zoya?"

Zoya's wide silver eyes bulged like Asta's. Oh well.

Gram sipped her drink and twinkled at us. "Oh, I remember! Melski and Kargol."

Tyler blinked and I'm pretty sure I did too. Zoya's eyes narrowed like slits, her bright red lips thin and angry.

Gram tapped her forehead and chuckled. "William's nieces. Those were their married names. I knew they were in there somewhere."

JUST ONE TINY piece of information before we could involve the police.

"No luck, Jordie. They haven't left," Uncle Kev said when I called.

"Unless they went out the back entrance or left in a car."

"Why would they do that? They don't know that we're following them."

"They know something's up. But here's the good news. Check the names of the occupants for Kargol and Melski."

"Why?"

"Because there's a good chance that they're Tyler's cousins and those are their last names."

"Oh. Hang on."

A minute later, Kev said, "Nope."

"Nope?"

"No one named Melski there."

"And Kargol?"

"Oh right. I forgot about that part."

"Are you still there?"

"No, I'm back outside now."

"Go back in and look."

I paced and waited.

Uncle Kev said, "I don't remember that name. Oh. There is it. Kargol, just like we said. Unit 310."

"Right."

"Good. Now we know that, I also need you to tell me something without any fibbing—"

You always have to say "need" with Uncle Kev and sometimes that's not enough.

"Me fib? LOL, Jordie."

"Just tell me what you are doing in San Francisco."

"Well, I came out here to help you, 'course. Didn't I just find those sneaky Kargols?"

I felt my eye begin to twitch. "Indeed. But you didn't know about the sneaky Kargols or that I might need help when you flew out here, Kev."

"Oh yeah. Well, you know. Lucky hunch."

I waited. After a minute I said, "So as you didn't know that I would need help—"

"But you did need help, Jordie. In a big way."

"Agree, but you couldn't have known that when you made your arrangements to come to San Francisco to help me."

"Exactly."

"No. Not *exactly*. Why did you decide to do that?"

Uncle Kev was quiet. "Tell me now," I said. "And you'll feel better."

"Maybe not, Jordie."

"Oh, hello!" A woman's voice trilled in the background. Sounded like Uncle Kev's new friend with the poodle. "Any luck?"

"Not now, Uncle Kev. You have to answer me. What are you doing here?"

Silence. Then, "We need to talk, Jordie."

"We really do. And before we talk, I need you to go back

to that house where you found the dog and check the blue bedroom closet. Don't get caught."

"Jordie. As if!"

"No offense, but don't. You're looking for a bag with trash, taco tray, coffee cups, that kind of thing. Oh, and of course, Jolly Rancher wrappers. Bring that. Then go behind the garbage can in the side yard and see if there's another bag with a uniform. Got that?"

"Easy stuff."

"Right. I need them and I need them soon. Then I need you to call me here and let me know when you have it. I'll meet you outside by the back deck. Don't let anybody see you."

"But—"

"No buts. I need the bags. I need them soon. Call me when you have them or if they're not there. Meet me by the back deck here, at Tyler's grandmother's house. Then you can tell me why you're in San Francisco. And make it good."

CHAPTER TWENTY-THREE

Someone will always believe you.
—THE KELLY RULES

I STUCK MY head into the sunroom and beckoned to Tyler. He joined me and we headed back to the parlor, our special place to plot and reveal secrets.

"Fine, Officer. I'm ready to talk. You know I made friends with that woman with the baby? Sierra."

"So far pretty tame."

"Yep. Well, I mentioned to her that Asta had disappeared the first time and how upsetting that was."

"Okay."

"Well, she and her husband, who I think is actually her brother or cousin in real life, actually abducted Asta and kept her in the house across the street." I pointed at Mr. Himmelfarb's place. "They were spying on us and I think they were also behind the home invasion and—"

"And you know this how?"

"Not, um, by exactly legal methods."

He raised an eyebrow. "Probably better if I don't know."

"You should really know." I sighed. I'd been doing way too much sighing lately. "Don't get too mad until I'm finished."

He watched, grim-faced, as I went through my unauthorized entry (I may have suggested the door was possibly somewhat open) into Gram's neighbor's house, my hiding out in the closet, and then my shadowing of Jessica and Josh to their apartment building.

"Never mind the illegality of it all, these were really dangerous steps, Jordan. Breaking into a house—"

"Not exactly breaking into."

He held up his hand to silence me and oddly enough it worked for a minute. "The law wouldn't see it that way. And aside from the law, you could have been hurt. Or killed. Think of all the bizarre and dangerous events that have occurred since we've been here. You were alone in a house and none of us had any idea."

I said, "It's true. I didn't think it through. I didn't know they'd be there. When I found out she wasn't who she pretended to be, I had to follow up."

"It was across the street, Jordan."

"In retrospect, I see I should have found a way to get here. I was worried about being followed to Gram's."

"I understand why you were worried, but it was a ridiculous course of action."

"In a way, it's like we've been hexed by Hammett."

He glared at me. "That is unfair. You can't blame Dashiell Hammett for you breaking into a house."

"Unfair? Of course I can blame him. Those Pinkerton operatives would stop at nothing. Neither did I. Did you not read the books?"

"Can I remind you that you are a book researcher, not a Pinkerton operative?"

"Don't patronize me. Okay, I know that. But let's remember that I'm all right and I did get to overhear them and I have their real names."

"What are they?"

"Jessica and Josh. One of them is a Kargol and the other

one will turn out to be a Melski. They were talking about getting us out of the picture. The main point is that we now know what they're up to."

"You make my head pound. What exactly are they up to?"

"If I understand their conversation right, they're trying to alienate you from Gram and to scare us away."

"But why?"

"Money. Greed. Gram will be worth a bundle . . . at some point. You are her heir."

"We have never talked about that kind of stuff. We're just getting reacquainted. It's not about money."

"Not about money for you. You really love her, but her brother-in-law's descendants won't have the same warm and fuzzies. They referred to you as 'the so-called grandson' and me as 'the nasty girlfriend.' "

"I am not 'so-called.' "

"They're probably thinking of Gram's assets as Huddy money and you as coming from the other side. I'm betting they feel not only entitled but cheated out of a potential inheritance."

"So get me and you out of the way."

"Then they can cozy up to her and get her to change her will."

Smiley was flame-red by this time. I wouldn't have given much for those cousins and their chances if he ran into them. We'd have to get him calmed down when we did involve the local police.

Finally, he said, "You think that they were responsible for everything?"

"We don't know how many cousins there are." I fished out my camera and flipped through. It was the last of many photos I'd taken that day. "But here's a shot of these two. Have you seen them around?"

He shook his head. "I recognize her from our walk, but I haven't seen him. I know him now."

"Jessica and Josh look a lot like those photos of William's nieces, same noses, tall, slender, all-American good looks, great hair. Almost annoying. And now, as it turns out, dangerous."

"And when the cousins were across the street watching the house, they would have known when Gram was alone."

"Exactly. She was in danger because of that. They must have staged that home invasion, to scare us away."

"And they dognapped Asta. They don't know who they're dealing with. It made us more determined not to leave Gram. It was actually a bizarre bonding moment for us. She's pretty gutsy."

I expected a chuckle, but he said in a dejected tone, "And this is all because of me."

"What? No. Nothing that's happened is because of you. It's because Howard Huddy's family is greedy and wants what isn't theirs."

"They must have been behind it all."

"Looks that way. And now we just have to prove it."

He straightened up and got his cop face on. "One thing we do really well together is—"

I was ahead of him. I grinned. "We set traps."

CHAPTER TWENTY-FOUR

Make sure they trust you.
—THE KELLY RULES

YES INDEED, SOME of our most romantic moments
had grown out of traps set successfully. I'll fill you in
on the daring details sometime.

"These people are dangerous," he said. "We know that
because of the lengths they're willing to go to and their
access to weapons. Dangerous and maybe even unhinged.
With wacky ideas."

I thought back to the stockings over the faces of the home
invaders and the weapons and shivered. "For sure. So we'll
have to be careful that no one gets hurt."

He nodded. "If we stage our trap here, Gram could be
hurt. We'd have to make sure she was somewhere safe."

I had a memory flash of Gram facing down the invaders.
"She'd hate to miss out on the excitement."

"Jordan, she's old. What if she had a heart attack?"

"She would have had it already with what she's been
through. But she'll probably resent it. Maybe we could tape
the whole sting and play it for her. That's worked well for
us in the past."

"We need some allies."

"Right. Too bad my uncles and Cherie are not here. They're always so—"

He shot me a look. "I'll assume you're kidding."

So, this wasn't the perfect time to tell him about Uncle Kev. Once I found out what Kev's actual reason for being in San Francisco was, that would have to be the right time. Some revelations are best left for the future. "Not Zoya," I said, deflecting the conversation. "I'm still not sure what's going on with her. What if she was feeding them information from the inside?"

He scowled in the direction of the sunroom and Zoya. "Do you really believe that?"

"No. Not really. But I don't really understand her relationship with Gram and I don't think we should let Zoya in on whatever plan we develop."

"Agreed. But we will need the police."

"The police! Are you out of your—"

"Keep in mind, I *am* the police."

"That's not the point. You're not the police *here*."

"What is your problem with the police? Don't you like Officer Martinez?"

To my surprise, I had to admit that I did like Jennifer Martinez. She was smart and sympathetic and most likely going places.

But quite aside from the Uncle Kev aspect—back-burnered in the talk department—there were issues. "Maybe I'm a bit worried about my, um, visit to the Himmelfarb house."

"I can see where that might be a hurdle. We just have to put the right spin on it."

"I suppose." What kind of spin that might be, I had no idea. But I did have the glimmer of a plan.

I said, "If we talk the cousins into revealing themselves, how I found out wouldn't be an issue."

He nodded. "If I can keep my hands off them."

"We will use Gram to build their trust. They think they're manipulating her. They think they're pretty smart. They'll never suspect she's tricking them. It will work like a charm."

"You know as well as I do that Officer Martinez won't be part of a sting without involving her superiors. "

"We'll just have to find the right way to set it up. It could be good for her career. As you say, these are dangerous people. And we don't know how many there are. And we only know what two of them look like. I guess the pudgy fake cop must be part of it and the guys with the guns at the hotel."

He said, "Here's an idea. Let's take the weak links, the two cousins. Let's invite them in and trick the truth out of them, and then we'll let the cops go after the thuggish ones."

"That's what we'll do."

I had a nagging worry that before anything was set up. I needed to talk to Uncle Kev again and get the story of why he was here.

He said, "But we'll have to let Gram in on the plan."

"Right. You'll have to tell her, Tyler."

He nodded.

"I'll get Zoya out of the way when you do. Then we'll have to arrange to meet with Officer Martinez away from here and bring her up to speed."

"Good point. I'll set that up."

"She could meet us at the hotel."

"And we'll need some reinforcements here. I have an idea or two."

We ambled back to the sunroom, holding hands. There's nothing like planning a sting to perk up a relationship.

"Tyler, pet, come here," Gram said. I noticed she was holding a fresh G and T. I hoped she'd remember what he told her. I hated to miss that conversation, but I had to lure Zoya away.

I headed toward the kitchen, where Zoya was slinging together dinner with her usual look of irritation. "I think Asta really needs a walk. She's circling in that way. Would you come with me, Zoya? I'm worried that someone would try to take her again."

Zoya gasped. Her hands shot to her face. "No!" One thing was for sure, Zoya was not faking her concern for Asta. She loved that little pug. If she had been involved with the cousins or the nieces or anyone else, she sure hadn't been party to Asta's dognapping.

"But with two of us right in the neighborhood, she'd be safe."

Zoya whipped off her flowered apron and stepped forward. "Asta! Valk!"

So that went well.

I wish I could say that Zoya and I bonded watching Asta scamper from bush to bush around the block, but you can't have everything. At least I got her out of the way.

BACK IN THE sunroom, Gram and Smiley were grinning like a couple of kids who'd found the hiding place for their gifts from Santa.

Zoya glanced at them with grave suspicion. I was thrilled. From the look of things, they'd cooked up something very sneaky. I couldn't wait to hear all about it.

Never mind Zoya's surliness, she sure could produce a fast and tasty meal. Maybe she wasn't in the signora's league, but Gram was lucky to have her. The beef Stroganoff with egg noodles was nicely retro and totally delish. We ate casually at folding tables in the sunroom. Of course, it was hard to wait to find out if Gram had agreed and what they'd worked out. That wasn't possible with Zoya sitting there, giving us dirty looks every few minutes.

I was torn between smiling at her or ignoring the looks.

Gram and Smiley chitchatted happily through dinner. They looked so sweet and innocent with the little gap-toothed smiles, no one would ever suspect what they were plotting.

KEV DELIVERED THE uniform and the bag of trash.

I took them from him and said, "Now, the truth."

Smiley's voice broke through. "What are you doing out here? Haven't you taken enough chances, Jordan?"

Kev melted away into the shadows.

"I was just going to do a bit of laundry. I found the uniform. The bag must have slipped behind the chair when I got here."

"Just come inside. Please. I don't think you can get into any trouble doing laundry."

In the basement laundry area, I took out the uniform. I checked the pockets and found Ana Maria's telephone number. I wondered if she'd tried to reach me. She wouldn't have gotten far as I'd lost my original phone. I called her number. It went straight to a Spanish message. My own message started with "*Hola!*" and shifted straight to English.

"I have your uniform. I'll return it to you clean as soon as I have a chance. Thank you for all your help. I've had to get a new phone." I didn't give my name, but I did leave my new number.

As the first load whirled in the new front-loader washing machine, I sat in the corner and tried Uncle Kev.

"The thing of it is, Jordie, that I'm not really in a position to talk." I thought I heard a muffled giggle in the background. But he was just here!

Kev is the most frustrating and distractible person in the world and he does love to drag it out. If you get mad, he gets spooked.

"I'm sorry that our conversation got cut off, Kev. I need to know why you are in San Francisco, who paid, and I really need to know now."

"No problem. I'll talk to you tomorrow then."

"No! Don't hang up on—"

I banged the phone on the washing machine in frustration. So much for filling in the blanks on Uncle Kev's mission.

The phone rang again just as I was putting the clothes in the dryer.

"It is Ana Maria."

"Great. You got my message. Look, I'll deliver your uniform, but I wasn't sure if anything had happened at work because you helped me."

She hesitated. "Not really. But I need to tell you I found your phone in the pocket of your jeans just after you left. There was a can of talcum powder there too and your big earrings. That's probably why I didn't feel it when I put them on."

"Of course, *that's* where I put it. And since we were all in such a panic, no wonder you didn't notice that phone. I'm so glad you found it. I had to get a replacement and I don't have any of my information on it. How can I get it?"

"I am at night school."

"Can I send someone to get it after night school then?"

"Sure." She gave me the address. I recorded it.

"Thank you, Ana Maria. You took a chance for me and I'm grateful."

"I'll wait at the door by the west side of the school at nine o'clock."

I wasn't sure how our sting would play out so I needed to get Uncle Kev in on this. "Someone will be there. It probably won't be me. You can expect a man with red hair and blue eyes. He's okay, but whatever you do, do *not* fall in love with him."

She laughed. Not worried about that. But then again, she hadn't met Uncle Kev.

"Wait for a few minutes. If he doesn't show up, we can make a new plan tomorrow. I'll go to the hotel."

"Maybe not the hotel. I thought someone was watching me today. It was just a feeling."

HEADING UPSTAIRS CARRYING clean, dry laundry, I spotted Smiley and Gram grinning conspiratorially over a new three-thousand-piece puzzle. As far as I could tell, it was a picture of the Sahara, minus an oasis.

More interesting was a plate of chocolate chip meringues.

Zoya was keeping a wary eye on them while covering up the birds. I caught her yawning and she looked furtive.

"Zoya, dear, do go to bed," Gram said. "You'll have us yawning too, and then we'll never get a start on this."

"What about Asta? Does she need to go out?" I plunked down in one of the chintz-cushioned wicker chairs. Asta jumped up beside me and curled up.

"Zoya took her out for another evening visit. I kept an eye on them in the backyard," Smiley said. "She's a nervous little pooch, isn't she?"

"You'd be nervous too if people were kidnapping you," I said. "Right, Asta?"

Asta snuggled her little body closer.

Zoya snorted. "Iss no choke."

"Help yourself to the meringues, my dear," Gram said. "They were always Tyler's favorite. Zoya whips them up these days."

We all listened as Zoya climbed the stairs. For such a whippetlike figure, she sure could thump on the old treads. I went to the foot of the stairs after a minute, and when I heard the door close on the second floor, I dashed back.

"It's all settled," Smiley said. "Gram reached the nieces, Janet and Clara, when we were in the backyard and invited them to a tea party tomorrow."

"Tomorrow? Do we have time to plan our trap?"

Smiley glared at me. "Give us some credit, Jordan."

Gram said, "I called Clara, she's the older of the two, on the Melski side. I had a heart-to-heart with her and told her how things hadn't worked out the way I'd thought with my grandson. He'd turned out to be unstable and grasping and I suspected criminal connections. I told her I was sending him and his greedy girlfriend away."

I said, "What?"

"All part of the game, my dear."

"Hmm."

Smiley said, "Don't you complain. I'm the one who's unstable and grasping."

"Oh, that."

Gram was chortling away. "I told her I was going to update my will quickly because I was really worried about what my grasping grandson might do. I said we need to keep our money in the Huddy family, as William would have wanted, although they're not Huddys. I said I hoped I could reconnect with Clara and her sister sometime. I said I'd be willing to put them up in a hotel and host their meals here."

"That's very generous of you," I said.

Smiley chimed in as he reached for another meringue, "And it gets better."

Gram said, "Didn't it turn out that she and her sister are just winding up a tour in California and they will do every-thing in their power to make it tomorrow."

"What a coincidence," I said. I'd finished one meringue

and now another one had found its way into my possession. Like magic.

"Isn't it?" Tyler said.

Gram added, "I said what a shame that their dear children couldn't also join us and . . . you'll never believe it, my dear."

"Try me."

"Both their children are also in the area, working, and living not far from here."

"Wow. Isn't that the best luck?" I said with a grin.

Gram picked up a meringue and added with a twinkle. "I think we're in business."

Tyler said, "We have a great plan."

There was a rustle behind us and Zoya stood fuming. So much for keeping her out of it.

"This is crazy idea! No good. Dangerous!"

I asked myself if she could be right. But right or wrong, apparently Zoya would now be on the team. I just hoped that she wasn't actually part of some other team.

Tyler said, "They'll all be arriving here for tea tomorrow. They will be under the impression that we have left and that there are very hard feelings."

"I like it already," I said.

A knock on the door indicated that another member of the team had arrived.

Turns out every party needs a lawyer. Gram's was a lean and steely-looking woman of an uncertain age. Not only was she willing to arrive at the drop of a hat, but she lived in the neighborhood and could figure out how to get to Gram's back deck without being noticed. The lawyer's name was Nancy Mitchell and she definitely had Gram's back. She settled into one of the flowered chairs and gave us a cool, speculative glance over her platinum-rimmed glasses. "You know, I'll need to spend a bit of time with Jean to make sure everything is just as you say it is."

Smiley's back stiffened.

"This is my family, Nancy," Gram said with a flash of her bright blue eyes.

I said, "Ms. Mitchell's right. You can never be too careful. We'll be in the kitchen stealing more meringues."

Gram said, "There are people I have to be careful about and I'll fill you in on them."

Gram shooed Zoya away along with us. When we returned ten minutes later, Nancy was on board. Gram was saying, "And I think I'll leave the share that the nieces and their children would have gotten to an animal rescue charity. I just need to decide which one. There are so many good choices."

Tyler said, "What about the shelter where you got Asta?"

"California Pug Rescue."

Zoya nodded. "Iss good idea."

So, all systems were go.

I WAS SURE I saw the second-floor drapes twitching in the Himmelfarb house as Tyler and I stomped out the front door, carrying our belongings. We engaged in a lively discussion on the front step. Much stamping of feet and gesticulating. Great fun. Right at the key moment, Sierra emerged with the carriage. She was wearing an Adidas running hat with a dark acetate visor and sunglasses, a bit late in the day. To make the case a bit more dramatic, Tyler and I were both waving our arms and shouting in the direction of Gram's house. Gram's and Zoya's faces were pressed against the turret window looking out. Zoya opened the purple front door and shook her fist at us. Asta yipped.

The cab driver got out of his car and stared. I think he was already regretting picking up this fare.

Zoya, who was now in on the plan, stayed on the front

porch, gesticulating wildly and shouting things I took to be of the "don't come back" variety in Russian. I definitely understood *Nyet!*

I bellowed back at her, "Don't worry. We wouldn't come back here at gunpoint. You couldn't pay us to spend another minute in your company."

Gram teetered out onto the steps, holding a hanky and wailing, "You are such a disappointment. You broke my heart."

Tyler yelled, "You don't have a heart!"

Gram said, "And that scheming creature you call a girl-friend, she's brought nothing but trouble since you've been here."

I gasped. Was that really necessary?

Tyler took the stairs two at a time and tossed his bags into the waiting cab. I had managed to fake some pretty good tears, again a family talent. They were streaming down my cheeks as I called out to Sierra and said, "You can't believe how badly we've been treated. We've been blamed for . . . everything."

Tyler grabbed my bags and took me by the shoulder and pushed me toward the cab. Not the actions of a good guy and that was the idea. "Let's get as far away as we can from the old witch. What a nightmare."

I flopped on the backseat as the cabbie accelerated away. Tyler squeezed my hand, which I took to mean, "Don't say anything in case someone talks to the driver."

As if a Kelly would ever blow cover.

CHAPTER TWENTY-FIVE

Kill them with kindness.
—THE KELLY RULES

WE DIDN'T GO far. Our cabbie let us out a mile away in front of a small hotel. We waited until he was out of sight before catching another cab back to Nancy Mitchell's house, four doors up from Gram's and on the corner. We went in by Nancy's side entrance, confident that no one had followed us. Nancy had spoken to her neighbors to let them know we needed to traipse through their backyards to get back to Gram's without being seen. No one had a problem with that. And everyone offered whatever help we might need.

I was still a bit worried. I said to Smiley, "But how do we know that Gram will be safe? These people didn't mind terrorizing us. Who knows what they'll come up with when confronted."

He said, "They won't try anything until they think she's actually changed her will. We get the goods on them before that. Anyway, Gram's having the time of her life with this. Apparently, although she liked Howard, she was never a big fan of his family. But of course, she never said anything because she knew what it was like to be in a fractured family, thanks to my parents. And as far as safety, Zoya's there to help us too."

"Right, the same Zoya who was injured in the last break-in."

"And Gus and the boys should be there soon."

"What?"

"Gram and I cooked it up. Gus and the boys will be arriving from the back way too, from the other side as soon as it's dark. They'll spend the night and will stay there tomorrow until after the visit. We'll make sure we have witnesses as well as a recording."

"Well, that's just great, but how do we know you can trust any of them?"

"We're confident. They're all devoted to Gram and I'm banking on that."

But of course, except for Nancy Mitchell they'd all been on my list of suspects, hadn't they? Everyone had been on it, including Smiley and me. "We don't know everything yet, Tyler."

As we reached the back deck in Gram's yard, he pulled me close, taking me by surprise. I didn't think the danger to his grandmother was a romantic conversation starter. "We know everything that matters. We know how much we care about each other. We know we're the best team. We know we're going to be together."

Oh no. Not here. Not like this. Not while I had so much to feel guilty about, in other words, meaning "you know who" and whatever he was doing following me.

"But—"

"Gram loves you, Jordan."

"Well, I'm sure she—"

"Nope. She loves *you*. Loves your sense of humor and

your bravery and the way you bounce back and the way you care about me."

"That's really great but—"

He reached into his pocket. "No buts. That's why she wants to know if you would like to wear this as your engagement ring."

"As my—"

"Yeah. She got it in her head that you didn't have an engagement ring because I just couldn't afford one because of the new house and changing jobs and all that, and she wants us to have this heirloom ring that has real sentimental value to her. It was her mother's. She wants to keep it in the family."

"And the truth is that I don't have a ring because we're not engaged."

"Well, yeah. But let's change that. Right now. I'll never find anyone I like more that you, Jordan Kelly Bingham. You make me mad as hell and your family are all crooks and yet I can't live without you. That makes it love."

"That's extreme, isn't it? You probably could live without me."

"Did I mention you're exasperating in the extreme?"

"That's me." I stared at the ring, a large emerald-cut yellow citrine with two tiny diamonds at the edge of the setting. Like it had been made for me in 1926.

He said, "It's called a citrine."

"I know. It's beautiful."

"She said it represents good luck and prosperity and generosity."

He let his arms drop. "But if you don't want to marry me, no pressure and no hard feelings. I know you have your own plans and you've had some issues with relationships. Take your time."

I looked up at his pink face and surprised myself by

saying, "I do want to marry you. I'll never find anyone I like more than you, Tyler Dekker. And you make me even madder than I make you. It is possible that I can't live without you either. It could be love. But there's just one thing—"

Smiley pulled out his phone. "It's Gram. She wants us to come inside before someone spots us. Who knows where these crooked relatives of hers are watching from."

Gram opened the door and beckoned.

Tyler said, "Sorry, what was the one thing that interfered with my proposal and your acceptance?"

I cleared my throat. "Um, as you had been keeping things from me and not for the first time this trip, I have something to tell you." It was way past time to tell him about Uncle Kev. It had been weighing on me. So even if I didn't know why Kev was in San Francisco yet, if was time to come clean.

"Can it wait?"

"What?"

"It's just that she's obviously anxious. Take your time. Consider your answer. Tomorrow's a big day. We'll get these crooks."

He was on his way back into the house before I realized I was still wearing the ring. It was just the right size.

IT SEEMED LIKE forever before I was free to call Uncle Kev. Our trap was just the sort of activity that Kev could destabilize in a major way. He needed to be in the loop. He could still do some damage, but maybe less. And we did need reinforcements.

"Jordie! There's sure a lot going on around here."

"Why didn't you answer your phone, Kev?"

"People are coming and going from that apartment like crazy."

"What people? Where are you?"

"I'm still watching the apartment. There's a lot of action there."

"Describe the action, Kev."

As he did, I felt some answers click into place.

"Try to get some photos of the cousins." I also described some other suspects that might be around. "Watch for large, burly, sweaty men who look like they may be packing heat. Plus you need to go pick up my phone tonight, Kev, and you need to drop it off here. That's very important. Don't get into trouble and don't mess up." I told him to pick up the bag with Ana Maria's uniform from our backyard, and gave him the address and the time and place where he could meet Ana Maria to pick up the phone and return the uniform with my thanks. "And when you bring it back, you can tell me why you are here and no fooling around."

"Not my fault, Jordie. Your pet cop there keeps interrupting. You should show that guy the door."

"No changing the subject and no excuses. Call me when you have the phone and you're in the backyard. Don't be seen."

"Jordie," he said reproachfully.

I crept outside with the bag containing Ana Maria's uniform for Kev, then I went back to join our ever-expanding group of conspirators. We'd now been joined by Gus and the boys. Except for Zoya, who personified gloom, they were all in a party mood in Gram's sunroom, out of view of the street. Gus and the boys had brought a boatload of souvlaki and Greek salad and baklava, an unexpected treat for all.

Smiley seemed subdued. I was trying not to pace nervously. Plenty depended on Uncle Kev, never a good thing. I caught Smiley's eyes on me several times. I had no choice but to tell him, but I thought I might wait until I had my phone back and Kev was out of his reach.

Our plans unfurled slowly as the evening wore on. We made contingencies for every possible situation, it seemed. Gus and the boys would be out of sight, but positioned to arrive in case of any hostility by our targets. Smiley and I were to be hiding in the dining room. The grand pocket doors would be closed. We would be free to observe thanks to a couple of peepholes newly drilled at just the right height by Gus. I thought that Gram might have objected to having holes in the walls of her home, but she said, "Small price to pay."

Gus rumbled. "Easy to fix afterwards. Five minutes, bit of plaster and paint. Nothing to it. Me and my boys are happy to help Mrs. Jean."

It was nearly ten when my burner vibrated. I headed to the kitchen on the pretence of getting a cup of coffee.

"Jordie," Kev said.

"Where are you?"

"In the basement."

"What? You broke in here? That's—"

"I have your phone."

"On my way. Keep out of sight."

"Jordie."

I stuck my head back in, coffee mug in hand, and said that I'd like to do a bit more laundry, things I'd forgotten earlier. Would that be a problem?

"Be my guest," Gram said, turning away from the others briefly.

As I headed up the stairs with the coffee to get my fake laundry, I could feel Smiley's eyes boring into my back.

Minutes later, I was standing in front of the washing machine preparing to toss in my perfectly clean pair of shorts and T-shirt.

Where would he be? I needed not to yelp in surprise when he suddenly appeared. Being Uncle Kev, he could leap out of a laundry basket or slither from under a table. I looked up in case he was about to drop from the ductwork. When I lowered my glance, he was standing beside me. "Your phone, Jordie. Your friend, Ana Maria, was glad to get her uniform back. She sent back your jeans and top."

"Good work, Kev," I said.

"Oh sure," a voice behind us said. "Very good work."

"I can explain," I said.

"Make it good," Tyler said. It wasn't a moment where you could call him Smiley.

"Uncle Kev happened to be in San Francisco and he was willing to help us out."

"Was he indeed?" Usually Uncle Kev was able to vanish like a wisp of fog in the sunshine, but not when his arm was being held firmly by a large police officer.

"Yes." I noticed that old familiar chirp back in my voice. "I didn't want to tell you because I thought you might be bothered by it."

"You'd be right about that. Where your uncle goes, trouble always follows."

Uncle Kev said, "Hey, that's not fair."

It was completely and utterly fair, but I said, "But it's good news. Uncle Kev's managed to get my phone back from Ana Maria, the chambermaid. I think you'll want to see the photos I took on my way to the hotel before I ran into the men with guns and afterwards when I spotted your cousins. We need to show them to Gram too. All thanks to Kev."

"Don't go anywhere," Smiley said to Kev as I showed him the photos. I said, "After looking at those old photos, do you recognize any of these people?"

Tyler let go of Uncle Kev and glowered as he scrolled through the images on my iPhone. "So that's what it's about," he said with a grim, even Sam Spade–like set to his jaw.

He said, "We have to show them to Gram. Let's go." He nodded in Kev's direction. "I suppose we'd better have him where we can keep an eye on him."

"Always a good idea," I said. "Don't worry, Uncle Kev. There's lots of great Greek food."

That was how Uncle Kev came to join the party. As you can imagine, he was quite a hit with the ladies.

Everyone had a good look at the photos I'd snapped. Kev's eyes widened as he spotted a few people. He was trying to catch my attention and yet not willing to say what it was about out loud. I knew there was something to discuss with him when we had a minute alone.

Gram had the most emotional reaction when she saw them. I thought I spotted tears in her bright blue eyes.

"I am so sorry, pet," she said. "I brought this all upon us. What a foolish old woman I am."

NEXT TIME KEV went to refill his drink, I shoved him into the pantry and closed the door behind us. Sure, I no longer had to deal with the ominous threat of Smiley finding out about Kev, but I did still have the ominous threat of Kev himself. Kev's eyes were wide. He was scared. Rightfully so.

"Jeez, Jordie, you're strong!" He rubbed his arm where I'd gripped him.

"Spill it, spill it now, or so help me, Kev . . ." There was way too much depending on our little trap. It was going to be delicate and Kev was a giant ginger bull in a crowded china shop.

"Well, I just needed to be sure that you haven't mentioned Uncle Seamus to anyone, have you, since you've been here, Jordie? Remember I sent you that text?"

"Uncle Seamus? No, I haven't . . . why would I? Oh, wait!" I flashed back to Farley Tso, his silver fox mane flowing at the shop. He had definitely mentioned Seamus by name. At the time, it had even surprised me, because we're really not supposed to talk about Seamus outside the family. If the TV shot I'd seen was correct, then Farley Tso was dead. Is that what had gotten him killed? "Wait, what text did you send me?" I pulled out the phone he'd retrieved for me and scrolled back to our last texts.

I read it, "'Make sure not to mention SeaWorld. Trust me,'" and then I held it up—perhaps aggressively—close to his confused face.

"Oh man, that Autocorrect is gonna ruin my life." Kev's shoulders slumped.

"Not if I end it first." I flared my nostrils. "What did you do, Kev? You know that Farley Tso is probably dead, don't you? Does this have something to do with Seamus?"

"I know, but I had almost nothing to do with it!" *Almost nothing?* How comforting. "I couldn't tell you before. Not even Mick knows and I swore I'd never mention it. And you know how good I am at keeping promises, Jordie."

"Back in the day, Farley and Seamus did 'a little job' together. They thought they were robbing some bombshell socialite named Laurie Leff. She was a real stunner, but it turned out this Laurie Leff was not only rich, but she was also really well connected. And I do mean *connected*."

"Are we talking about the Mob here?" My stomach turned.

"Yeah, she liked to walk on the wild side with a mob guy named Les 'the Bat' Blatt. The story goes, this Laurie Leff had been seen at an after-hours club flashing one heck of a diamond necklace. Showing it off, ya know. I guess Seamus heard she was staying in a hotel that he'd already cased. *Batta-bing batta-boom!* When she was sleeping it off that night, they swiped it."

"When was this?" My temples were throbbing.

"Early eighties."

"And why is this all coming up now? Why wait all this time to kill Farley Tso?"

"Seamus knew they were going to get caught, once he realized what a mistake they'd made. He put the word out that he'd done the heist alone. Mick even thinks it was a solo job. But that was just to protect Farley. And it didn't work. Someone dropped Farley Tso's name. Next he gets cornered by some mobsters connected to Les Blatt and he ends up shooting one of them. Blatt pays off some cops and the cops make sure Farley goes down for twenty-five years. Out in twenty for good behavior."

"I think my brain is going to explode."

"Stay with me, Jordie. Here's where Seamus comes into it. He decides to leave the necklace for Farley, somewhere safe, for when he gets outta jail. He feels bad 'cause it was all his idea and there was way too much heat on to pawn the stupid thing."

Something in the back of my mind said, *Necklace? Like the one in the handkerchief box upstairs? The one that Farley gave me?*

"And then Seamus disappeared himself, and I helped him. I'm sorry, Jordan, I couldn't tell you, besides you weren't even born yet. Mick has no idea about any of this, otherwise he would've never sent you to see Farley. I didn't realize he made that connection. I think he just felt bad for the guy, 'cause he just got out of jail, and his business was slow."

"Mick and Lucky don't know about the robbery or the necklace?"

"They knew that Seamus was in the wind, because he stole something, but they never found out about Farley's part in it."

"Why do you think Farley didn't sell the necklace? He could have made out like a bandit, which he was, I suppose."

"Well, he was pretty sure that he would still be watched. That necklace is worth at least a hundred and fifty grand now, it would have been risky but—"

"What?"

"He wanted to give it back to Seamus, or at least back to his family. To thank him for taking the blame and for walking away from his own life to save Farley's, even though he got twenty-five. I talked to him right after he gave you the necklace, but by the time I got down to San Francisco, he was already dead." I guess there is some honor among thieves. "It's in that box he gave you, Jordan. That's what those guys in suits were after at the hotel. They were Les 'the Bat' Blatt's goons."

"I'm the reason Farley Tso is dead." I felt a lump in my throat.

"Don't feel bad, Jordie. Even if he'd had the necklace, and given it up, they woulda killed him. Just to make a point, ya know?"

"What about Laurie Leff? The necklace belongs to her."

"I guess, but she got caught in the crossfire one night she was out with Les Blatt, about twenty years ago, and that was it for her."

"She died."

"Yup. Too bad. She was a beauty."

"And that's why you came? To keep me from getting hurt?"

"Yeah, but I texted you not to mention Seamus to anyone."

I still had to go back to the planning party. How was I going to keep the burden of this information off my face? Tyler would pick up on it immediately. I had to hope he'd be too enveloped in the sting and attribute any weirdness I exuded to adrenaline.

How would I deal with the stolen necklace that belonged to a dead bombshell?

"Now what do we do?" Kev's huge blue saucer eyes stared into mine.

"One plan at a time, Kev."

GRAM WAS DRESSED to kill, a vision in fuchsia silk, her soft white waves shining, looking fragile and delicate with her bird-handled cane at her side. And yet, I knew, having the time of her life. Zoya had caved and served her a G and T in a flowered Shelley china cup.

Smiley and I were set up at our observation posts in the dining room with the pocket doors closed. The Chinese screen was set up to hide us on the off chance that someone took a trip to the powder room and decided to snoop around. The boys were posted in closets, on the back stairs and, in Gus's case, behind a wicker love seat. For his sins, Uncle Kev was also in position with a remote video camera setup and a special job when the trouble started.

Gram was stationed as hostess at a large, low table set up for afternoon tea in the wide, formal parlor with Zoya behind her. A silver samovar gleamed next to the rest of the tea service. Pretty, crustless party sandwiches—my favorite—were arranged to tempt on tiered plates, and cookies and chocolates sat flirtatiously in delicate china dishes. Asta was circling and obviously had a plan too.

Zoya was wearing a sober dark gray dress that emphasized her slim figure and angry silver eyes. She was also sporting a purely symbolic white maid's apron. Her jaw appeared to be clenched, if such a thing is anatomically possible.

Nancy Mitchell, also with a china teacup and saucer, was still and watchful in one of the deep rose velvet wingback chairs.

I quivered when the doorbell rang.

Zoya answered the door. The first batch of Huddy relatives had arrived—Janet Kargol and her son, Josh. I still thought of him as Michael. His mother obviously was in charge. He hung back and looked everywhere except at Gram. Zoya escorted them to the parlor, her wide silver eyes radiating daggers. Oh well. We can't all be as cool as Gram.

"Darling Auntie Jean," Janet said, sweeping close enough to give Gram a pair of air kisses. She was tall, with highlighted hair, well dressed and very confident.

Gram smiled a twinkling smile at her.

Asta scampered around snapping at Josh's ankles. Gram ignored her. It was one more way to ratchet up the tension.

My heart was thundering. We had been right. This niece was much more than she'd pretended to be. I tried to make eye contact with Smiley. But no luck there.

"I don't know what's keeping Clara, but let me say that it's been much too long and we have missed you. Haven't we, Josh?"

He shrugged. I noticed he couldn't bring himself to look at Gram.

Gram twinkled a bit more. "We're so glad you're here. Tea or champagne?"

Josh shook his head. Maybe he wanted an energy drink. Janet chose champagne and practically purred as Zoya poured it. From my perch, Zoya looked like she wanted to wrap her hands around Janet's throat. Luckily, she wasn't in charge.

Gram waved her hand toward the table. "Zoya has outdone herself with sandwiches and sweets."

The doorbell rang again. Josh jumped. I knew who Janet was and I knew I'd recognize Clara when she arrived too.

I hadn't been too worried about Josh, but it belatedly occurred to me that I should be much more worried about his mother. Josh was a twit and Jessica not much better.

The mothers were the ones to watch out for.

Was there a chance that I could alert Smiley and warn him? Apparently not. Zoya stormed in with a slightly shorter woman with equally expensive highlighted hair and the person we'd known as Sierra at her side. Clara raised her eyebrow to her sister. "Thought you could have waited the few seconds."

"No harm done, Clara. You might have kept up."

"Auntie Jean, it's lovely to see you," Clara said in a voice like poisoned syrup.

Gram must have practiced her most sugary responses. "Yes, after all this time, together again. Jessica, how you've grown up. I can't believe you and Josh are here. So wonderful."

Asta turned her attention to Jessica and yipped and even hurled herself. Jessica did her best to ignore the dog. Janet looked daggers at Jessica and at Asta.

"Now that you are all here, let me introduce my neighbor and good friend, Nancy Mitchell."

A round of greetings ensued.

Gram said, "Nancy is not only a wonderful neighbor and friend, but she's also my lawyer."

Eight eyes focused on Nancy, who nodded gravely, radiating calm, steely professionalism. I wouldn't have liked to be up against her in court.

Gram twittered. "We have a few estate planning things to discuss, now that we're mending fences."

Clara's head swiveled. "Mending fences?"

Oops. Zoya deflected attention by offering tea and champagne. Jessica's knuckles were white as she clutched but didn't sip her flute with the sparkling treat.

"I should have said reconnecting. Being family again. Please forgive me. I am terribly upset because of something that's happened to us."

"Oh? And what is that?" Janet asked. She couldn't quite suppress a gleam in her eye, visible even to me.

"My grandson, whom I told you about. Well, I explained to Clara when we spoke. He came to see me and stayed in the hotel Clara recommended. La Perla? A good choice in hotel but a bad reunion. I think he was just after money. We've had nothing but trouble since he and his girlfriend arrived. I finally had to show him the door, didn't I, Zoya?"

Zoya said, "Gone avay now. Good riddens."

In a rattly voice, Gram said, "So I really need to get him out of the will altogether. That's why Nancy is here."

Janet glowed. "I'm so glad you gave him the boot."

"Yes," said Clara. "There's nothing worse than a greedy relative."

Jessica smirked and took a gulp of her champers. Congratulating herself, I supposed. Josh reached for a glass himself.

"To the Huddys!" Gram said.

It was enough to make you hurl.

With perfect timing when they were all in mid-sip, Gram added, "You won't get everything, of course. Most of it will go to a home for pugs—"

I hoped no one heard me laugh out loud at the resulting spew of champagne. Smiley glowered at me, but his lips twitched. I thought Nancy Mitchell's might have too.

The doorbell pealed just in time to distract.

"Oh my," said Gram. "I think Gloria must be here."

"Who is Gloria?" Janet said with a frown. Of course, they'd be wanting to ingratiate themselves with Gram without competition.

"Gloria Zeller. Another lovely friend and neighbor, across the street."

"But shouldn't this just be a family affair?" Jessica squeaked.

"She'll remember your mother as a girl visiting here and Janet too," Gram said gaily. "I knew she'd be glad to come. And we'll need her as a witness for the will. Zoya can be the second one."

"Of course," Janet beamed. I figured she was already working on a plan to get rid of the pug charity.

We were getting close to our action moment.

I tried to signal Tyler without making any noise. No luck. He was staring quite murderously at the cousins. But he needed to be directing his anger at their mothers. He needed to see past the expensive honey-brown and blond highlights and remember them with silver hair and Tilley hats. He needed to know that they were not attractive and harmless ladies. I was remembering them always being nearby in the hotel, looking so innocuous when we were leaving for dinners, smiling at me on the cable car, passing by just before I was pushed. I was speculating that it had been Clara or Janet in the hallway behind me near the staircase when I pulled off the bedspread. Jessica and Josh were dolts, even if they were criminal dolts. But we needed to beware of their mothers.

Zoya arrived in the parlor with Gloria Zeller. She was in fine form.

Gram waved her greeting and Nancy nodded a welcome to the new arrival. But Josh stared and Jessica's hand shook as Gram introduced everyone.

Gloria played her part perfectly. "Don't I know you, dear?" she said to Jessica, a smile on her kind, generous face.

Jessica shook her head, ponytail swaying. "No. No, you don't."

Gloria looked startled. "Yes. I do. You are staying next to me in the Himmelfarb house. I recognize you. Of course, you are so very pretty, just like your mother was at that age."

"I wasn't there!" Jessica shrieked.

Clara reached over and clutched Jessica's hand, perhaps trying to squeeze some brains into her.

Jessica said, "Ouch. Mom!"

"Jessica is often mistaken for people in film and on television," Clara said.

Jessica's free hand went to her hair and she couldn't hold back a conceited smile. Of course, she somehow had evaded the glares that Tyler was aiming her way through the wall. "As if," he muttered.

"No, no, dear, it was the Himmelfarb house. You had your baby with you and your husband came and went too, but from the back door."

Josh whirled and yapped, "That's stupid. You didn't ever see me. Nobody could see anything back—"

His mother stepped forward. "You forget yourself, Josh. It's just a bit of mistaken identity."

Gram said. "Well, now I am confused, Jessica dear. Were you trying to visit the Himmelfarbs? Because they both died, you know, and I didn't think you'd ever even met them. Your mother would have been to that house as a child, wouldn't you, Clara?"

"Not that I remember. My memory's not what it used to be."

Gloria said, "Well, mine is as good as it ever was, and I know that I've seen this young lady go into my neighbor's empty house. I assumed she was a real estate agent. Where is the baby now?"

"There is no baby," Jessica snapped.

Gram said, "Gloria, my friend, please have some champagne or tea and a sandwich. We'll get all this confusion sorted out."

"Well, I'm not used to being spoken to in that tone," Gloria said. "Very unsettling, Jean."

"Yes, I'm a bit surprised to see that there's a bit of an issue with manners and these young people."

Janet stepped forward. "The children are just tired because they've been, um, hiking around the coast. They're very sorry for their tone. Aren't you, Jessica and Josh?"

I felt goose bumps rise on my arms. Smiley turned to me and we exchanged knowing glances. Gram, Gloria and Nancy managed to keep straight faces throughout. *That's quite a talent*, I thought. Zoya's wide silver eyes were like slits by now. Gram shot her a look and said, "Another round of champagne, Zoya. We all need to . . . *What* is it the young people say? Chill?"

I smothered a snicker.

It was almost time for my big number. Stealthily I made my way out the back and around through the neighbor's yards to the corner and then hurried along the sidewalk. I approached the front veranda, crouching down without being visible through either the bay or the turret windows. I rang the doorbell and took a deep breath.

Zoya seemed to enjoy pretending to prevent me from joining the group in the parlor. *"Nyet! Nyet!* Go away! Not welcome!" She gave me a couple of shoves to make her point. I gave her a dirty look and pushed my way in.

"Gram!" I shouted. "You must listen to me. Nothing was Tyler's fault. The attacks were set up by—" I stopped and stared at Jessica and Josh. "Sierra? Michael? What are you doing here?"

"Leave at once," Janet said, standing to block me from Gram. Jessica stood behind her and said, "I don't know what you're talking about."

"Yes. I know you from across the street."

"You so do not!" Jessica said.

"And you never even saw me," said Josh.

Gotcha.

"What did he say?" Gram said, leaning forward.

Nancy pursed her lips and said, "Perhaps you should hold off on the will a bit, Jean. Just until we figure out what's going on."

Gloria said, "I'd like to know too. But you see, I'm not the only person who recognizes this young woman."

"This is all ridiculous," Janet said. "This girl is trying to cause trouble because she's after your money, Auntie Jean. Would you like me to call the police? You don't have to let her in your house. If you ask her to leave and she doesn't, it's against the law, you know."

"I'll show her to the door," Clara said grimly.

Tyler's voice took them by surprise. "While we're

showing things, why don't I show her these photos of two ladies who were staying at La Perla when we had our troubles."

"How did he get in here?" Janet yelped.

Tyler strode across the room and thrust my phone into Gram's waiting hands. Nancy got up and stood behind her to get a look.

Gram said, "But that's you, Janet, and you too, Clara. Why is your hair gray? Are you wearing wigs? Or are you wearing wigs now?"

Clara went to snatch the phone from Gram. Not a good move. Zoya was between them with Gram's cane in her hands, the metal bird handle aimed at Clara's temple.

"This is an outrage," Clara huffed. "Auntie Jean, you must tell these people to leave. We are your family. They are trying to—get away from me with that thing!"

Zoya must have lunged.

Smiley said, "Don't stop now, Gram. You'll find a photo of your so-called nieces still in disguise on the cable car on the trip where Jordan was pushed and almost killed."

I said, "And didn't you say that Clara gave you the name of the hotel where we stayed? The same hotel where our rooms were trashed and I was pushed down the stairs. Those were violent attacks, and yet look who was right there."

Gram's narrowed. "I told you that my grandson would be staying there and so you took it upon yourselves to attack him and his—"

Janet said, "That's enough. We're leaving and you'll be hearing from our lawyer. This is an outrage."

Tyler said, "The police will want to talk to you all. These are serious offenses, felonies, and will almost certainly lead to jail time."

Jessica began to wail. "It's not my fault. It's Aunt Janet! She came up with the idea. She made us do it. She said we'd make a lot of money and the old lady probably wouldn't live long after"—Jessica's shaky finger pointed at Gram—"all the fuss!"

Josh yelled, "That's a lie, you witch. It was you that decided to break into that house and pretend to be friends with her." He pointed at me as his mother said, "Shut up, Josh. You too, Jessica. Stop talking right now."

Jessica chose instead to scream at Josh. "Oh yeah, you doofus. It was your idea to kidnap the dog. You said that would really set her off."

Tyler barely managed to stop Zoya before she reached Josh with the cane. I stayed out of the way. Didn't want to get in the middle.

Clare said, "We will have the police investigate you people. We'll tell them."

Uncle Kev chose that moment to pop his head in through the door. "That's great because they're on their way."

Janet forced her way past Gloria and Tyler and even the seething Zoya. "Come. We're leaving."

I said, "They'll be particularly interested in your using a false name at La Perla and I think they can probably tie you to the black Prius that tried to hit us on our way home from the restaurant on our second night."

"You can't prove a thing," Janet said. She was pretty good with the haughty looks. "We're leaving."

"We can certainly prove that Jessica and Josh were both in the Himmelfarb house. Gloria can confirm it and we have evidence with DNA and fingerprints from your vantage point on the second floor. You should be more careful with your coffee cups, cousins."

Jessica shrieked, "I told you the trash was gone, you idiot. Now we'll all go to jail."

Josh bellowed back, "No, you're the idiot, not me."

Nancy Mitchell shook her head. "This is beyond belief. Jean, my friend, you've had a very close call."

Uncle Kev said, "That's why we have it all on tape. Nice confession. You're both doofuses."

I shook my head and suggested that Kev zip his lip.

Janet and Clara pushed their way from the room. "Let's go," Clara bellowed. "They can't stop four of us, and if that crazy Russian woman hurts anyone, she will be going to jail, and better yet, she'll be deported back to whatever hell-hole she came from."

I whirled to look at Zoya, who turned almost transparent and slumped against the table. Tyler and I barely caught her in time. Janet and Clara headed for the front door while Jessica and Josh, pushing and slapping at each other, raced toward the back.

Nobody was expecting Gus and the boys. One per perpetrator. Soon all our fleeing felons were squirming under a surprising amount of weight.

Officer Martinez stepped through the front door, looked at the wriggling bodies, listened to the shrill protests and said, "Well, this has been interesting. I hate to think I missed some other good stuff too."

Kev unzipped his lip long enough to say, "You'll like the video, Officer. Hope you brought lots of cuffs with you."

Tyler and I took Officer Martinez aside as her backup team walked the four pathetic would-be heirs to the waiting squad cars.

He said, "And you'll find some more evidence in the cameras that we planted in the ninth-floor suite at La Perla. We couldn't go back to get them, but after the attacks, we wanted to be sure. They'll be date stamped and I think you'll find the shooters who were after Jordan. Then you can tie them all together."

"And we won't have to worry about the chain of evidence," she said. "Unlike your coffee cups and trash that you're not sure how you came to have. Listen to them. They can't wait to turn on each other. I'd say we've got 'em. Let's see if the cousins will turn on the thugs."

I said, "The shooters may have been hired professionals. They had that look."

She nodded. "That's what I thought when you sent the photo you shot through the hotel door peephole, but it was too distorted to ID them. We'll keep at it. But at least you guys can relax and enjoy the rest of your holiday without worrying now. And I just want to say, if I'd listened to you, Jordan, and tracked down Jessica, she might have cracked under the strain earlier, saving a lot of trouble."

I shrugged. "We were grateful that you believed us about everything."

Smiley said, "Amen to that." As awful as the hired professionals were, I think he was relieved the attacks had nothing to do with his hidden photo album.

CHAPTER TWENTY-SIX

It ain't over 'til it's over.
—THE KELLY RULES

OFFICER MARTINEZ WAS in a very good mood when we spoke to her the next time. Apparently, Jessica and Josh were so happy to implicate each other and each other's mothers that they'd spilled all.

"The plan was to scare Tyler and you away, by various attacks. The dognapping was a last minute addition to stress Mrs. Huddy. It was sort of goofy, but they had cooked up this conspiracy to get their mitts on the Huddy money. They were convinced they were entitled to it, and if Mrs. Huddy had a heart attack from the stress of everything that went on, that was just tough."

Tyler shook his head.

I said, "What about the other guys?"

"Nothing yet. We've been digging and they look a bit like a pair of low-level mobsters. But we don't have proof and all four relatives keep insisting they know nothing. We can't shake them, and believe me, they were easily shaken on all the other stuff: The Prius attack was Janet. We have proof of rental. The cable car was Clara. Your photos helped there.

Too bad you didn't report those. The break-in across the street and dognapping were Jessica and Josh. But no one will admit to the violent home invasion or either incident at the hotel."

"I don't think it was any of them. I'm pretty sure they're connected."

"We've been all over that, and we believe they're mob goons, but old guys, who should be retiring in Vegas by now. No one's seen them around for years. They're connected all right, but not to your gang of four."

"Any names come up?"

"Some guy named Les 'the Bat' Blatt was supposed to run them back in the day."

Uh-oh. "Still alive, though. Keep us posted."

"Sure thing. They may have had you mixed up with someone else."

"Let's hope," Tyler said.

I had a funny feeling in my stomach.

"HERE." KEV HANDED me a parcel. It was a book wrapped in plain brown paper, with a simple twine bow. Inside was the *Red Harvest* that Farley Tso had promised me.

"How did you get this?" Don't get me wrong. I was ecstatic that I wasn't going to face the wrath of Vera for having lost her money plus "failure to acquire," as she would put it, the *Red Harvest*.

"I don't think you want to know, Jordie." Of course I didn't *want* to know. I needed to know for my own peace of mind. "I think you had better tell me anyway."

"Don't be mad."

"Don't be mad" was never followed by anything good. "You don't have to worry about Blatt's guys anymore. They're, uh, taken care of."

What? I gulped. "Kevin, no!"

"Not me, you know I couldn't ever, um, take care of things like that. It was Seamus. I sent him a message, said we needed his help. Don't ask me how, Jordie, I don't want to lie to ya." He shifted uncomfortably under my horrified gaze. "He wasn't gonna let you get hurt, even though he never met you, you're family. He risked everything coming back here, dealing with those guys and then making it look like the thugs ran off with the diamonds. That Blatt's not gonna keep looking for you. Now he'll be looking for them."

"I feel sick." Another two people whose lives ended because I was just doing my job.

"I don't know why, Jordie. These were really bad guys. They never got to you, but they got to poor old Farley Tso and they got to the manager at the hotel. Seamus found out they threatened his wife and kids—and the guys in that restaurant. People were really scared of Blatt's thugs. There are a lotta other people in California that are pushing up daisies thanks to them. They would have killed you without blinkin'."

I guess I didn't have to feel entirely awful about the missing goons. But I was still conflicted.

"Where's Seamus now?" But I already knew he was in the wind.

"Halfway back to nowhere." I could see a sadness creep into Uncle Kev's bright eyes. He truly missed his brother, and that was obviously a bond that would never die. I was lucky enough to have the same bond with Kev and Mick and Lucky and even with Seamus. I pulled Kev's jean-jacket-clad body to me and gave him a bear hug.

"What's that for?"

"For being you, Kev." He seemed to accept that and hugged me back.

THE MOONLIGHT GLITTERED on San Francisco Bay. We glittered a bit ourselves. I was wearing my red dress

again and my cute little dress boots. I'd been warned that
the air on the bay would be chilly, so I had artfully arranged
a pair of pashminas from Gram's collection around my neck
and shoulders. Under the pashminas I wore the necklace
from Farley's shop. I thought I'd wear it just one time. I had
a twinge about poor Farley and what had happened to him.

But this was a night to celebrate. It was our last evening
in San Francisco after seven days of incredible and unexpected adventures. Gram had chartered a party boat for us
to have what she called a "belated celebration" of our engagement and the ousting of the reptile cousins. Once again
there was champagne, but this time Tyler and I were able to
enjoy it.

In my small evening bag, I had an old-fashioned telegram
from Vera.

> **Understand congratulations in order STOP Don't
> dawdle STOP Bring Red Harvest STOP VVA**

Nothing had changed, except that I now had to repay the
money I'd borrowed for my replacement phone. I'd gotten
off lightly.

Officer Martinez had been able to join us, although that
had involved getting permission from up the line. She was
in her civvies and looked amazing in a slinky black dress
and four-inch silver heels. Her hair was long and loosely
curled and her large silver hoop earrings suited her, as did
her silver arm party.

Although it wouldn't have been my first choice for our
champagne party, Gram had catered Chinese food for the
event, following, I believe, a suggestion from Uncle Kev,
who was in everyone's good books except mine. He would
have been in Tyler's very bad books if he knew everything
there was to know.

Nancy Mitchell had joined us as had Gloria Zeller. Ana

Maria had claimed a night school commitment, but maybe she was just too shy to come.

We all enjoyed the floating festivities and the Chinese food was perfect, as it turned out. I loved the little take-out boxes that you could eat right out of. Even Zoya and Asta seemed to be having a good time over sweet and sour chicken balls.

My wish for a three-flavor gelato cake had also been honored. While everyone was clinking glasses and chatting pleasantly about whether double chocolate, hazelnut or pistachio was the perfect flavor, I slipped away and sent a group text to Tiff and Lance.

Haven't chatted in a while, thought I would give you guys a "ring." I snapped a picture of my gorgeous heirloom citrine and sent it along with the text.

Lance was first to reply. OMG!!! Congratulations, Jordan. Officer Smiley has great taste in jewelry AND women. I am only entirely jealous. And then, of course, a winky face.

This was topped by Tiff's response. I hope you realize I can only support this union under the following conditions. 1. I get to be the maid of honor, and 2. We get to go to Vegas for your bachelorette party.

Wedding bell and bride emojis were followed by a dozen martini glasses to let me know she was happy about it.

I knew she would be; any doubts in either of their minds would have been put aside when I decided to say "yes," because that's what friends do. And I had some great ones. As I wandered back to the party, I wondered if there could be a librarian of honor in a wedding party and also if I could give Vegas a miss.

I sat down near Gram and commented, "Zoya seems a bit more relaxed."

"The poor girl. I know she can be a bit difficult but I am very fond of her. I suppose I should explain. She was here as a so-called Russian bride for a man in his fifties, and she found herself in a terribly abusive relationship with no one to turn to. She was fleeing from him and happened to come across me when I'd fallen in the street while shopping. She took a big chance to stop and help me. And I took a chance to help her. I gave her a home and she has given me a comfortable life. It's good for both of us."

"What happened to him? Did she ever see him again?"

She shook her head. "He spotted her again not long after and chased her right through heavy traffic. She got across, but he didn't."

"What a shame," I murmured. "You're sure?"

"We both made the trip to the morgue. You can never be too careful."

"Words to live by." But of course, I hadn't been living by them.

I turned as there was a roar of laughter as Gus and the boys traded stories with Uncle Kev. Nancy Mitchell was able to throw in a few of her own. And Gloria said that she regretted being so respectable all her life.

Everyone toasted our engagement. I showed off my citrine ring. And Smiley showed off his Guy Noir Bobblehead, my engagement gift to him, which he was equally proud of.

I enjoyed wearing the diamond necklace, just one time before I mailed it back anonymously to whoever I found were Laurie Leff's rightful heirs. No one would ever think it was real, except me. Wherever he was, Uncle Seamus might enjoy that idea.

We had survived our adventure stronger than when we'd begun. We would continue to survive and we might even thrive. But like the great Dashiell Hammett, I would reserve the right to have my little secrets.

Smiley and I raised our glasses and said in stereo, "To us. Whatever that brings with it."

RECIPES

GRAM'S BEST FRIED CHICKEN

Enjoy this old time treat with family or friends.

1 chicken, about 3 ½–4 pounds
4 cups fresh buttermilk
4 tsp Dijon mustard
1 tsp sea salt
½ tsp ground pepper
1 cup flour
¼–½ tsp cayenne pepper (depending on how spicy you like it!)
2 tsp paprika
2 tsp dried thyme
2 cups Canola or corn oil
½ cup butter
Additional salt and pepper to taste

Cut the chicken into eight to ten pieces. Gram cuts each breast in half if the chicken is large. Combine buttermilk with Dijon, salt and pepper. Cover chicken with buttermilk mixture and marinate overnight if you can.

Add flour, paprika, dried thyme and cayenne to a large plastic bag with a zipper closing. Shake well. Add chicken piece by piece and shake to coat. Remove and place on a dish until ready to cook.

In a large cast iron skillet (or regular skillet if you don't have cast iron) heat oil and butter until very hot. Cook half the chicken at a time, covered, reducing heat to medium or medium-high to keep it from smoking. Turn when brown (eight to eleven minutes depending on the size of the pieces) and cook about ten minutes until done.

Place on a platter with paper towels to soak up excess oil.

Serves four.

TYLER'S FAVORITE LEMON DESSERT

Memories of childhood desserts will come flooding back with this, a favorite for all ages.

1 ½ tablespoons butter
2 tablespoons flour
⅞ cup sugar
1 tablespoon lemon zest (1 large lemon)
¼ cup lemon juice
¼ tsp salt
3 extra large eggs, at room temperature, separated
1 ½ cup milk or cream

Preheat oven to 350°F for 30–35 minutes.

Beat butter and sugar until well combined. Add lemon

RECIPES 297

zest, lemon juice, egg yolks, salt and flour. Beat until light and fluffy. Gradually add milk and blend well.

Beat egg whites until stiff. Fold into lemon mixture. Pour into GREASED 6-cup baking dish or casserole.

Bake at 350°F for about 35 minutes until puffed and golden.

Serve warm or at room temperature.

Serves four (or six small portions).

Chocolate Chip Meringue Kisses

These are the meringue kisses that Smiley remembers from his childhood. They're very easy, as long as your eggs are at room temperature and there's not a speck of anything greasy near bowl or beaters and that means not a single drop of yolk, according to Gram.

4 egg whites (from extra-large eggs, at room temperature)
1 cup minus 1 tablespoon granulated sugar
1 tsp good quality vanilla
½ tsp almond extract (optional)
⅛ tsp cream of tartar
¾–1 cup semi-sweet chocolate chips

Preheat oven to 225°F.

Beat the egg white with cream of tartar until soft peaks form. Add vanilla and almond. Slowly add sugar tablespoon by tablespoon, beating well after every addition, until stiff peaks have formed.

Line a cookie sheet with parchment paper. Scoop out meringue and shape into "kisses." Bake in pre-heated oven

at 225°F for about 50 minutes. Turn off oven and let kisses
dry for at least an hour. Don't let them brown at the edges.
If your oven runs hot, reduce temperature.

Store in a cookie tin in a cool, dry place.

*Makes about eighteen depending on size of kisses. They keep
well if no one finds them.*

The Woman has crush
on her boss